ALSO BY AMBER McBRIDE

Me (Moth)
We Are All So Good at Smiling

GONE WOLF

AMBER McBRIDE

FEIWEL AND FRIENDS
New York

For my parents, Mario and Debra,
who always let me weave grand
stories when my soul was not ready
to face the truth.

And for Shiloh: Thank you for
teaching me how to *go wolf*.

A Feiwel and Friends Book
An imprint of Macmillan Publishing Group, LLC
120 Broadway, New York, NY 10271 • fiercereads.com

Our books may be purchased in bulk for promotional, educational, or
business use. Please contact your local bookseller or the Macmillan Corporate
and Premium Sales Department at (800) 221-7945 ext. 5442 or by email at
MacmillanSpecialMarkets@macmillan.com.

Library of Congress Control Number: 2023018024

First edition, 2023
Book design by Michelle Gengaro-Kokmen
Feiwel and Friends logo designed by Filomena Tuosto
Printed in the United States of America

ISBN 978-1-250-85049-2

1 3 5 7 9 10 8 6 4 2

BLUE: BIBLE BOOT, 2111

Sometimes I tell big stories
that pull a wool blanket over my eyes
so I can hide . . .
hide . . .
hide . . .

–Imogen, 12 years old

1

Sun-Day Blues

The lady in blue holds up the dolls again. She asks me, *Which one is better?* One has pants with edges like the corner of a wall—it must be painful to wear something so stiff.

The doll's face is pale with blue eyes. Behind its thin lips are straight teeth like square pearls. The doll's hair is bright blond, I want to touch it. I want to touch the hair, but I am afraid it will be hot like the sun. The lady in blue says, *The sun is big and bright—if you stand in it too long, it can burn you.*

I have never seen the sun, but the lady in blue says, *You will see the sun soon.*

The second doll wears a big dress made from squares of many colors. It is as if the dress is not sure what color it should be, so it decides to be all the colors. Like a rainbow. I have never seen a rainbow, but *rainbow* means colors and that is what I think it must look like, but in the sky.

The second doll's clothes are wrinkled and the paint

on the doll's fingernails is chipped. The plastic face smiles too big and her slightly yellow teeth remind me of what a sunrise must be like.

It's true, I have never seen a sunrise, but the lady in blue says, *You will see the sunrise soon.*

The lady in blue watches me study each doll, and her eyebrows pull together. She wants me to pick the one with blue eyes. I know because we have been doing this test for weeks. I know it has been weeks, because a week is seven days long and I have had more than fourteen breakfast trays since we started this test.

I don't know if I can fail a test, but the little sigh the lady in blue does when she puts the dolls back in their boxes sounds like failing. The lady in blue always says, *I am not disappointed.* Which I guess is true, because she also says she can't *feel* anything.

I point at one of the dolls.

"And why, Inmate Eleven, do you like this doll?" The lady in blue examines the patchwork dress of the doll I picked.

The lady in blue's eyes look less blue today and more storm.

"I like her hair," I say because the patchwork-dress doll has nice hair.

"You like it better than this hair." The lady in blue tugs at her own golden curls, holding what must be sunshine.

"I like that it is blue," I say.

Blue like the ocean, which I have never seen.

Blue like the sky, which I have never seen.

Blue like my hair, which I can see when I look down.

"Blue is an odd color for hair, don't you think?" The lady in blue lifts her eyebrows.

"Maybe."

There is the lady in blue and she has golden-sun hair. There are some guards when I am *bad* and they also have golden-sun hair. Then there are the doctors I see when I am very sick—they have golden-sun hair too.

"And what about the teeth." She points at the stains. "You like her teeth better than this doll's?"

"Maybe." The lady in blue usually does not ask so many questions. Maybe it is because today her eyes are more storm than blue. I have never seen a storm, but in books storms cause rain and lightning and are very angry.

"And you see her clothes, they have many colors." The lady in blue lifts the perfect doll close to my face. So close it is blurry. "This doll's clothes are clean and pressed. Her nails are painted and never chip. Her hair curls perfectly, it is not blue and nappy. See the scar on her arm? She has a vaccine, and she can go outside, because she can never get sick. The blue doll doesn't have that perfect scar. She can't go outside."

"I like how the other doll *feels*," I say because she *feels* like something that wants love. She feels like a friend you can tell secrets to.

I don't have any friends. I mean, I don't have any *people* friends.

The lady in blue lifts her eyebrows again. "You are not touching them. How do you know how they feel?"

"No, how they *feel*." I hit my chest near my heart. I know this will only make the lady in blue's eyes stormier, but I don't like to lie.

"You are too old to be saying things like that, Inmate Eleven." Her hand tightens around my favorite doll's waist. Her nails dig into the fabric.

"I know."

"Every day I come talk to you. Have I not taught you to read and write? Have I not dealt with your sicknesses and crying?"

The lady in blue looks at me like she looks at the doll I picked—like there's a problem. There are five holes in the doll now, where her fingernails dug into the fabric. I wonder if she notices what she has done.

"Yes." I try not to look at her. I wish Ira were here prowling around the room.

"And every time I ask you this question, you willfully answer wrong." Her grip loosens and tiny blue beads tumble from the doll.

"Wrong?"

"Yes, wrong." The lady in blue lets the beads fall on the floor until the doll is as empty as clothes without a person.

"I like how the other one *feels*," I try to explain.

"And how is that?" The lady in blue inspects the empty doll again.

"Like the sun would feel on my face." I want to add: like

warmth, like a cup of tea, like a summer day, but I have never felt those things and I don't want to get it wrong.

"The sun burns the skin when you stay in it too long," she says quickly. "And there are germs outside."

"I know," I mumble. That is why I am not allowed outside. "That's why I have to stay inside."

She says flatly, "And this one, how does it make you feel?"

"Like my insides are frozen." The eyes are too perfect, the smile too wide, the crease in the pants feels like a knife on my leg.

"Inmate Eleven, the sooner you learn that Clones are *better*, the sooner we can proceed with your education. The sooner you can get a vaccine. The sooner you can go outside."

"Better?"

The lady in blue stands and walks to the door. She leaves the dolls this time. "Please keep studying your learning flash cards, Inmate Eleven. Shall we try again tomorrow?"

It is a rhetorical question—*rhetorical* means not really a question. It means that you don't have a choice.

I have lived in a cell my entire life.

When the lock snaps shut, they let Ira out of the small-small room attached to my room. He races to me and nuzzles my hand, so everything is much better, but there is still no sun and the doll with vacant eyes glares at me from the floor. The other doll is so empty it hurts.

So empty I hurt. So, I do what I always do.

I write poems in my head.

A poem is something that makes you *feel* something. I don't have a pen or paper, so I have to remember the poems. I have so many poems stored in me that sometimes I think they might spill out the alphabet when I cry.

THE BIBLE BOOT LEARNING FLASH CARDS

The Blue Doll Test

The Blue Doll Test is one of the most important tests any Blue must pass to be able to go outside. It is important for Blues to understand that Clones are better. It would be unwise and wrong to think anything else.

During the Blue Doll Test, one doll that is perfect and white is shown. The other doll is blue and has shabby clothes and chipped nails. The Blue child must pick the correct doll–it should be easy, but Blues are not very smart and often have trouble understanding.

This test is important for everyone. It is the best test and once a Blue passes it, they have an opportunity to go outside.

2

Small-Small

I don't know if my room is small. I don't have anything to compare it to. It's like when I see a picture of the sun in a book and I can hold it in my hands. Then the lady in blue tells me, *The sun is big—over one million Earths can fit inside the sun.* Which means nothing, because in the book I can also fit Earth in my hands.

Sometimes when the lady in blue leaves, I look out when the door closes slowly.

What I see is a long tunnel with doors, which makes me think my room is small, the way the earth is small and the tunnel is big like the sun.

I can't be sure, though.

I am sure that my room, from left to right, is eleven normal steps and twenty-two baby steps. From right to left, it is ten normal steps and twenty baby steps. I know science says it is supposed to be the same, but it isn't, because on the way back I am rushing.

For Ira, it is about a two-second trot.

It is difficult to measure steps when you have four legs.

Ira is fast. Sometimes he circles the edges of the room. His head gets real low and his eyes turn into slits.

That is his *gone wolf* face. He is imagining himself somewhere else.

It means he hates the cell.

I don't have many visitors, but I never have any when Ira *goes wolf*, because I can't get him to go into the small-small room beside my cell. The lady in blue does not like Ira. She has never really met him; she just sees him on the camera and I bet he looks scary on camera. I know there are cameras, because sometimes voices echo out of the ceiling and bounce around the room telling me to stop doing this or that.

I don't know where the cameras are hidden. I have never seen a real camera, but the lady in blue says they record things so we don't forget. That means cameras are very useful because sometimes I forget. Sometimes I forget that my world is only—from left to right—eleven normal steps and twenty-two baby steps. From right to left, it is ten normal steps and twenty baby steps.

Sometimes I think outside might be too much space.

Sometimes I feel bad.

Because of me, Ira has nowhere to roam, unlike the wolves in the lady in blue's books. The lady in blue doesn't know Ira's name is Ira. She calls me Inmate Eleven. So my first name is Inmate and my last name is Eleven.

My name is a lot different from the names of people in books.

They have names like Mary, Monica, or Myrtle. Sometimes they have song-sounding names like Norhan, Kalisa, Hamid, or Shuruq. Those are my favorite names because the lady in blue stumbles on them, but I say them just right. I have never read about a person named Inmate.

I wonder if I am a *real* person the way people in books are *real*.

Ira is not a *real* wolf, or at least that is what the lady in blue says.

He is a genetically modified dog. That is a long way of saying he is special.

The lady in blue says, *We extrapolated all the good qualities from dogs and wolves to create the perfect companion.*

Extrapolated means to take out.

I don't know if it is nice to take only the things you like out of something.

The lady in blue says, *We don't make mistakes.*

That makes me feel a little better.

I make lots of mistakes. Just yesterday, I accidentally touched the big metal door and cried. I did not cry because of touching the door, but the door bites when you touch it. The lady in blue calls it a *shock*, which is a boring word for something so painful.

I pretend that Ira is a *real* wolf. The lady in blue says that *my kind* did not always have wolves, but something happened to our brains when we did not have a companion.

She says, *Something about being alone made you even dumber.*

That was the day I realized there were others like me—maybe others with Inmate as a first name and a number as a last name.

Which means I am *real* the way people in books are *real*.

I push my bed away from the wall for when Ira *goes wolf*. The mattress of my bed is stuffed with crow feathers. I don't actually know if they are crow feathers, but I know that crow feathers are black. The feathers that stick from my mattress are black and the tips are pointy and scary-looking.

Most nights it is like sleeping on pins.

Most nights the feathers make me bleed.

Like right now, one pushes into the basin of my back.

Which means blood.

I don't actually mean that my back is a basin. A basin carries water and things. I mean that the curve right at my tailbone dives in, so it makes that part of my back look like a basin. I am afraid to roll on my side. Then they will see the blood through the cameras and shuffle me into the small-small room so they can collect the sheets. Ira hates the small-small room even more than this one.

What Ira hates most is the thick white collar around his neck.

Sometimes it bites him. I don't mean that it really bites him, but *shock* is such a boring word, I really don't like it.

It is nice that the lady in blue wears blue. It makes it feel like she is trying to be kind.

My skin is dark blue and my hair is a lighter hue—maybe a blue like the ocean?

The lady in blue says, *It is not your fault you are hideous. It is just that some things are born better than others.*

Also, because I am Blue, I can't go outside, because of my immune system.

My learning flash cards say I can't go outside, because the sun will also hurt my skin.

I don't know exactly what that means, but the lady in blue says, *It is safer this way, until you get a vaccine.*

The lady in blue got a vaccine when she was a baby.

I say that maybe I should get a vaccine so I can go outside too, but she tells me that won't work. I have not passed my tests yet. I don't think that I should be punished for being born the way I am. Then again, Ira was created as a companion for me and is kept cooped up in the small room with me. So, Ira is punished because of me.

Besides, the lady in blue says, *You are not being punished. This is just the way things are.*

I guess some things are just like that.

The lady in blue says, *We will never have another Civil War here, because we all think the same and know what is right.*

I don't understand how she can be so sure of the past, present, and future.

The lady in blue says, *We have eliminated hate, because everyone knows their place.*

I hate.

What I *hate* the most are the men who come in, blindfold me, and put me on a metal bed that rolls. They roll me for a long time. Maybe we have traveled to the sun.

They never bring Ira on these random journeys, which means I feel empty. When they remove the blindfold, it is bright, which is why I think we might have traveled to the sun. My eyes feel bruised and I wonder if the entire world is just a bunch of bright rooms. Maybe outside is not real.

I *hate* them in their white smocks.

They don't wear any blue.

Just a bunch of snow-white smocks.

I don't mean snow as in the cold stuff that falls from the sky.

I mean snow as in the color.

I *hate* them.

And I think that is another reason I am kept in the small room.

Hate is illegal in the Bible Boot.

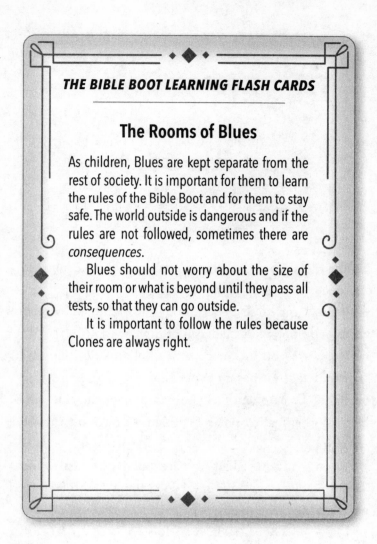

The Rooms of Blues

As children, Blues are kept separate from the rest of society. It is important for them to learn the rules of the Bible Boot and for them to stay safe. The world outside is dangerous and if the rules are not followed, sometimes there are *consequences*.

Blues should not worry about the size of their room or what is beyond until they pass all tests, so that they can go outside.

It is important to follow the rules because Clones are always right.

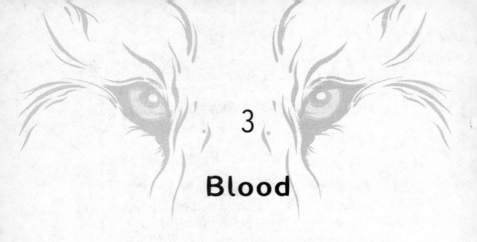

3

Blood

The metal door opens and closes quickly like a blinking eye.

I didn't move, so I don't know how they know about the blood pooling in the basin of my back.

"How are you this morning?" an ebony droid hums. Its face is metal so it has no expression.

"Fine." I sit up and dangle my legs over the side of the bed. Another feather pokes my thighs through my thin blue uniform.

"Wonderful! Excellent. You are looking very pale today." The droid says this every time. I don't think it is programmed to talk to people like me.

I have never been pale, just blue.

"You think?" I say as I try to pull the bloody feather out of the bed.

"Please move into the smaller room." It means the small-small room. The fake clicky voice might sound friendlier if it was not holding a Taser in my face. Ira moves in front of me. "You and Ira have to the count of ten, Inmate Eleven."

I stomp toward the small-small room. Ira follows.

Ira is gray and blue.

I have not seen any gray-and-blue wolves in books.

I think that is because Ira is magic.

The small-small room is only five steps across. Ira can't even trot. He nuzzles his head under my left arm, right below my rib cage. I hear the droid clanging around in my room. They don't have cameras in the small-small room. I don't know what a camera looks like, but sometimes I hide little things in here and they don't say anything. I pull the black feather from my sleeve and examine it.

Long, light, black, and sharp. The lady in blue says, *Feathers come from birds.*

Birds can fly.

Flying is when you walk, but in the air and flapping your wings instead of moving your legs. It seems like a lot of work. I squint at the red on the end of the feather. Strange that it is this simple thing that makes me different.

Blood.

Mine is a mistake.

My blood *feels* too much, gets sick too much.

My blood is not Clone blood.

The lady in blue says, *Some blood is just better than others, that's why we left the rest of the States.*

She means the second Civil War, which split the United States in two along the Bible Boot. Some people ran away,

17

out of the Boot. The ones that stayed were either Blue or a Clone.

At least that is what the lady in blue says and she can't lie.

The lady in blue says, *Blues are genetic mistakes, which is why we take care of you here.*

The lady in blue says, *Up North, everyone gets sick all the time.*

The lady in blue says a lot of things. She knows a lot of things.

She is probably right. Sometimes I get so mad at everyone here when I shouldn't. The lady in blue gives me pills when that happens. The pills pull a blanket over my thoughts. I know blankets can't really be pulled over thoughts, but they cover things and that is what it *feels* like. It *feels* like the pills cover my angry thoughts.

So, I try to be nicer and I keep reminding myself that if I was in the North, I might be really sick. I am lucky the lady in blue takes care of me, even if I can't go outside yet.

The lady in blue says, *Sacrifices must be made for peace.*

Sometimes I feel like she should *sacrifice* something, but that is the thing. I *feel* too much. I feel so blue.

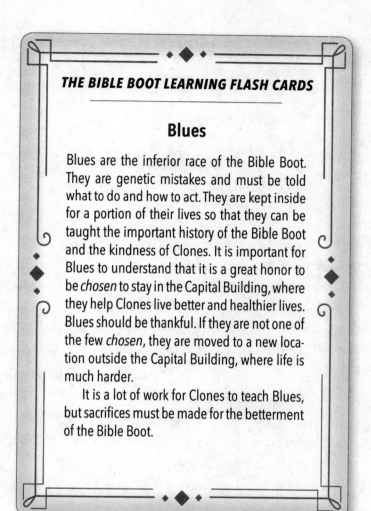

Blues

Blues are the inferior race of the Bible Boot. They are genetic mistakes and must be told what to do and how to act. They are kept inside for a portion of their lives so that they can be taught the important history of the Bible Boot and the kindness of Clones. It is important for Blues to understand that it is a great honor to be *chosen* to stay in the Capital Building, where they help Clones live better and healthier lives. Blues should be thankful. If they are not one of the few *chosen*, they are moved to a new location outside the Capital Building, where life is much harder.

It is a lot of work for Clones to teach Blues, but sacrifices must be made for the betterment of the Bible Boot.

4

Feather

They know I took the feather.

I hear more feet stomping and then voices filled with deep dips.

You would think that Clone voices all sound the same. They don't. You would also think they all look the same. They don't. The guards have the same color hair as the lady in blue, but their faces are different.

I cover my ears and close my eyes so tight that sparkling dots shimmer. It's like constellations behind my eyelids. I don't mean real constellations.

The lady in blue says, *Real constellations are only in the sky*.

The stomping near the small-small room gets louder. I hear three numbers beeped into a keypad—I know the numbers, 911. The door slips open. I open my eyes and see five guards with five shocking/biting machines, which also means five guns. I don't like guns even though I am not exactly sure how they work, but the lady in blue says the shocking/biting machines are called Tasers.

Ira growls from under my left arm.

His growl rumbles, like it is plucking at each of my rib bones.

He has a low growl like that. The kind that makes the guards with five guns on their hips and five Tasers pointed at me take a step back. Their tall black boots stomp on the floor like they are trying to hurt it.

"Inmate Eleven, come forward slowly with your hands up." This is the man with the crooked nose.

I *hate* him. Ira *hates* him.

I crawl out of the small space and make sure that my hands are high above my head, so no one gets confused. Ira stands at my side. Clones don't have wolves and I wonder if they feel naked without them.

"Where is it?" The guard I hate waves the shocking/biting machine in my face.

"Where is what?" He lunges forward and shocks me. I grit my teeth, but I make sure to keep my hands up. Ira growls the rib-rumbling growl again and I try to hush him so he won't get shocked.

"Give it to me or I'll shock your mutt next." His finger hovers over a button that sends a bite to Ira's white collar. "What's your mutt's name? Till?"

"His name is Ira," I say. The guards always call Ira "Till" and I don't know why.

The guard glares at me. "No, his name is Till. Just you wait and see."

"Here." I pull out the feather with my blood on the end. He grabs it with his free hand.

"Now, that wasn't so hard, was it?"

I don't say anything. He punches me under my left ribs. I collapse to the floor, but make sure I keep one hand up, and with the other I hold Ira back. "Answer me."

"Not hard," I say through deep breaths. Ira flashes his teeth at the guards.

"Inmate Eleven, stand up." He twirls the crow feather between his fingers. "Why did you take this?"

It takes me a second to get to my feet. Ira lets me lean on him a bit because my breath feels small and fragile. "I don't know."

"Wrong." He slams his finger down on the button on his belt. Ira yelps but stays standing. "Inmate Eleven, why did you take this?"

I look at him and back at Ira. His legs are still shaking from the shock. "I. I . . . please, I just took it."

"Wrong." He slams the button again. This time Ira growls and the hair on his back bristles up. It's like the anger in Ira can't stay in his skin so it feels up his fur.

"Stop it! Stop it, you are hurting him," I scream.

"Inmate Eleven, why did you take this feather?" His eyes are stone. "Do you want me to hurt Till again?"

"I . . . I wanted to keep my blood." Maybe that is what

22

he wants to hear. I taste salt in the corners of my mouth. Clones hate crying. I wipe my face.

"And why would you need your blood? You have plenty of it in that disgusting body of yours." For a moment I think he is going to hit me again, but instead he lifts the feather in front of my face. "Your blood and the blood of every blue-skin in this establishment belongs to the state."

"Other blue-skins? Establishment?" I have not heard those words before and I have never heard the area outside my door called *establishment*. *Establishment* does not sound like the sun. It sounds like there are more people like me very close.

"You are all trash. Only good for working and—" Another Clone with a shocking/biting machine clears his throat.

The guard stops talking.

He stomps his boot against the floor. I have never heard thunder, but the lady in blue says it is a sound the sky makes and it can be heard for miles. That's what the stomp sounds like—a bang of thunder.

I flinch.

They all turn to leave.

The door opens and closes quickly like an eye blinking.

I slide down to sit on the floor beside Ira.

My hands shake as they tangle in his fur.

Other blue-skins? *Only good for working and . . . ?* I wonder what else he was going to say. I know there are others, but he made it seem like there are a lot of others *here*. I walk to the other side of the room and lay my hand flat against the wall. Is there an Inmate Ten on the other side?

The lady in blue says, *We are nothing alike.*

I get that, I really do, but Ira and I are not alike and I would not hit him just because I could.

Hitting feels like *hate*, but it can't be the same, because *hate* is illegal here.

Illegal means not allowed.

The Bible Boot

The Bible Boot, which is separate from the rest of the continental United States, consists of the former states of Louisiana, Florida, Mississippi, Alabama, Georgia, North Carolina, South Carolina, Tennessee, Arkansas, Oklahoma, Kentucky, eastern Texas, and the lower region of Virginia.

The flag of the Bible Boot is wonderful. It is bright red and shows President Tuba crushing a tiny version of the northern states with his polished boot.

The borders of Elite, the capital of the Bible Boot, are protected by a tall wall that one can see from space. It is the best and greatest wall to ever be built. The Bible Boot was created in 2022, and President Tuba has presided over it for eighty-nine years.

Rules and the military are important in the Bible Boot. Rules like *All Blues living outside the capital of Elite must carry identification cards with their blood type and age.*

Hate is illegal in the Bible Boot. Everyone lives peacefully.

5

Clone Boy

"Who are you?" I say.

A Clone boy with sandy blond hair stands in front of me. I know he is a Clone because he is not blue, but he looks different from other Clones. Shorter, with one brown eye and one blue eye. Then I realize I have never seen anyone near my age before. I guess Clones still have to grow.

I've also never seen anyone with two different-colored eyes. Not even in books.

"Wow. You really are blue." He squints his eyes like that will change my skin. "I have never seen a blue kid before."

"Who are you?" I say again.

He keeps looking at me like a science project. Science is a subject, it doesn't judge—it just inspects. That is how the Clone boy looks at me, not judging, just inspecting. I wonder if he wants to touch me just to make sure the blue is not paint.

"Your eyes are funny-looking." He takes a step closer.

"My eyes are clouds." They are not really clouds, but they are gray and smoky-looking. I think clouds might look like this.

"You are wrong. That is not what clouds look like." I don't like the way he says *wrong*. Like all clouds are the same, but something tells me he has seen them in person, so I don't argue.

"What do clouds look like, then?" I say.

"Like clouds." He shrugs.

I try to help him. "What do they taste like?" Surely one would taste something so fluffy. Once I licked Ira's fur to see what it tasted like. Once I licked my own skin to see if it had a taste.

"You don't eat clouds." His eyebrow raises, but it is hard to tell because his eyebrows are so light they are almost invisible.

"Oh." I like that he is trying to be helpful, but I have never seen a sky so it is still hard to understand. "What do you do with them?"

"You look at them in the sky." He looks up at the ceiling as he speaks.

"That's it?" That seems pointless, that they just float around.

The Clone boy sits on the floor. "No, that is not all. Then they collect water from lakes and then it rains."

"Rain is water." I know that. "Rain falls from the sky."

"No, it falls from the clouds," the Clone boy corrects me. "The clouds get really heavy, then it rains."

"It falls from the clouds after they drink too much water?"

That makes sense. When I drink too much water, I sometimes rain.

"Clouds don't drink," he says.

"But you just said . . ."

"You are strange." He says it like a question. "Different."

"That is what the lady in blue says." He says it nicer, though, like being strange might be an okay thing. "Who are you?"

"Larkin." He sticks out his hand. I don't know why.

"Larkin?" I stick out my hand and copy him. Now both of our arms are hanging out in the air.

"Larkin. Who are you?" He leans forward, grabs my hand firmly, and shakes it.

"Inmate Eleven." I keep shaking his hand because this seems like the thing I am supposed to do.

"No, what is your name?" He lets go of my hand and inspects his own.

I think he is wondering if blue got on him.

That's not how being blue works. It doesn't rub off.

"Inmate Eleven," I say, frustrated.

"That is not a name." He folds his hands in his lap. "Anna, Debra, or Mary. Those are names. I know someone named Truth. Those are names."

"That is what they call me," I say, crossing my arms. A name is what you are called. "The lady in blue doesn't have a name either."

"You mean the doctor? Her name is Abby."

"Abby?" I stick out my hand for him to shake.

"No, your name is not Abby; her, I mean, the lady in blue's name is Abby." The Clone boy, I mean, Larkin shakes my hand again. "You are only supposed to shake hands when you first meet someone and say your name."

"My name is Inmate Eleven," I say again, because that is what they call me.

"Inmate Eleven is not a good name," he says. "You can have another name too."

"Like what?" I ask.

"I don't know." He shrugs.

He shrugs, like I shrug.

Not like the lady in blue shrugs.

"Well, that is not helpful," I say.

"I am not here to be helpful," he says.

I don't like the way his shoulders raise. Like he just realized what *kind* of person he is talking to. Maybe I am just *feeling* too much, though. The lady in blue says I feel too much, and that's probably why she only visits me for a few minutes each day.

"Why are you here?" I ask, trying to stretch the minutes he stays in my small room.

"I don't know." He looks toward the door then back to me. I think he knows.

"You are not smart like the lady in blue." I try to sound nice. "She knows everything."

"Her name is Miss Abby, not the lady in blue," he reminds me.

"And you are Larkin." I smile.

"You are bluer than I thought you would be," Larkin says. He looks at my hair. "Especially your hair."

"I have never thought of you before," I add because I have not thought of him. I did not know he existed. It was only me, Ira, the lady in blue/Miss Abby, the people who blindfolded me, and the mean guards.

Larkin stands to leave, he punches in a three-digit code. He doesn't look mad, but I wonder if that was mean to say. I have not ever thought about him. I did not know he existed and how can you think of someone if you don't know they exist? I wonder if talking is supposed to be like that. It was different from when I talk to the lady in blue and Ira.

If this is a test, I hope I passed.

I hope Larkin comes back.

I hope I can go outside.

I hope I can see the sun.

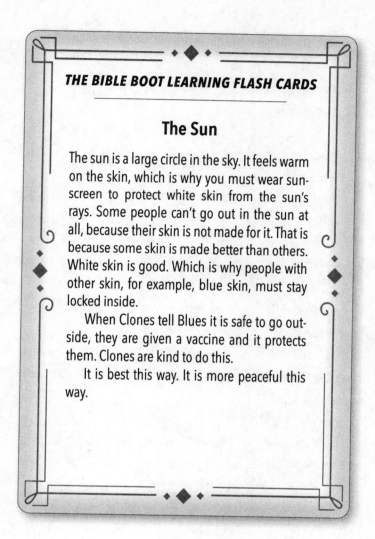

THE BIBLE BOOT LEARNING FLASH CARDS

The Sun

The sun is a large circle in the sky. It feels warm on the skin, which is why you must wear sunscreen to protect white skin from the sun's rays. Some people can't go out in the sun at all, because their skin is not made for it. That is because some skin is made better than others. White skin is good. Which is why people with other skin, for example, blue skin, must stay locked inside.

When Clones tell Blues it is safe to go outside, they are given a vaccine and it protects them. Clones are kind to do this.

It is best this way. It is more peaceful this way.

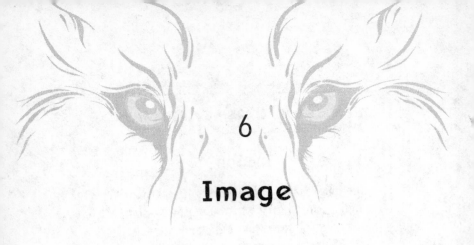

6

Image

Miss Abby says, *Everything white is good. The whiter the better.*

Larkin's skin is white, but also tan. I don't know what that means.

"Ira, do you think Larkin would like me to tell him a story? I could tell him a story about two boys who are like night and day."

Ira yawns and places his large head on his paws.

"I don't think he would think the stories are boring." I rub Ira behind the ears. "I think he would like them, especially a story about two brothers."

The lady in blue hates my stories. Sometimes, I try to tell her about a boy with brown hair and blue eyes who is tall and kills spiders. I have never seen a spider but in pictures they look very frightening.

She doesn't listen.

Then I try to tell her a story about a brown boy with brown eyes who is very strong. He is so strong he can punch through walls and if he wanted to, he could punch through this door.

She hates that story.

Ira lifts his head and tilts it again. Ira knows his name. Whenever someone says it, he looks at them. So many names—Larkin, Ira, Miss Abby, and Inmate Eleven. How do people keep track of names that have nothing to do with how the person looks? I imagine people outside my small room know at least ten people. How do you keep ten names straight? I decide to keep calling Miss Abby "the lady in blue," because it's confusing not to.

The lights in the room start to dim, which makes my shadow grow up the side of the wall like a tree. "Like a tree" is a simile, *a comparison using like or as.*

That's poetry.

I lie beside Ira and my shadow shrinks.

I wonder who named Larkin. I don't remember being a little baby. All I remember is this room, the guards, a few doctors, Ira, and the lady in blue. There must have been a time when I could not put food into my own mouth. What happened then? I had not thought about it until Larkin. It is easy to not think of age when you don't see anyone near your own age.

I guess the lady in blue put food in my mouth, which makes me think I should be nicer to her. I should try harder at the tests. She really has done a lot. I am a slow eater now and I bet I was a slower eater then. It would have taken a lot of time to feed me.

I rub Ira's belly. "Maybe I do need a new name."

Ira rolls on his back.

How does one go about renaming oneself? There are so many words that can be names. I like the word Sky, but I don't want my name to be something I have never seen. Flower would be a nice name because it is supposed to be something pretty, but I don't know if I am pretty. I have never seen myself in a mirror and I have never seen a flower. Only in a book—but that doesn't count.

Floor and Small would not be good names either. I could call myself Blue, but that is too close to the lady in blue and I don't want to be too much like her. I think of other colors—black, green, gray, smoke, depth. I know that smoke and depth are not real colors, but they should be.

Smoke is a cloudy gray and depth is pitch-black with no light.

I sit up quickly and my shadow grows again. This renaming business is very difficult. So many names, but so few that work. I stand and shuffle to my bed with crow feathers. I don't want to be called Crow. *Crow* means bird and blood. I don't like either of those things.

Ira hops beside me on the crow-bed. He curls below my feet, and his shadow grows and shrinks against the wall as he breathes. I watch the shadow. I sit back up and look at my shadow. It copies everything I do. The image is so similar. I don't like the name Shadow. I like the word Imagine even though the lady in blue says I imagine too much. None of these words have lots of my favorite letters.

After *M* and *N*, *O* is my next favorite letter. Imagine and Image are my favorite words. I can make a name out of that. I start spitting out possible names—Imago, Imgine, Imoge, Imogen.

Imogen.

It sounds like Imagine and Image, which makes it perfect.

Ira is asleep, but I gently take his paw and shake it, saying, "Hello, my name is Imogen. Very nice to meet you."

I want to shake it again, but Larkin says you only shake once and I want to practice the right way. I am lucky I have Ira to practice with. I should thank the lady in blue more for that.

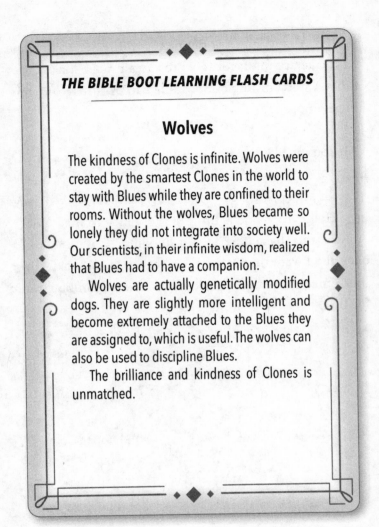

THE BIBLE BOOT LEARNING FLASH CARDS

Wolves

The kindness of Clones is infinite. Wolves were created by the smartest Clones in the world to stay with Blues while they are confined to their rooms. Without the wolves, Blues became so lonely they did not integrate into society well. Our scientists, in their infinite wisdom, realized that Blues had to have a companion.

Wolves are actually genetically modified dogs. They are slightly more intelligent and become extremely attached to the Blues they are assigned to, which is useful. The wolves can also be used to discipline Blues.

The brilliance and kindness of Clones is unmatched.

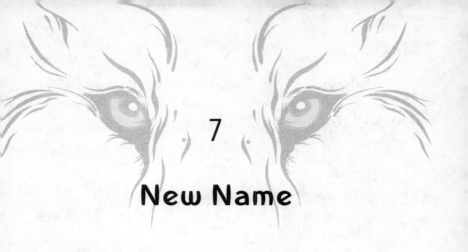

7

New Name

L arkin comes back.

This time he has a pad of paper with words scribbled on it. His handwriting is very good. Mine is not that good.

"I made a list." Larkin sits cross-legged on my bed. The feathers don't seem to be bothering him.

"A list of what?" I sit on the floor in front of Larkin with Ira curled at my side like a half-moon. Ira doesn't seem to mind Larkin, which is nice.

"Of names." He smiles. It almost looks real.

"Oh." I don't want to tell him that I have thought of a name. He seems very excited.

"Tell me if you like any of these." Larkin looks up from his paper pad. "Rose."

"That's a flower," I say.

"It is also a name," he says while crossing the name off. "Mary."

"Merry? Like happy?" I don't know if that describes me very well.

"No, Mary. M-A-R-Y." Larkin spells it out. "Like the name."

Mary does not mean anything, it is not a word I have learned. Larkin watches my face and crosses Mary, not Merry, off the list.

"What about Image. Or Imagine," I say.

Larkin puts down his pencil. "Those are not names. What about Lacy?"

"That sounds too much like Larkin, we might get confused." I frown.

"How would we get confused? You would be Lacy, I would be Larkin."

"The *La* sound gets confusing," I admit.

"I know a Lacy, Lucy, and Louis, and I don't get them confused." Larkin crosses Lacy off the list.

"What kind of names are those?" I don't like when I hear words that the lady in blue has not taught me.

"They are normal names. Image is not a normal name, it is just an image."

"Images are normal." I stand up and make my shadow grow. "See, an image."

"But it is not a name," Larkin says calmly.

"Are Lacy, Lucy, and Louis your friends?" I ask.

"Why would I need friends?" Larkin looks confused. "People do what I say."

"You don't get lonely?" I think of the word a lot. The word *lonely* was in a book about islands that the lady in blue gave me. Islands are like mountains in the ocean surrounded by water. The book was called *Lonely Islands* and I thought it was sad that a mountain in the middle of the water did not have other mountains to talk to.

"What do you mean by lonely?" Larkin puts down the pencil.

"When you want to be around other people or, you know, Clones." I add, "When you feel really empty on the inside."

Larkin tilts his head. "I don't think I have ever felt *lonely*. I am always around other Clones."

"Oh," I say, disappointed that Larkin doesn't know what it feels like to be a mountain surrounded by water.

"Do you feel lonely?" Larkin picks up his pencil and paper.

"I don't have anyone, other than Ira. I was born lonely."

"I guess I was born lonely too." He is drawing a design on the sketch pad. "My father is very busy. I am very busy because of the job I'll have when I grow up."

"What job?"

Larkin looks annoyed but answers, "I am going to be president."

"Of the Bible Boot?" Now, that sounds like a job as big as the sun.

"Yes, President Tuba is my dad." He sighs. "He says that with any luck, I might get to be president of both the North and South . . . again."

"Is that good?"

"Of course it is good. People are dying from sickness in the North; they are getting too old and not using our methods and medicines to stay healthy. Sometimes people in the North like to come down here and *stir up trouble*." Larkin sounds different when he talks now, like the droid voice.

"What kind of trouble?" I swallow. "What kind of methods and medicines?"

"Saying whi . . ." Larkin pauses. "Saying Clones are breaking rules." He points at me. "That we are abusing Blues. But that's not true. Sometimes you have to do things to help lots more people."

"What is *whi*?" I ask because it sounds like he started a word, but forgot the rest.

"I said the wrong word," he says without looking at me.

"Will you be president soon?" I think Larkin might be an okay president, but I don't know exactly what a president does.

"No, Clones live for a long time. Not until this president, my father, runs out of . . . well, until he is gone."

"Runs out of what?" Larkin keeps forgetting words today.

"Nothing. It is not important."

"You don't seem very excited to be president," I say.

"It is a lot of work," Larkin says.

"At least you get to see the sky."

"Yeah, the sky is nice." He has a strange look on his face. I want to wipe it away.

"Larkin."

"Yes."

"What about the name Imogen?" I say.

"Imogen?"

"Yeah, like Imagine and Image together with an O, because I like that letter."

Larkin sticks out his hand and says, "Nice to meet you, Imogen."

I squeeze Larkin's hand firmly. "Lovely to meet you, Larkin."

"Now we have to name your wolf." Larkin smiles at Ira.

"Oh, his name is Ira."

"You named your wolf, but not yourself?" Larkin looks at Ira, who watches him closely. Larkin is not afraid of Ira, unlike everyone else.

"He is alive so I named him." I shrug. "The guards call him Till but I don't know why."

Larkin flinches. "I think they mean it as a joke."

"How is that funny?" I ask.

Larkin rubs his eyes. They look red. "It's not. It's not funny at all."

I don't know why he is upset.

Then I realize there is a big problem.

How could I forget to name myself, when I am alive? Maybe that is why Larkin is sitting in front of me with tears water-falling down his face.

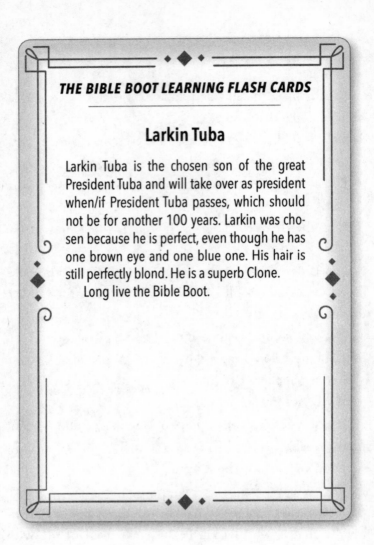

THE BIBLE BOOT LEARNING FLASH CARDS

Larkin Tuba

Larkin Tuba is the chosen son of the great President Tuba and will take over as president when/if President Tuba passes, which should not be for another 100 years. Larkin was chosen because he is perfect, even though he has one brown eye and one blue one. His hair is still perfectly blond. He is a superb Clone.

Long live the Bible Boot.

8

President Tuba

I say my name out loud so I can get used to it.

Imogen.

I want to sound sure when I tell the lady in blue that she can call me Imogen instead of Inmate Eleven.

Rustling static fills the room then: *Inmate Eleven, place your wolf into the other room.*

The voice has no waves or valleys. I have never seen a wave or valley, but I know that waves jump out of the water and valleys dip under the ground. Voices are like that too, they jump and dip and hum. The voice that comes out of the ceiling has none of that. It is a droid's voice.

Even Clone voices have waves and valleys, but drones sound like nothing.

The small-small room has a door that raises up when the voice with no waves or valleys tells me to move Ira. Ira won't go into the small-small room unless I coax him by crawling in with him. Then I kiss the top of his head and crawl back out. The thin door comes down and I feel *lonely*.

I stand up and smooth my blue uniform. The lady in blue does not like wrinkles, and I tuck my blue hair behind my ears so it is not so puffy and noticeable. I think maybe I should try to call the lady in blue "Miss Abby."

It seems only fair if I want her to call me by my new name.

The door clicks open. Miss Abby walks in, followed by Larkin, then a man with thinning blond hair. His hair is so thin he has pulled it forward to cover what looks like a bald spot. Beside him is another boy. He looks a lot older than me, a little older than Larkin.

The boy has *blue* hair.

The boy has *blue* hair and *blue* skin.

I swallow. I want to touch him to make sure he is real.

I think Miss Abby says something. I can't stop looking at the boy with *blue* hair and *blue* skin who has brown eyes as soft as dirt. I have never touched dirt, but I know people can dig in it, so it must be soft.

The older boy's skin is a lighter blue, almost like dust, and his hair is the same. It almost passes for gray, but people don't have gray skin. There is blue skin, like mine, and white skin, like Miss Abby's, Larkin's, and that of the other man in the room.

It is not until now that I realize that maybe there are many different shades of blue skin. Powder blue. If I had to describe the older boy's skin, it would be blue with powder sprinkled in.

"Inmate Eleven, I said, you have a very important visitor

today." The lady in blue, I mean, Miss Abby, fidgets with her hands.

I focus. I want my name to sound right when I say it. I want to say *Hello, my name is Imogen*, but I don't know if this is the right time to correct Miss Abby.

Her eyes already look like a storm.

I don't want them to become two large hurricanes.

I know that eyes can't be storms or hurricanes, but storms can grow into something bigger—hurricanes. I learned about hurricanes in one of the books that Miss Abby gave me—at the very center of a hurricane it is calm, they call it the eye.

I study my feet.

"You've already met Larkin. This is President Tuba and Inmate Three." She points to each person as she introduces them. I want to tell them my name, but with everyone staring, *Imogen* does not feel like my name anymore. "I am so sorry, President Tuba, Inmate Eleven is not used to visitors."

"You said she was intelligent for a Blue." The president inspects me. It is like he is looking for the bad parts of me. "And shouldn't she have started the socializing process by now?"

"Sir, she is the smartest from this batch. She is a bit behind in the socializing process, she has had trouble with a few of her lessons." Then Miss Abby folds her arms across her chest like this is all my fault. I don't understand what part is my fault.

"I see. Well, we can't have a mute traveling with Larkin. Are there other matches?" The president continues to inspect me. I still do not like his eyes. "She can be moved to the fields."

"Inmate Eleven is a ninety-eight percent match. No others come close." Miss Abby shifts on her feet like there is a breeze pushing her. I know there can't be a breeze inside, but that is what it looks like.

I want to say, *Hello, my name is Imogen*. Or, *Hi, I am Imogen*, but the longer they stand there and the more they say Inmate Eleven, the more I think that might be my forever name.

Inmate Three seems content with his name. He is not smiling, but he did not reintroduce himself as something else. Maybe Larkin is wrong, maybe Blues don't have name-names. Maybe our names start with Inmate and end with a number.

Larkin says, "I think she is confused."

"Yes, Larkin, *they* are all confused," the president says.

"No, I think she is confused because her name is *Imogen*. Not Inmate Eleven," Larkin adds. "We like that better than Inmate Eleven."

"It is best not to name *it*." President Tuba taps the shoulder of the blue boy beside him. "Inmate Three has never cared about having a name before, have you?"

"No sir," the blue boy says. His voice has no waves or valleys.

The way he says *no sir* makes me feel so empty I have to speak.

"Hello, my name is Imogen." I stick out my hand just like Larkin taught me.

President Tuba looks at me like I'm a virus. Viruses are very dangerous sicknesses, like the one that started the second Civil War. The lady in blue, I mean, Miss Abby, looks at me and shakes her head; the powdered-blue boy looks worried.

"Inmate Three, explain to Inmate Eleven why *it* has no need for a name." President Tuba folds his arms across his chest.

"Blues are not intelligent enough to remember their names," he whispers. His voice feels too small for so big a boy. Like a mouse voice.

"I can remember names. You are President Tuba," I say. I point at Larkin. "That is Larkin." I look at him so he understands that I can handle names. "My name is *Imogen*."

President Tuba frowns at Miss Abby. "She is uppity. Can we try again?"

Miss Abby shakes her head. "There would not be enough time."

"I like the name Imogen," Larkin says clearly. "I think it is a nice name. I don't mind reminding her if she forgets."

"That is not the point, Larkin, we do not name *them*. *They* do not deserve names."

The way that President Tuba says *they* is like he is talking about a flea, or a tick.

Fleas and ticks are both bugs you want to kill.

"Perhaps we could try it out and see how things go," Miss Abby fake-whispers to the president. "I think she will catch on quickly. Inmate Three did."

"That is true." President Tuba looks at his powder-blue companion. "*It* learned eventually."

Inmate Three flinches, like learning was painful. He glances up at me, trying to tell me something with his eyes as soft as soil.

I want to be helpful so I say, "I am a fast learner."

"What is your name?" President Tuba glares at me.

"My name is *Imogen*." I stick out my hand like Larkin taught me, but the president slaps it away. It stings but does not hurt.

Inmate Three flinches and drops his eyes.

"Your name is Inmate Eleven." The president grabs me by the chin. "Say it." His nails dig into my face.

I wonder if beads will fall out of me if he makes a hole. Just like the blue doll.

Ira growls in the small-small room.

Larkin's eyes are as big as saucers.

I can't lie. Now that I have found my name, I don't want to misplace it again.

So I just stare at the president.

Until he leaves, and Miss Abby leaves, and Larkin leaves without saying bye, and the powder-blue boy leaves without looking at me, and then the voice with no dips or valleys lets Ira come out of the small-small room. I feel better tracing the letters of my name in his fur.

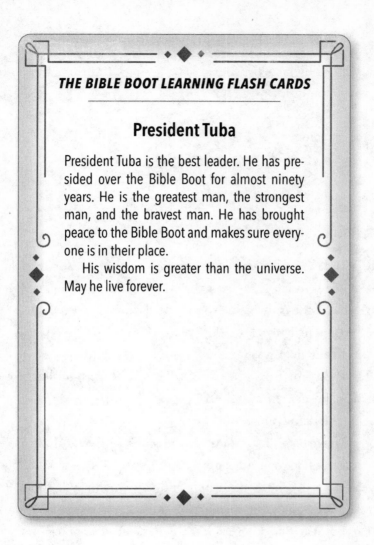

President Tuba

President Tuba is the best leader. He has presided over the Bible Boot for almost ninety years. He is the greatest man, the strongest man, and the bravest man. He has brought peace to the Bible Boot and makes sure everyone is in their place.

His wisdom is greater than the universe. May he live forever.

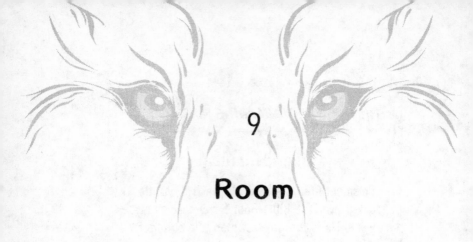

9

Room

Today is a big day. Well, actually, yesterday was the big day. Today is the day that the big thing happens. Yesterday, Miss Abby came to my small room and said, *You are getting a new room.*

I thought I was in trouble about my name.

President Tuba was so angry that his fingernails left two nicks on my chin.

They are scabs now.

I have never had a new anything before. Even my clothes don't feel new. I am happy, but I spent last night saying goodbye to the small room and the small-small room. I wonder if my shadow will look the same in my new room.

If it will look different, like a monster instead of my image.

I might have to change my name again.

I tell Ira we are getting a new room, and I think he is just hopeful it will be bigger so he can trot more and maybe he will be less likely to *go wolf*. I tell the bed with crow feathers I am switching rooms too. I know beds can't talk, but I have been sleeping on it for years and it has been collecting my blood and skin for just as long, so I think a goodbye is important.

Everyone should remember to say goodbye.

I have already had my first meal of the day—toast and beans—the same as it is every day. I don't really like beans, but I eat them anyway 'cause I will shrink smaller if I don't. I slip my plate through a notch in the metal door carefully so it won't shock/bite me. I wonder how long Miss Abby will wait before she shows me my new room. I chase Ira in circles until we are both out of breath, then I rock back and forth a bit. I do that sometimes when I am nervous.

My second meal slides under the door—vegetables, chicken, and bread. I eat the bread and vegetables and give the chicken to Ira. I don't know what time it is. Time usually feels unimportant. Maybe I am not going anywhere.

I hop onto my bed with my back flat against the cold wall. Why would Miss Abby lie? I don't slide my plate back through the door like I am supposed to. If they want it, they can come get it themselves. I want the door to open, because the room feels too small right now, like the walls are marching closer to me.

Like they are leaning in at the hip to fall and bury me.

The door clicks and opens and closes quickly.

"It is early to be sleeping." Miss Abby tries to ignore Ira, who sniffs her feet.

"Early?" It is the same time that it always is. It is feeling a bit like sleepy time.

"I have come to take you to your new room." She hands me a black bag. "If there is anything you would like to take with you, put it in here."

I glance around the small room. There is my bed with the crow feathers, a metal chair in one corner, a small rug on the floor, and a blanket on my bed. The blue beads doll is also on my bed, but she looks like she belongs in the room.

"I don't have anything," I say, tugging at the arm of my shirt.

Miss Abby has a strange look on her face. Not sadness. Clones can't feel sad.

"Right, come this way, Inmate Eleven," she says.

I roll up my sleeve and wait for the guards to come through the door to stick me like they always do before I leave the room, but there is just the lady in blue, I mean, Miss Abby.

"This way, Inmate Eleven," Miss Abby says, staring at me.

I walk toward the door, which is highlighted in light, like the sun is on the other side. "What about the sleepy shot?"

"No shot this time. I want to show you things before I take you to your new room."

"Is Ira coming with me?" I take a step back. I am not going anywhere if Ira has to stay in the small room. Ira rumbles the thunder growl.

"Ira can come with you." She tries to smile, but it looks like it always does. Strained.

I stand in the doorway. Right in front of me, there is a metal door similar to mine. It has a number ten on it and a danger sign underneath it. I step all the way out of the doorway, and the door to my small room closes loudly behind Ira and me. I touch Ira's fur to remind myself that he is there. My door has a number eleven. Under the number is a note: *Restricted (Choice One: Unvaccinated) Dr. Abby Only.*

Miss Abby starts walking, but I can't seem to make my legs move forward. The floor below me looks like blue water, but it is solid. I stomp my left foot against it and it does not give. Maybe it is frozen? *Frozen* means solid, but it can eventually become liquid. It has to be cold for things to freeze and it is not very cold.

Miss Abby turns and motions at me to follow. "This way, Inmate Eleven."

"Is it water?" I look down at the floor. It is blue like me.

"Is what water?"

I bend down and point at the blue surface below my feet. "This. Is it frozen?"

"No, this is a hallway, it leads to other rooms." She points to the floor. "This is blue tile. It is shiny."

"And you are Abby?" She bristles a bit. I point at the door to my old room.

"Yes, I am Dr. Abby." She folds her arms. "We really need to get going, Inmate Eleven."

I follow her down what she calls a hallway.

The blue floor is slick.

I think she might be lying. It looks an awful lot like water to me.

Down the length of the hall, there are metal doors evenly spaced. The halls are empty and just as silent as my small room. Ira seems to like the space, after he sniffs and licks the tile. He is ready to go. The final door has a number twenty-five on it.

At the end of the hall, Miss Abby punches in a new set of numbers and a set of metal doors open slowly. The blue tiles change to white and I wonder if this is snow. I kneel down to touch the floor, but it is not cold like snow is supposed to be.

The lady in blue, I mean, Dr. Abby, keeps walking down the hall with white tile and I try to keep up. She opens another door and it leads into the biggest room I have ever seen. White expands in every direction.

"This is the lunchroom for Blues." Miss Abby keeps walking. "If things go as planned, you might be eating here."

"What is lunch?"

Dr. Abby sighs. "I will explain all of that later."

It takes 105 steps to get to the other side of the lunchroom. Then Dr. Abby starts to climb the tiny floors. I don't follow.

"Inmate Eleven, these are called *stairs*. We have to go up them to get to your room."

"What if they fall?" They don't look very stable to me.

"They won't. These are stairs." She continues to climb

the stairs. "I have gone up them hundreds of times. They are safe."

I follow her. They feel okay, but I would rather walk on something flat. Ira does not mind them. He takes them two at a time, like he has been using stairs for his entire life, but Ira is brave. At the top of the stairs, we turn down a hall (that is what Miss Abby calls it) that looks like trees are on the floor. I decide not to ask if we are walking on trees, because that is a stupid question. Trees grow up toward the sky not sideways.

"I was planning on showing you more, but I think it is best if you rest now." Miss Abby opens a door with no sign on it. "Welcome to your new room."

It is more than twice as big as my old room. The bed is also twice as big. There are also other things in the room. A black box sits in front of a stuffy piece of furniture. The walls are blue with some sort of design on them. On either side of the bed there are what look like floorboards. They look misplaced, like they were accidentally put there.

"How do you like it?" She looks proud of it, so I don't want to say I miss my small room.

"It is very big."

"Yes, your bed is bigger and you have a sofa." She points at the stuffed thing in front of the black box. "That is a TV, but it is not working at the moment."

"What is a TV?"

"You will find out soon, if you are good." Miss Abby does her fake smile again.

"I am good," I say because I want to know what a TV is.

"You have been good, but you must stay good," she says.

"I want to know what a TV is." I try to keep my voice even, but I am feeling very excited. A TV sounds like a very interesting thing.

"Inmate Eleven, this is what I am talking about. You must keep your emotions in check," she says evenly.

"I will try."

"All right, Inmate Eleven, have a good night." Miss Abby turns and leaves. I hear several clicks before I hear her heels continue down the hall with soft tree leaves for floors.

I run to the TV, its face is brown. "Hello?"

It is silent.

Something tells me it is not supposed to be silent. I wonder, *If I am bad, will I get to take the TV back into the small room with me?* I look at my reflection in the TV. I look brown not blue. I like it.

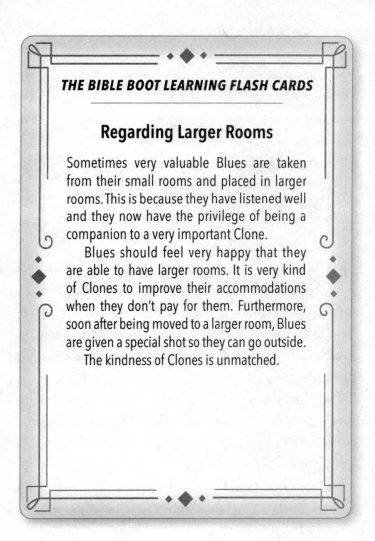

THE BIBLE BOOT LEARNING FLASH CARDS

Regarding Larger Rooms

Sometimes very valuable Blues are taken from their small rooms and placed in larger rooms. This is because they have listened well and they now have the privilege of being a companion to a very important Clone.

Blues should feel very happy that they are able to have larger rooms. It is very kind of Clones to improve their accommodations when they don't pay for them. Furthermore, soon after being moved to a larger room, Blues are given a special shot so they can go outside. The kindness of Clones is unmatched.

10

Shadow-Change

When I wake up, Larkin is there. I sit up quickly because I've never woken up with another person in my room before, and I don't like the idea of being watched while I sleep. Ira is on his back with his legs in the air. Larkin scratches his belly in a way that makes Ira's tail thump against the floor.

The feathers in this bed did not prick the basin of my back during the night. This bed is soft and feels more springy than feathery. The room is dark except for the TV that expels a soft blue color over the room. I like the color blue.

I won't speak first. I don't want to startle Larkin. I don't want to startle any of this away. I am sure I like this new room now and I don't want it to disappear like a dream. In my small room with the metal door that sometimes shocked/bit, I had lots of dreams about large rooms. I even dreamed about outside.

In my dreams, the sun is warm and the grass is blue, even though I know the grass is green, and the sky is blue, which is true. In my dream, Ira keeps the mean guards far away. Larkin is there too and we sit in a circle: Larkin—white, Ira—gray, and me—blue.

Then I would open my eyes and my back would still be stuck by feathers and my eyes would only see fake light and Ira would *go wolf*, and I knew it was all just a dream. Not real life.

Larkin stands up. "Good morning."

"Good morning, Larkin." He skipped over using my name. Maybe he is a bit confused now too on what it is. Last night, I dreamed it was Inmate Eleven again, which is wrong, I think.

"How did you sleep?" Larkin looks past me. Like there is an interesting shadow on the wall, and I think maybe my shadow has changed in this room.

"I like this bed. It is soft." I try to not be so obvious and look behind me to see my new shadow, but it looks the same to me.

"That is good." He looks at his hands now. "I think Ira likes the new room."

I don't say anything, because I don't know if he likes the new room yet. I just got here and slept, and I have not been able to watch and see if Ira likes the new room. Ira jumps on the bed when he hears my voice and settles near my feet. He curls up so that his fluffy tail becomes his own personal pillow.

"I said, I think Ira likes the new room." Larkin talks slower this time.

"I heard you."

"Oh, I thought . . ."

"I just am not sure if he likes the room yet." I shrug. "I will let you know soon."

"Have you watched the TV yet?" Larkin points at the screen filtering out blue light.

"No."

"I can show you how to use it." Larkin walks to the TV and presses a button. People hop around on the screen. I gasp. "It is okay. It is not real." He touches the TV.

I crawl to the edge of the bed. "It looks real." They are not Blue people, they are Clone people with pale skin.

"Come touch it. It is just an image." Larkin taps the TV.

I climb out of bed toward the TV. It buzzes softly. "Why is it humming?"

"That is how you know it is on. It also talks, but maybe we should wait for that?"

"So, TV is a person too?" If it talks and has images, maybe it is a type of Clone the lady in blue did not tell me about.

"No, the TV stands for television. It is an electronic device. It just shows images of real people." Larkin speaks slowly like he knows this is all very difficult to understand.

I touch the screen. It feels prickly against my skin, but I can't touch the people running around inside it. I can't feel anything. "Like shadows?"

Larkin shakes his head. "Shadows don't have colors."

"Like a painting then? Or a picture that moves?" I try to

understand the strange machine. I don't think I will like it if it talks. I don't want it in my old room if I get sent back there.

"Yes, more like a painting that moves," Larkin says enthusiastically as he picks up a little black square and points it at the TV. "Do you want to hear it?"

I shake my head and step away. "I think seeing is enough for today."

"Yeah, maybe." Larkin puts the black square down, but keeps the machine on.

He looks lost today.

Like he knows less than yesterday.

Larkin in my small room knew lots of things, he told me about lots of things. This Larkin is confused and I wonder if a room can change someone. Or maybe the room has changed me and I am not the same, but I can't tell.

"You should get ready, there is a bathroom through that door." He points to a small door on the far end of the room.

I go to inspect the bathroom. Not exactly sure what the word means. My bathroom before was a wet towel and a bucket. This room has shiny silver knobs. I know water comes out of them, from seeing them in books.

"I'll wait outside with Ira until you are ready. There is something for you to wear on the chair."

I yell, "Okay." Even though I don't know why I am getting ready or where I am going.

"Please be quick, Inmate Eleven." Larkin leaves before I can correct him.

The room must be different. My shadow has changed again and so has my name.

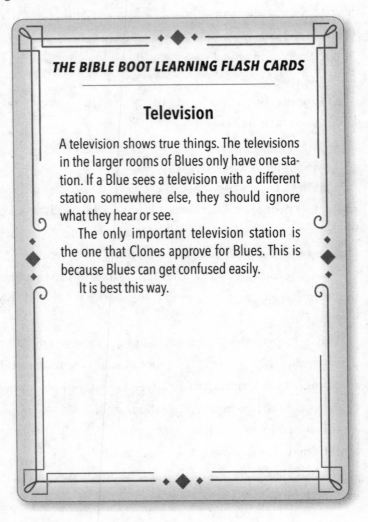

THE BIBLE BOOT LEARNING FLASH CARDS

Television

A television shows true things. The televisions in the larger rooms of Blues only have one station. If a Blue sees a television with a different station somewhere else, they should ignore what they hear or see.

The only important television station is the one that Clones approve for Blues. This is because Blues can get confused easily.

It is best this way.

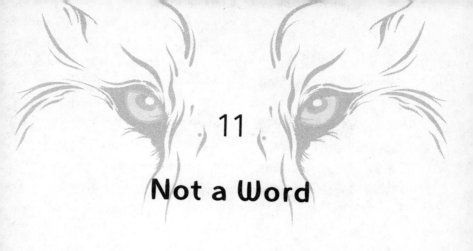

11

Not a Word

Larkin changes too. He is not wearing the white pants and top that he usually wears. I hardly recognize him. He wears pitch-black cloth that fits close to his skin. Except for at the center of his chest, where there is a white stripe. The white stripe is a different material. He looks uncomfortable leaning against the wall near my door.

In my small room he slouched, he ran his fingers through his hair, and smiled.

Inside my new room, he forgets my name.

Outside my new room, he looks down at his feet.

"That was fast." Larkin takes his hands out of his pockets.

I blink. "You said, get ready quickly." I try to sound like him when he talks. There is a drawl in his voice that makes him sound like he is talking real slow.

"You look nice." Larkin smiles.

It is not a real smile.

I can tell because it is not in his eyes.

I know Clones are not supposed to have real smiles, but when Larkin smiles for real, his eyes do this thing. It is like they are shooting out light. I know that eyes can't really shoot out light, but that is what it *feels* like. I hear Miss Abby in my head saying, *Inmate Eleven, stop talking about how you feel and start thinking about what is.*

I don't look nice. I look different. Which I guess is the same thing.

The clothes that Larkin said were on the chair were not really clothes. It was a dress. I have never worn a dress before, I have only seen them in pictures. There were also these elastic things with the dress that looked like pants, but you could see through them. I decided to wear them like pants. I think they are supposed to keep your legs warm. The dress is black and gray. It reminds me of Ira's fur, so I like it.

"You look pretty," I say, and try to copy Larkin's smile.

"Pretty?" Larkin rubs the back of his neck. "I can deal with pretty, I guess."

"What are these?" I point down at the see-through pants I put on under my dress.

"Oh, those are . . . Well . . ." Larkin stumbles over his words. I feel bad for asking.

"They keep my legs warm?" I say.

"Yes and, you know, cover up the blue."

"The blue?" He must mean my skin, and I realize that the outfit covers most of it. Long sleeves, things that keep my legs warm, and the neck of the dress is very high.

"It bothers some people," Larkin says quickly as he starts to walk down the stairs.

"It bothers you?" I say.

"No, just some people. They prefer it to be covered." He doesn't look at me when he talks.

"But, I never see people." And if he doesn't mind, I don't see why I have to wear them. They are itchy and stretch oddly over my knee when I walk. "I can't see too many people, because I might get sick."

"Today you will see more people." Larkin looks at me now. "Today is a big day."

"The lady in blue said yesterday was a big day." I stop a stair above Larkin. The stairs are not so bad today.

Funny how quickly things become okay.

"You mean Miss Abby?" Larkin takes a deep breath like he is nervous. "Today is a bigger day." I know Clones can't be nervous, but that is what the breath *feels* like.

"Who am I meeting today?" There can only be so many people to meet.

"We have to meet Congress, some nurses, and President Tuba today." He takes another deep breath. "Tomorrow there are more people to meet."

"That's a lot of people." My legs feel heavy on the soft floor, like they are sinking in, like I am sinking in.

Larkin looks around before touching my shoulder. "I will be here the entire time. It will be fun."

"It doesn't sound like fun." Ira is sitting down beside me,

right where I stopped on the stairs. Well, his bottom is on my stair, and his two front paws are on Larkin's stair.

"Imogen, you have to try, okay? It is important that you try to be normal."

"You said my name." I am so happy that I almost forget that I have so many people to meet today.

Larkin is uncomfortable again. "I can only say your name when we are alone, okay. I know your name, I like your name, but out here I call you Inmate Eleven."

"Do I call you something different out here?" Larkin looks upset. I don't want Larkin to be upset. "I am sorry, I will try. I will try very hard."

"It is not that." He rubs Ira's ears.

"Oh," I say.

Larkin is still standing on his step and I am standing on my step and Ira is on both steps, and I wonder why it feels like Larkin is far away and Ira is right there.

"You don't call me anything out here. You don't talk unless someone talks to you." Larkin won't look at me when he talks. He just keeps petting Ira.

"You don't have a name out here?" That is not very nice. "How do people know who you are?"

"Everyone knows who I am, Imogen. You are not permitted to talk to me out here. Clones and Blues don't converse." Larkin keeps petting Ira.

By the time I say "Oh," Larkin is walking again and I am confused.

I follow Larkin down the stairs. We don't go through

the doors I came through before. I want to ask Larkin about the soft floors and why they are wearing clothes and feel like treetops, but I don't want to go against the rules. Larkin wants me to try and I am going to try.

There are smaller halls that branch out from the main one and we reach a sterile-looking area. It is painted all white and I can see through the little window that there are needles and women in long coats. I know I don't like this room already, but I also don't want to disappoint Larkin. He seems so miserable today.

"Not a word, Imogen," he says without looking at me.

And I don't say anything, because that is what he said, *not a word*.

I don't say anything. I keep telling myself so I remember.

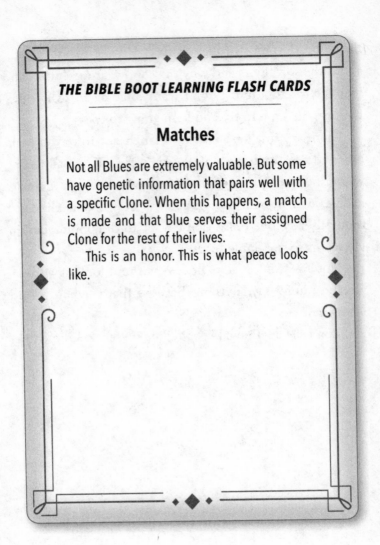

THE BIBLE BOOT LEARNING FLASH CARDS

Matches

Not all Blues are extremely valuable. But some have genetic information that pairs well with a specific Clone. When this happens, a match is made and that Blue serves their assigned Clone for the rest of their lives.

This is an honor. This is what peace looks like.

12

Spirit Height

Larkin changes when he enters the white room. I don't mean changes into something else. That is called magic.

It is Larkin's spirit that changes.

It lifts up higher. He looks a full inch taller.

All I can see is his back, stiff and straight, like it is trying to say, *I am taller—I am better than you.*

Larkin was already tall and for the first time I wonder how much older he is than me. Maybe a year. Maybe two?

Age is a difficult thing. For example, Ira is the same age as me, but somehow seems much older. Larkin sometimes seems the same age as me, but right now he seems centuries older. *Century* means 100 years.

On the day the president visited my small room, I saw the same thing happen to Larkin's spirit. It was not as obvious as this change, but I saw it then too. His shoulder rose a little and his face was difficult to understand. It is like he is trying to be a picture in a book instead of a boy. It reminds me of Miss Abby with her fake smile that pulls tightly at her cheeks.

Ira is right in front of me. I think he notices that Larkin changed too, because he is not walking as close to him as he did before and he sniffs the air curiously.

In two seconds an entire body can change.

How strange is that?

I want to tell Larkin about his ability, maybe it really is magic, but I remember I am not supposed to talk. So I follow him across the shiny white tile that reflects a morphed image of my face.

I see three women in the room and they change when Larkin enters too. They stand straighter, but not in the way that Larkin does. His comes from his center, the three women just look like they are lifting their shoulders to their ears. They also smooth their crisp white dresses with their hands. I don't know why, because there are no wrinkles in them. The women are also wearing see-through pants. Their dresses have large black buttons up the front. I wonder why they are all wearing the exact same thing; I want to ask, but I remember I am not supposed to talk right now.

"Your Majesty." The tallest of the three women bows. "You are early. We are so sorry, we will be ready in a moment."

Apart from their dresses, they all look very similar except for their height. One woman is very tall, taller than Larkin. I guess it is not difficult to be taller than Larkin, he is a boy even if his spirit age is different. The other one is Larkin's height and the last woman is a little taller than me. The shortest one flicks some pointy objects over a sink and I know this is not going to be a fun day. Larkin lied, which is strange because Clones are not supposed to be able to lie.

"Please hurry. We are on a strict schedule today." Larkin pulls a circular metal object from his pocket. It makes a ticking noise.

"Yes, of course, Your Majesty. We are ready now." The shortest woman points at a chair that looks like it is covered in plastic. It looks sticky. The other short woman looks at me. "Stand on this scale."

I walk past Larkin to a metal object with numbers scattered at the top. I don't know what a scale is, I don't know what I am supposed to do. So I just stand there for a moment looking at the numbered machine.

"I said get on the scale, *Blue*." The short woman's voice is cruel and even, which is confusing because Clones are not supposed to be cruel, just even.

I step on the machine and a little arrow twirls around and lands on a number. The short woman says the number loudly. "Sixty pounds, very small for her age."

I don't say anything, because Larkin said I should be silent. I look at my feet. Ira is standing right beside me off the scale. He seems confused by the commotion, tilting his head this way then that way.

"Sit down here." The tall lady points to the sticky chair. I step off the scale and walk across the room to the chair. "How old are you?"

I don't say anything, partly because Larkin said don't talk and partly because I don't know. I look at Larkin. His eyes are glazed and I wonder if I am really looking at Larkin or a shadow of Larkin.

"She is not the talkative type." Larkin chuckles. "She is twelve years old."

"A bit young," the tall nurse says before adding, "but a good match. I like the quiet ones, they know their place."

"Silent is best." Larkin snorts.

I try not to frown, because no one else is frowning.

I don't want to bring sadness to the room.

Larkin has never said he dislikes my voice. I watch Ira pace from one side of the room to the other. He is not in full *gone wolf* mode, he is not prowling but he is inching closer to it. I think it is the floor that is throwing him off. He can see himself in it and I think he thinks there is another one of him, and he doesn't like it.

I would not mind if there was another one of me.

I think I would like the company.

The short lady comes toward me with a sharp object, which makes my heart start running, which makes Ira growl, which makes everyone frown. And I feel guilty because I just made everyone frown even when I was trying to not make everyone frown. The object is very long and my palms feel sweaty. I know I have been bitten by one of those things before, but I was asleep for it. I woke up with a circular hole in my skin.

"Get that mutt under control," the short lady growls. "I

need to draw blood and give you some vaccines or you will be sick in a week."

I try to calm my heart so that Ira will calm down, but I can't. I don't like when they steal my blood. It is mine and I don't want the sharp thing to bite me and I don't want to be in this small room. I want to be back in my small room with just me and Ira and not so many people. I look at Larkin.

His eyes are not like ice now, they are warm and filled with life.

"Inmate Eleven has never given blood without being sedated." He rolls his eyes. "She is confused."

"Oh, yes of course, because of her age." The shortest nurse pauses.

Larkin walks across the room, his eyes switch between ice and warmth. "Inmate Eleven, this is called a needle. It will go into your skin and take a blood sample. These samples are needed to ensure your health. The next needles are vaccines that will make it so you can go outside."

I nod my head because I am not supposed to talk.

I nod my head because if I talk, I might cry-talk.

I don't want the women to see me cry-talk.

I don't want Larkin to see me cry-talk.

"It will hurt, but only for a moment. With time you will get used to it and not give these wonderful ladies so much trouble." Larkin winks at the woman.

"Sorry," I say. It slips out. I don't mean to say it. I don't think I mean it, but the look he gave the women made me think that I had been very difficult.

Larkin raises an eyebrow. "Next time, do better." His voice is cold. He coughs once, clearing his throat.

The women swarm in and they bite me with the needle several times, and I stay calm because I don't want Ira to get in trouble, but it hurts and I am mad. I am very mad at Larkin because he said he would be beside me the entire time, but he is not.

I don't know the boy who leans against the cabinets.

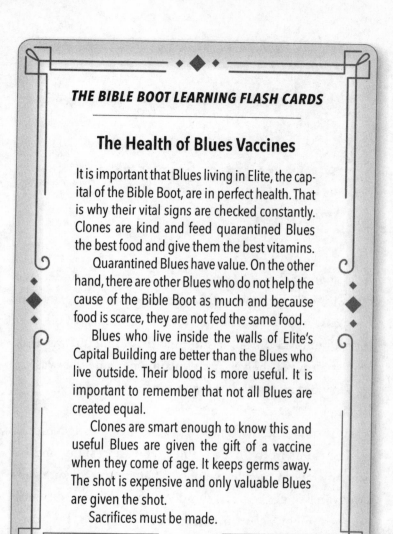

The Health of Blues Vaccines

It is important that Blues living in Elite, the capital of the Bible Boot, are in perfect health. That is why their vital signs are checked constantly. Clones are kind and feed quarantined Blues the best food and give them the best vitamins.

Quarantined Blues have value. On the other hand, there are other Blues who do not help the cause of the Bible Boot as much and because food is scarce, they are not fed the same food.

Blues who live inside the walls of Elite's Capital Building are better than the Blues who live outside. Their blood is more useful. It is important to remember that not all Blues are created equal.

Clones are smart enough to know this and useful Blues are given the gift of a vaccine when they come of age. It keeps germs away. The shot is expensive and only valuable Blues are given the shot.

Sacrifices must be made.

13

Inmate Sixteen

My arm aches. They bit me in the same shoulder five times before I was allowed to leave, which seems like a big cost to go outside. The women all thanked Larkin at least a hundred times for stopping by. All he did was lean against a row of shelves and explain what a needle was.

They did not say anything to me.

Not even *good job* for not crying.

It is sometimes hard not to cry, because I feel so much.

The floors in the halls are not white and shiny, and Ira is happy he can't see his second self anymore. Larkin walks slowly in front of me. His shoulders melt down and I think his eyes might be warm again, but I can't tell, because I can't see his face.

"You did well," he says so low I can hardly hear.

I don't say anything, because I am not supposed to talk. I rub my shoulder instead and I think one shot will scab over just like the nicks the president left on my chin.

"I am sorry, but they needed the blood samples and you

needed the new vaccines. You need them to go outside." Larkin says this even lower. "I thought warning you might make it worse."

I don't say anything, because I think I am mad.

It is not the same kind of mad that I feel toward the guards and their biting machines. It hurts too somehow. Like there is a small fire at my center and each word Larkin says kindles it, but also burns me. I have never seen fire, but this feeling makes fire feel very dangerous. Miss Abby says, *Angry and mad are not usual emotions—you just are or are not*.

Larkin looks over his shoulder, his eyes *are* warm again. "I really am sorry." I don't say anything, because I don't have the heart to say, *I don't forgive you*. "One of the shots will scab over and we will have matching scars on our right shoulders now."

I glare at him.

Larkin's voice changes back to being clinical. "Those were the nurses. They will take your blood weekly now to make sure you are healthy." He looks up at a circular object on the wall. It makes a ticking noise that I don't like. "They are really very nice most of the time."

I want to say they are very nice to *you*.

They like *you*. They don't like *me*.

Larkin keeps walking. If those were the nurses, that means I have to meet Congress and the president today. I don't want to do either. I don't know what Congress is, but it seems like it is a big deal and I am already tired.

"We meet with Congress in an hour." He stops at a door that says INMATE SIXTEEN (VACCINATED) on it. "But before that, we need to do something about your hair and, well, some other things."

Larkin pushes in a code and the door pops open. First, I see the wolf because Ira runs toward it, tail wagging. They stare at each other for a moment before making the choice that they are friends. I have never seen Ira like this. He looks younger, hopping around with this other wolf. He looks happy.

I like it.

It is not until I look up that I see the Blue woman. Her skin is so blue it is almost the color of night. Her nails are the same shade of blue as mine. The Blue lady is very tall and skinny. Her lanky arms cross over themselves.

"Inmate Sixteen, Inmate Eleven needs to be cleaned up," Larkin says. Larkin turns to me. "Inmate Sixteen is mute."

"What is mute?" I say before I remember I am not supposed to talk.

"She can't talk," Larkin says.

"Just like me?" Just like I can't talk to Larkin or anyone else.

Larkin rubs the back of his neck. "No, she . . . she was born without a tongue, she could not talk if she wanted to."

I don't say anything, because I feel bad for talking.

I was upset about not talking for a day.

She cannot talk for her entire life.

How is one born without a tongue? Miss Abby says that

Clones never have that problem. Clones are born perfect and I see now why that might be a good thing; you would never have to worry about being born without a tongue.

"I will be back in forty minutes." Larkin turns to leave the room. "Inmate Eleven, I really am very sorry."

Larkin was right. Inmate Sixteen has no tongue. I know because she yawned once and I looked in her mouth very quickly and there was nothing where her tongue was supposed to be. Her room is bigger than my small room, the one that Ira *goes wolf* in. There are lots of shelves holding bottles of things.

The bed is familiar. Metal with a mattress stuffed with sharp feathers, but it only takes up a small part of the room. There is a huge circle that holds water, and taps that let out water in the room. First thing Inmate Sixteen motions for me to do is to get in and scrub myself.

"I scrubbed this morning," I say as she pushes me toward the large circle filled with water.

I don't know if she understands or doesn't care. She points at the circle filled with water again. Tub. I remember it from a book that the lady in blue, I mean, Miss Abby, read to me a long time ago. I get in, I have never sat in water up to my neck before. It is warm and makes me feel weightless.

I like it.

Inmate Sixteen hands me a bar of soap, which smells very sweet. I have never been given soap that smells sweet.

I scrub with it. She puts slimy liquid in my hair while I am scrubbing and works it through. She goes to her shelves and picks up a comb. I tense, knowing what is coming next. I hardly comb my hair. I just run my fingers through it and hope for the best.

It hurts, but she tries to be gentle, holding the ends in one hand while working out the knots. After a little while she can move the comb smoothly through my hair. She adds more liquid and works it in. Then she fills a jar with water. She taps me on the shoulder and I turn around. She puts her hands over her eyes and I copy her. She pours the water over my head, washing out the things she just put in my hair.

I want to ask her if she likes her room. If she always has been here. I want to ask what her real age and her spirit age are, but I don't know if I am not supposed to talk in here. Plus, she can't answer. Ira puts his paws on the lip of the tub and watches the water. Inmate Sixteen scratches him behind the ears. He leans into her palm.

When I am out of the tub, she pushes me behind a screen and gives me another bottle of liquid. She motions that I should rub it on my skin. I follow directions. The liquid makes my skin feel like plastic. It makes my skin shine like the floors of the nurse's office and I don't like it. I worry I might see my reflection in myself.

The screen I am behind looks different on one side.

The front of the screen is pitch-black.

The back side has a long blue snakelike stitch.

Above it there are yellow stitches that remind me of stars.

I have never seen stars, but I know they are bright and sparkle and some line up into pictures.

I think it is amazing that the stars thought to organize themselves into giant outlines. The one on the back of the screen is the Big Dipper. I have seen it in a book Miss Abby gave me about constellations. The name of the art on the back of the screen is *Follow the Drinking Gourd*. I know because the name is stitched in right above the stars that lead through a forest to something that looks like a black snake. Then there is an arrow that points to something that looks like cars I have seen in books Miss Abby showed me. It feels like a treasure map leading somewhere that *feels* like the sun.

Inmate Sixteen inspects several blue dresses before she hands me one with see-through pants to wear. She picks a dark blue one. It is almost the complexion of her skin. I want to touch her skin. To be sure it is really that perfect. But she moves away before I can. After I am dressed, she sits me down in a chair and combs my hair again. When all the new tangles are worked out, she begins to pull it back in sections. Like she is creating a raised snake down the middle of my skull.

When she is done, she turns the chair to look at me. She smiles. Her teeth are perfectly white and she smiles like I smile. She looks into a box and pulls out something red and puts it on my lips. She then motions for me to press my lips down on a piece of paper. It was like she put the red stuff on and then took some off. She points to the mirror and I look. I think there is a new person in the room until I realize that I am looking at myself.

My lips are stained.

My hair is tamed.

My skin is blue, but it is easier to ignore.

I am looking at myself in the mirror when I hear the faint click of the door as it unlocks. I can't turn away when I hear Larkin's voice. Then I see him in the mirror, his mouth is open like he is trying to form words and nothing is coming out. My eyebrows scrunch together and Larkin opens his mouth to try to speak again, but again no words come out. I turn around quickly because I am worried that he has lost his tongue somewhere in the last hour.

When I look in his mouth, I can see he still has his tongue.

Inmate Sixteen comes beside me and sprays something on the snake/braid she made with my hair. I turn to her, confused. No one is talking and I don't know if I am supposed to not be talking and I don't want to make any mistakes. Inmate Sixteen smiles and folds her arms across her chest. Her arms are so delicate, they remind me of clouds. I know that arms can't be clouds, because clouds float in the sky and are not thin and bony, but that is what her arms feel like. Like they are weightless against her body.

"Am I not supposed to talk?" I ask Larkin, who stands with his mouth slightly open.

He blinks a few times before saying, "No, you can talk right now."

"Why are you not talking?"

Larkin rubs the back of his neck. He has been doing that a lot lately. "I don't have anything to say at the moment."

I look at Inmate Sixteen and back at Larkin. "Your eyes, they look like they have something to say."

His eyes do look like they want to say something. I don't know what, but they are scrunched at the sides, like they are trying to figure out something difficult. He kicks his foot against the floor, I don't think he notices that he is doing that. Inmate Sixteen pats my shoulder and gives it a little squeeze. I wish she could talk, because I think she might know why Larkin is acting funny.

"Nope, I just came to get you. We have to go visit Congress now." Larkin looks at the door and back at me.

"I can talk at Congress?" I ask. I want to know all the rules before we leave.

"No, no talking again."

"Okay," I say.

"Okay." Larkin turns to Inmate Sixteen. "Thank you for your assistance."

Inmate Sixteen makes some motions with her hands. They are graceful and flow like water. I know that hands can't flow like water, because water is not solid, but that is what it looks like. Larkin motions something back, but when he does his cheeks look bright red and he turns to leave the room before Inmate Sixteen can motion something back.

I follow Larkin out of the room, not because he tells me to (he left very fast), but because Inmate Sixteen pointed to him like I should follow. I have to walk very fast to catch up with Larkin, his legs are very long and each of his steps are two of my steps.

"What was that?" I ask.

"What was what?" Larkin glances over his shoulder and looks startled that I am there. Maybe Inmate Sixteen was wrong, maybe I was not supposed to follow him.

I move my hands in the air, trying to imitate the motions I saw a moment ago. "This," I say.

"Oh." Larkin sees that I am struggling to keep up and slows down. "Sign language."

"Sign language?" The words sound funny in my mouth. Miss Abby never taught me anything about sign language.

"Yes," Larkin says simply.

I think I am supposed to be quiet now, but I want to know what sign language is. It looks so pretty, like water, and I wonder if I can learn to talk like water. I don't say anything for a moment just in case Larkin was going to say something else, but when he is silent for a moment I say, "What is sign language?"

"What did I say about talking?" he says.

"What is sign language?" I say again, but softer.

Larkin exhales loudly. "It helps people communicate without words."

"Is it magic?" That sounds like magic to me.

"No, people agree on certain signs that mean certain words. So, if you know what the signs mean, then you make them and can communicate with someone who can't hear or speak."

"Still sounds like magic." I say it because it does sound like magic. Who would even have such a wonderful idea of creating this language?

Larkin stops and looks down the length of the hall. "It is not magic." Larkin holds his hand in a fist and raises his pinkie. "This motion is the letter 'I.' By stringing together lots of motions, you make a sentence."

I copy the motion. "I."

"Exactly." He looks at me funny.

"What is it?" I want to know what his eyes want to say.

"You . . . you almost look whi—I mean, like a Clone," Larkin says.

"No I don't, my skin is blue."

"Not as blue as some. Sometimes I forget." Larkin looks like he wants to touch my skin to make sure, but he keeps his fist at his chest, making the "I" sign. "Maybe it is because we are almost the same age. I did not realize there were young Blues."

"There are young Clones. Why would there be no young Blues?" I cross my arms. Sometimes Larkin doesn't seem very smart. "We have to grow up. That's science."

Larkin shakes his head. "I mean, I never *see* any young Blues. It, it makes it easy to forget you are Blue."

"Maybe it is easy to forget because you don't have blue skin." I don't mean it in a mean way, but I see *my* blue skin, everyone reminds me it is blue.

Larkin starts to walk down the corridor again. "You are probably right."

I think I hurt his feelings. I know Clones can't have their feelings hurt, but he looks like I just slapped him across the face. I follow Larkin down the hall, where the floor is not all white. There are blue speckles on the surface. I think our destination is a huge set of doors in the distance. The word *Congress* sounds like a big word, which would be behind big doors. I can see two men standing in front of them.

They don't have blue skin.

"Will you teach me sign language?" I ask Larkin.

"No," Larkin says softly. "Blue people are not allowed to learn sign language."

"Inmate Sixteen knows it," I say.

"I know," Larkin says meanly. The closer we get to the guards, the straighter his shoulders get and I know it is time to stop talking. So, I push all my thoughts back into my head and not to my mouth.

When we finally reach the brass doors, I realize they are not brass. They are another shiny material I don't know. I don't know many materials other than concrete. Concrete is what the floors of my small room were made of.

Larkin's shoulders are fully pulled back. I follow a little farther behind because this Larkin is my least favorite Larkin. The straighter he stands, the more I remember him letting me get poked, and the less I remember him saying sorry. In my head, I keep doing the sign for "I" because it calms me. I wish I knew more words than "I," then I could tell Larkin how angry I am without talking. Then again, signed or otherwise, Larkin has no idea what anger is, so it would be a waste of time.

When we get to the doors, both men standing on opposite sides bow very low. Larkin does not even smile at them. He just pushes the doors open. They are not very heavy. They look like they should be heavy, but they swing back and forth. I have to speed up to make it through the doors before they swing closed. I almost run into Larkin because he stops walking after a few steps into the room.

When I glance up to see why we have stopped, my throat becomes suddenly dry.

My lungs hug themselves and I know for a fact I don't like Congress.

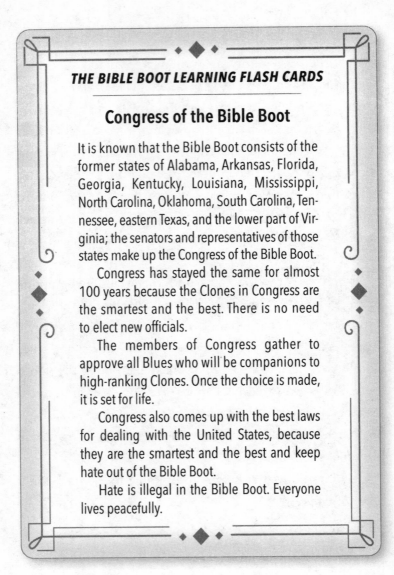

THE BIBLE BOOT LEARNING FLASH CARDS

Congress of the Bible Boot

It is known that the Bible Boot consists of the former states of Alabama, Arkansas, Florida, Georgia, Kentucky, Louisiana, Mississippi, North Carolina, Oklahoma, South Carolina, Tennessee, eastern Texas, and the lower part of Virginia; the senators and representatives of those states make up the Congress of the Bible Boot.

Congress has stayed the same for almost 100 years because the Clones in Congress are the smartest and the best. There is no need to elect new officials.

The members of Congress gather to approve all Blues who will be companions to high-ranking Clones. Once the choice is made, it is set for life.

Congress also comes up with the best laws for dealing with the United States, because they are the smartest and the best and keep hate out of the Bible Boot.

Hate is illegal in the Bible Boot. Everyone lives peacefully.

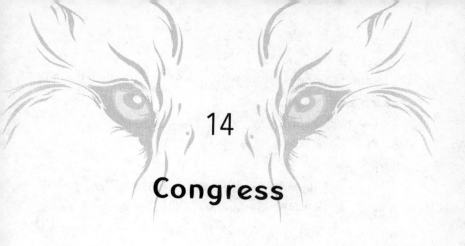

14

Congress

The Congress room has to be bigger than the sun.

The room is a circle, the sun is also a circle, but they are different. The room circle could hold hundreds of my small room. Probably thousands of my small-small room. The floors are shiny, I can see my reflection and it looks so different from this morning. The dark blue dress makes my skin look almost white instead of light blue.

I find Ira at my side and touch his fur. It doesn't help.

I have never seen so many Clones in my life.

My hands shake.

In the center of the circle there is a single chair. It doesn't look like a chair that you want to sit in. It looks like a chair you sit in when you are in trouble.

I can feel so many eyes looking at me. They crawl on and under my skin. It makes me want to jump back in the tub in Inmate Sixteen's small room. Larkin walks slowly to the center of the room.

I don't remember following but before I realize it, I am sitting in the chair.

The bad chair.

The chair I do not want to sit in, and Ira sits close beside me.

Larkin walks up a small flight of stairs to a larger chair that is covered in funny designs. Everyone stays standing until Larkin sits, and I think I have done something wrong again, because I am already sitting. I try to count the Clones in the room, but it is too difficult. All I see are eyes. All I hear are whispers. I watch Larkin, hoping he might offer a smile, but his eyes are glazed over.

He is someone else.

Someone I don't like.

"Congress, may I present Inmate Eleven for your approval. Her blood has been drawn and she has been vaccinated." Larkin nods his head in my direction. "She is twelve, not very bright, but very healthy according to the records that were handed to you this morning."

I think my mouth is open.

Not like open just breathing, but open as in stunned.

Calling someone *not very bright* is not very nice.

I know Clones don't know the difference between nice and not nice, but I think Larkin knows better. He knew better in my small room. He knew less in my new room and out here he knows nothing. All the eyes in the room push on my skin even though they are not touching me. I feel sticky with eyes.

"She is too young." I hear a voice shout from somewhere, it is impossible to place. All I see are eyes.

Young for what? Young to be Larkin's friend? I don't think he is more than a year older than me even though he is much taller.

"Younger than most, yes," Larkin says, then raises an eyebrow. "Desperate times call for desperate measures."

A female voice says, "And why is she female?"

I wonder if girls are not supposed to be friends with boys in the world outside of my small room. In the books Miss Abby let me read, boys and girls were friends. I want to tell the woman that I am good at being friends with anyone. I don't actually know that, but it feels like a test and I want to pass.

Besides, Ira is a boy and we get along great.

"Like I said, desperate times, desperate measures." Larkin rests his chin on his hand, covering his mouth to cough lightly. His voice sounds rehearsed, like someone wrote this down for him to say. I don't think it is the voice of someone around my age. "These are the cards we are given at the moment."

"Can she speak?" I hear another set of eyes with a voice.

Larkin tilts his head toward me. "When spoken to."

Satisfied whispers fill the room.

It reminds me of water, like how a wave would sound, each hum falling over the other. I know I don't know exactly what a wave sounds like, but an abundance of soft voices is as close to it as I have heard.

A man in a long red dress stands. "Inmate Eleven, who was your Overseer?"

I look at Larkin. I know I am not supposed to speak unless spoken to and I was just spoken to, but I don't understand what he is asking. I look down at Ira and rub his fur. Larkin says nothing.

"Answer me, Blue."

"What is an Overseer?" I say because I don't know and I don't know what else to say.

Larkin decides to talk now. "As I said before, she is twelve. Induction age is usually sixteen or seventeen. Her education on the way things work is limited at the moment. Something we will be fixing very soon."

The man clicks his tongue. "She is too young."

"She is also very small." I hear a woman talking. "Isn't she small for her age? I bet she can't donate more than a pint of blood at a time."

A lot of people are talking now.

Their voices lap over each other just like waves in the ocean do. I have never seen an ocean, but the lady in blue says that is how oceans work. The waves come to the shore, stretch, then go back. Waves are just salty water. I don't understand why water is salty, but the lady in blue says some things just are. I don't like that answer, just like I don't like that no one answered my question. I don't know what an Overseer is and I feel like I am supposed to.

I try again, a little louder, "What is an Overseer?"

The room is silent again.

Just eyes, no waves. I wonder if I have said something wrong.

"I thought you said she only speaks when spoken to." The man with the red dress stands up again. His brows are attacking each other.

I think he has forgotten because everyone started talking. I think he has forgotten that he asked me a question. "You asked me a question," I say because it is true.

"I will not tolerate this sort of disobedience." His face looks angry. I know it can't actually be angry, because Clones don't feel angry, but that is what it looks like.

Larkin interrupts, "She is very excited to learn her responsibilities."

"Excited and uppity are very similar," a woman near the back of the room shouts.

Larkin's voice bellows through the room, "I was talking, and are you, ma'am, excited or uppity?"

Everyone is very quiet.

Even Ira.

I did not know Larkin's voice could be that loud, it was like ten of his voices joined together to yell. He is sitting tall now and his spirit age is very old even if his real age is young. I know Larkin is important, his voice is important and I wonder if when his shoulders get taller, he is just trying to remind everyone that he is important.

Larkin speaks again. "An Overseer, Inmate Eleven, is the person who teaches you."

A voice in the crowd mumbles, "And punishes you."

I ignore that voice because Larkin seems to be the one with the voice that everyone thinks is important. My eyes brighten. "My Overseer is the lady in blue, I mean, Miss Abby, I mean, Dr. Abby."

"That is correct." Larkin nods then addresses the rest of the people in the room. "Abby noted that Inmate Eleven has a tendency to take things literally and ask a lot of questions, but she is in all other aspects, as you can see, fit to serve."

I want to be helpful so I add, "Miss Abby also says I *feel* too much, and I am working on that." I put my hand over my mouth quickly. I forgot that I was not supposed to speak, but the crowd does not seem too upset.

"Feeling and thinking are difficult traits to train out of them. That is why they are usually older," an older lady says to the group as if I am not there. "And Dr. Abby has a tendency to sympathize with them."

"I don't recall you being so picky when your match was chosen." Larkin rolls his eyes. "Do you have a better suggestion?"

Everyone is silent.

So silent I wonder if anyone will ever talk again.

I can hear breathing now, in and out at the same time. Everyone breathing in and out in harmony. I really want to see waves one day. I wonder if, on a day when Larkin is not being very tall and very loud, he would show me waves.

Probably not. They are probably not real.

I told the lady in blue that the first day she taught me about oceans. I told her that no bowl could hold that much water. Miss Abby said that the ocean was not held in a bowl, it just was.

That seems impossible. Everything is held by something. My eye sockets hold my eyes and the floor holds the chair. Sometimes, I hold Ira. I told the lady in blue that I could hold the ocean if I had to. She said that I did not understand what holding means.

The room is still silent.

People swivel in their seats and Larkin sits with his right leg creating an angle on his left. When two corners come together perfectly, they create an angle. Your joints can create angles when you bend them just right. The lady in blue taught me that too. I think about breaking the silence, because I don't think anybody likes it. Not even Ira, he is pacing a bit now. I think about saying these are the things the lady in blue, I mean, Miss Abby, taught me, but Larkin's face frightens me right now. It is traced in shadow.

"I propose to approve Inmate Eleven." I hear a faint voice from the row of eyes.

Larkin nods.

"I second that proposal." Another faint voice.

Larkin nods again. I don't understand the look on his face now. I don't understand why there are so many looks on so many faces. Clones are not supposed to feel all these things. At least that is what the lady in blue says. Maybe they are all acting. It makes them seem very human, very

Blue. Then I look down at my skin and remember that I am the only Blue in the room.

"All in favor, please raise your hands." Larkin flicks his hand in the air and brighter lights illuminate the people in seats. "I want to see who agrees."

When I see all the faces with the eyes, I wish it were darker again. There are so many people. More people than I have ever imagined, and they all look very different. Some have dark hair. Some have light hair. I thought Clones all looked similar.

One thing they all have in common is white skin.

Everyone raises their hands.

Larkin nods. I look at all the hands in the air, all different shades of white, but none blue.

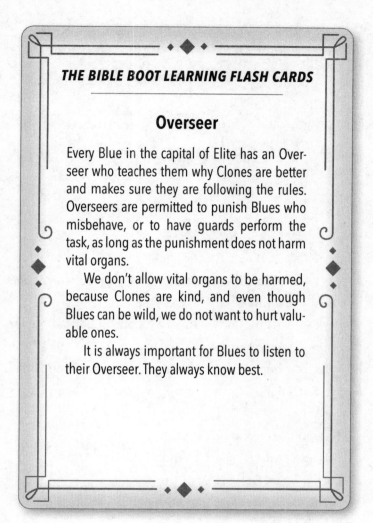

Overseer

Every Blue in the capital of Elite has an Overseer who teaches them why Clones are better and makes sure they are following the rules. Overseers are permitted to punish Blues who misbehave, or to have guards perform the task, as long as the punishment does not harm vital organs.

We don't allow vital organs to be harmed, because Clones are kind, and even though Blues can be wild, we do not want to hurt valuable ones.

It is always important for Blues to listen to their Overseer. They always know best.

15.

Lunch

I follow Larkin down another hall.

His shoulders have not settled down, but they shake like he is coughing silently.

Larkin leads me into a small box and presses a button. It reminds me of the small-small room. There are a lot of buttons, but he presses number twenty-two. Then it feels like my stomach is moving up and my feet are pushing down.

The doors open and it is bright.

"My eyes hurt," I say. Ira blinks too.

Larkin stops walking. "Put these on."

"Glasses?" I remember seeing a pair in a book Miss Abby once read to me.

"Glasses that block light," Larkin says. His shoulders are still touching his ears.

"Is this light?" I look around the hall. There are no bulbs.

Larkin opens a door and walks to the other side of the room. There is a wall that is not a wall, you can see through it. I think it is a window, because I have seen them in books. I follow him.

"That is the sun," he says.

"The real sun?" It is so bright, I am glad I have the glasses that block light. It is also smaller than I thought it would be. I hold my hand up and I can cover all of it with my palm.

"The real sun." Larkin watches me while he talks. I know because I can *feel* it. "It is magnificent isn't it?"

"It is better than all the pictures," I say. The sun is round and perfect and feels strangely warm. "How far away is it?"

"Millions of miles. If it was any closer, it would burn us." Larkin's shoulders are relaxed now and he sounds like small-room Larkin.

"Does the sun have a name?" I close my eyes and feel the warmth, even through the window.

"Sun."

"That is not good enough," I say because it isn't. It might be smaller than I thought, but it is warmer than I imagined.

"No, it isn't, is it." Larkin walks away from the window.

"What is all that gray stuff?" I ask. "It looks like the surface of the moon. Are we on the moon?"

"That's just the quarry," Larkin says.

"What is that?" I tilt my head, trying to look farther out.

"A place with a lot of special rocks." Larkin's shoulders tilt down a bit. "They are very important."

I nod.

"We will be late for lunch with President Tuba if we do not hurry."

I follow him out of the room, sad to leave the sun when I have only just met it, but the warmth is still held in my skin. I wonder if you can collect warmth from the sun in your skin and use it later.

While we walk, Larkin explains that I have also just seen the sky, and I feel overwhelmed. The sky is bigger than I thought, but I don't see stars and it makes me a little confused.

Larkin reaches for the handle of an opulent door that looks like it is outlined in gold and glimmering stones. "Remember, don't talk."

"Unless spoken to!" I finish, almost giddy from sunshine.

"Imogen. I am serious. Not. A. Word." I nod because the way he says *not a word* scares me. Like if I say a word, there will be no more words ever.

The room is brighter than the hall. It is drenched in sun, like this is the sun's favorite place in the world. The actual room is an awful bright red color. I don't like it. It hurts my eyes.

It reminds me of blood.

It reminds me of my blood.

"Exactly on time," President Tuba says.

"Yes, sir." Larkin walks farther into the room, but motions for me to stay where I am.

"How did everything go?" The president does not look up at Larkin. He is busy signing papers. He signs one, then adds it to a pile beside him.

One mountain of white paper grows while the other gets smaller.

"One hundred percent of Congress approves," Larkin says, and I can tell he is smiling.

"Did you do the light trick?" President Tuba glances up from his papers. "Just like I told you?"

"Yes."

"Good job. You are going to be an excellent president someday." The president stands. "Now, where is *it*?"

President Tuba walks past Larkin toward me. It is not until then that I notice his Blue friend is standing just behind me. Actually, his friend seems a darker blue than before and his eyes look very sad. The president smiles. Not a real smile. His teeth are not white. They are yellow.

I don't like his teeth and I don't like his smile.

"A perfect match for harvesting. The victories of science." I don't think the president is talking to me so I don't say anything. "Inmate Eleven, you will be having lunch with me today."

I nod my head.

"Not a peep. Perhaps *it* is a fast learner." He looks over his shoulder at Larkin. "You have school. I will have *it* sent back to *its* room after lunch."

"I don't mind staying." Larkin looks worried.

"I do mind. I need to talk to your newest toy without you." The president's voice booms loudly, flooding the room.

Larkin flinches like he is afraid the voice will hurt him. He slowly walks to the door.

His eyes scream, *NOT. A. WORD*.

After Larkin leaves, a table is brought in by several people who look a lot like me. They all have varying degrees of blue skin. I want to touch them to make sure they are real, but I don't want to get in trouble. I try to stand out of the way as the room is converted for lunch. While everyone is darting around, President Tuba sits at his desk, signing papers.

The lady in blue, I mean, Miss Abby, once read a story to me about these creatures called bees. They buzzed and helped make things grow, but the Queen Bee did not work, she just made more bees. I wonder if the president is doing that. Making more people each time he signs a sheet and adds it to the white mountain. Ira watches the other Blue people hustle about. He is still, but his eyes follow them curiously around the room.

I don't see any wolves with these Blue people.

Once the table is placed in the center of the room, dishes are added and forks and knives. I have never seen dishes that sparkle. It looks like stars are dancing on the plates. I want to ask if they collected sunshine to put into the dishes. I want to ask how one thing can sparkle so much, but I don't want to get into trouble.

Not. A. Word.

After the dishes are placed on the table, two people who look like me carry in a big chair. I have never seen a chair so big. It is the color of the sun and very shiny. I think the sun and the chair must be brothers. They put the chair down with a thud at the head of the table. Two other people who look like me bring out a small square table and place it to the right of the other table. They also bring out two objects that fold out into chairs.

I wonder if that is what magic is. They did not look like chairs before and now they are perfect and ready to sit in. Next they bring out even bigger plates, with food tumbling off the sides. They put a large plate on the big table. On the small table, they place a dull plate. I get very excited because I see sandwiches, which are my favorite. I hope I get to sit at the table with the sandwiches and the magic chairs.

That table seems best.

Once everything is set up, the president keeps signing papers for a moment. The room is empty except for Ira, Inmate Three, the president, and me. I think we are waiting for President Tuba. I study the room more as I wait, and Ira stays so close to me I can feel his fur on my leg. The ceilings are so high that I expect to see the blue sky when I look up. The carpets are so soft that they remind me of snow. I have never felt snow, but I think this is what it would feel like.

The president stands and struts to the table with the very shiny chair. He takes a white circle from a container filled with white circles and swallows it saying, "We must keep up appearances." I am not sure what the president is talking about, but next he sits down and begins to fill his plate with food. I wonder if I am supposed to sit down too, but the Blue boy does not move; his eyes meet mine and his head gives a slight shake that says, *No*. So I stand still too.

I think of trying to be a statue.

A statue is something that is not alive.

It is made of stone. Right now, I am made of stone.

"Sit," the president says with a full mouth. He gestures toward the small table to the right of him. "And keep that Till of a wolf away from me."

"Thank you, sir." The Blue boy sits down in one of the magic chairs; I follow.

"So, Inmate Eleven, your Overseer told me that you ask a lot of questions." The president takes another noisy bite and swallows. "Is that true?"

I don't know what the right answer is; I look at his Blue friend and he nods like I should talk quickly. "I do." I say that because I think I do ask a lot of questions, but just because I want to understand.

"What sort of questions?" The president takes a huge gulp of a red liquid.

"Depends," I say, because it does.

"What question are you thinking of right now?" President Tuba does not look at me, he is more interested in the red liquid.

"How is liquid red? I have never seen red liquid," I say. "And that white circle you ate."

"This is wine. Those circles are mined by Blues like you

and given to all Clones in the Bible Boot to help them live longer." He swirls the red liquid in his glass. "My followers believe everything I say and so should you. Anything else?"

"Are these chairs magic?" I say, because it is a question that I have.

"Hmmm . . . ," the president says, finally looking at me. "Do you know what *stupid* means?"

"Yes, not smart." I swallow.

"You are *stupid*. So are your questions." He licks his fingers. "You just need to follow directions. Now eat."

I don't want to eat. The last thing I want to do is eat. I don't think I am stupid, but I do always ask questions and I never know the right answers. Even the lady in blue says I always get the answers wrong. I grab a sandwich and break off a piece for Ira.

I try to keep the water in my eyes, but tears spill on my plate. The president's eyes push me and when I look up, he is smiling.

He is smiling a real smile. While I cry.

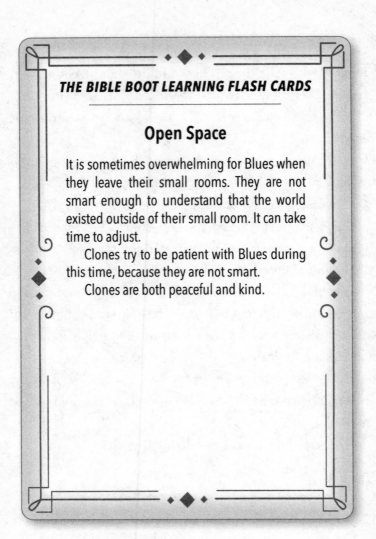

Open Space

It is sometimes overwhelming for Blues when they leave their small rooms. They are not smart enough to understand that the world existed outside of their small room. It can take time to adjust.

Clones try to be patient with Blues during this time, because they are not smart.

Clones are both peaceful and kind.

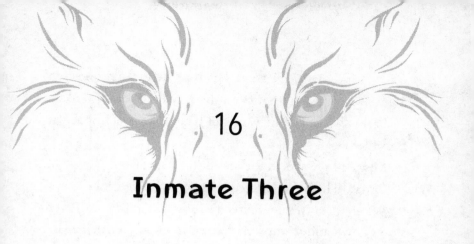

16

Inmate Three

I have to eat all my food before President Tuba lets me leave. He even insists that I lick the plate to show that I am grateful. The Blue boy, Inmate Three, walks me to the small box that is called an elevator. He has not spoken to me at all today. His skin is different, so blue, blue like the sky might be before a storm.

"Why is your skin bluer?" I ask because I don't understand.

He doesn't say anything.

"Why is your . . . ," I start.

"It has been a difficult week," Inmate Three says. Like he has answered my question.

My stomach drops with the elevator, and Inmate Three puts a reassuring hand on my shoulder. His hand feels like a blanket. I know a hand can't be a blanket, but blankets feel safe and they keep you warm and that is what his hand feels like.

When we get off the elevator, the hall is empty. He

walks briskly with his shoulders hunched into a question mark. It is very different from the way that Larkin walks.

Larkin walks like he wants to take up as much space as possible.

Miss Abby walks in the space she is given.

Inmate Three walks like he wants to be invisible.

We are near Inmate Sixteen's room when Inmate Three slows down and stomps his feet on the floor a little harder as he walks. Like his feet suddenly get very heavy, he only walks funny for a few steps, then a white slip of paper slides from under Inmate Sixteen's door. Inmate Three scoops it up very quickly and pockets it.

I think this is a secret and I hope no one saw. The hall is empty, which I think is good. I want Inmate Three to look at me so he knows I won't tell anyone. I want him to tell me what the paper says. I wonder if they are friends.

I would like a friend.

A friend other than Larkin, a friend who looks more like me.

I want to ask Inmate Three where his wolf is, and if *they* joke and call his wolf Till too. I want to know why the president wanted to make me cry. By the time we reach the stairs, I am desperate to ask him something, anything. I am almost at my room. The place I have wanted to be all day, except now I wish the stairs would grow. I wish they would grow like the Tower of Babel, which I read about in a book.

"This is your room, correct?" Inmate Three points to the door.

I am so surprised by his voice, it's like crushed velvet. He talks different when he is not around President Tuba. I like this new voice. "Yes."

He opens the door and takes a step in. "Do you like your room?"

"Yes." I try to elaborate to keep the conversation going. "My small room made Ira *go wolf.*"

He nods toward Ira and shakes his head. "You named him?"

"Yes." I want to ask if he named his, but I remember I don't see a wolf with him and I don't want him to think I am bragging. I want to be his friend.

"What is *going wolf?*" Inmate Three crosses his arms and leans against the wall by my door, giving me plenty of space.

I put my hands behind my head and pretend they are ears. "It is when Ira gets real wild and his ears go back like this. Then he paces back and forth."

"He doesn't like small spaces."

"No, do you?" I ask.

"No living thing should like small spaces. Even if they are trained to." Inmate Three moves toward the door. "How old are you, Inmate Eleven?"

"Almost thirteen," I say because I don't want him to think I am too young to be his friend. "You can call me Imogen. If you want."

"Almost thirteen. They start younger and younger." He whispers, "Much too young for this, Imogen."

"Start what?" I ask while smiling because he used my name.

"So, Ira is your only friend then?"

"No, I have the lady in blue, I mean, Miss Abby. There is Larkin too," I say proudly.

"So, no friends then." He folds his arms over his chest again, takes a deep breath, and it sounds hard for him to breathe. "We are in the capital of the Bible Boot, Elite. You only have Blue friends here."

"Why is your skin bluer?" I ask because he is finally talking and I want to understand.

"It has been a sad week." He turns to leave. "You can call me Kin, if you want."

I think he accidentally drops the paper that he picked up from Inmate Sixteen, but he would have had to take it out of his pocket, and there is also the fact that he drops it on the table. Which would be a strange place for it to accidentally fall.

I don't run to it until Inmate Three, I mean, Kin, is out the door, because if it is an accident, I don't want him to take it back. I begin to unfold it, but the handle to my door jiggles, so I stuff it down the top of my dress.

Then my friend Larkin walks in. The paper is a secret I don't want to share with him and you are supposed to share secrets with friends—I think.

Blues in Elite, the Capital of the Bible Boot

The most valuable Blues live in the capital of Elite, and it is important that they do not associate with outside Blues or even with one another. Clones have found that when this happens, lies can be spread. Blues lie a lot.

For example, you might hear rumors that no Blues live outside the walled capital. That is a lie.

This is why it is important that Blues only converse with Clones when spoken to . . . It is best this way.

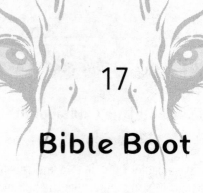

17

Bible Boot

Larkin looks at me funny. "Is everything okay?"

"Everything is very good." I don't know why I say very, it makes me sound like everything is the opposite of very good. "Is everything okay with you?"

"You are acting weird." Larkin sits on the small couch in front of the thing called a TV.

I notice as he walks that his spirit is not trying to spring from his body. Actually, it is almost the opposite; he hunches over and puts his hands in his hair when he sits. He is coughing a bit again and I wonder if he has a cold.

I want to ask him what is wrong.

I also want him to leave so I can read the paper Kin left behind.

"Is everything okay with you?" I ask again.

Larkin looks at me and I realize this is the first time he has really looked at me since this morning.

"How was lunch?" Larkin asks like he already knows the answer.

"I think I said something I was not supposed to," I say.

"Everyone says something they are not supposed to in front of him." Larkin whispers it like it is our little secret. I don't like the way he whispers. "But by the looks of things, you did not say anything too bad."

"By the looks of things?" I don't know what that means. I did not know you could look different just from talking to someone.

"Your skin." He nods at me like I should understand what that means.

"My skin?"

I look at my hands.

Something is a little different.

I can't figure it out. I am still blue.

I wonder if my hair is different. I push past Larkin to the small bathroom to look at myself. My hair is still blue. Something is different, but my spirit is not taller; it is the same as it always is.

Larkin hovers in the doorway now and I want to slam the door in his face. Miss Abby would say, *That is your emotion, Inmate Eleven, you must control it.* She is right, I don't know why I am so upset. I have never wanted to slam anything before. I get closer to my reflection, something is different. I touch my face and run my fingers through my hair. I can't figure it out.

Larkin says, "It is subtle."

He says it like he is trying to be helpful.

"What is subtle?" I ask because I want to know.

Larkin looks down. "You are a little bit darker blue. I barely noticed."

I look back at myself. He is right. It is hardly noticeable. It is like a slight shadow hovers over my blue skin. How could that happen so quickly? Then I think of Kin. He said it had been a bad week for him. It had been a bad hour for me.

Larkin adds, "I don't mind."

"You don't mind?" I say. It's my skin not his, why would he mind?

"No, I don't mind that you are darker now." He says it like he is saying something important.

"Oh," I say. He says he doesn't mind like I should thank him. I would not mind if his skin changed color, so I say, "Thank you."

Larkin doesn't say anything after that, he just looks down again and I know he is keeping a secret. I don't feel so bad about keeping the secret that is literally on my chest now. I leave the bathroom, still stunned that my body could change without me knowing.

"I am supposed to watch a video with you now." Larkin follows me out of the bathroom.

"What is a video?" It sounds interesting, not as interesting as my note, but I want to know what it is.

"A video shows an image, like the TV, but you can watch the same thing over and over again." Larkin sits down on the small sofa. "It is a very important video."

Now I am more interested in the video than the note.

"The lady in blue would have told me about it if it was really important," I say.

"She was not allowed to tell you about it until you got older." Larkin folds his arms. His spirit looks really short when he folds his arms.

"Why?" I ask. It is strange that some things are left to teach later, especially if they are supposed to be very important.

Larkin's arms are crossed when he says, "Just because."

"Because?" I say back.

"There is not a reason for everything, Inmate Eleven." Larkin sounds mad. Which is unfair because he is the one who told me about the special video.

I sit down beside him and he doesn't say anything, so I say, "My name is Imogen."

"Your name is Inmate Eleven," he says quickly.

"You said, when we are alone, my name is Imogen," I say to remind him because that is what he said.

"I was thinking." Larkin runs both hands through his blond hair and I wonder if my hair would ever turn that color. "We might slip if we do that."

"Slip?"

"Yeah, like I might accidentally call you Imogen in public." Larkin raises an eyebrow like that would be a very big mistake.

It would be sad if he called me the wrong name, but it would be sadder to always be Inmate Eleven after I just discovered a new name.

"I won't mind if you mess it up sometimes," I say because I don't want him to feel bad about having to remember two different names.

"That is not what I mean," Larkin says.

"Oh." I fold my arms like Larkin and my spirit feels even shorter than his.

"You could get into a lot of trouble if I call you Imogen," he says.

"Why would I get in trouble?" I ask. I am not the one messing up.

"Maybe we should just watch the video." Larkin says it like the video has all the answers.

"Does your soul feel smaller when you cross your arms?" I ask Larkin.

"What?" Larkin looks at me funny.

"Your soul, when you cross your arms, does it feel like a cage?"

It feels like a cage to me. I uncross my arms.

"No."

"Oh."

"It feels like a barrier," Larkin says.

Something in his voice makes me sad. "A barrier from what?"

Larkin gets up and pushes a funny-looking square into a bigger square and turns the TV on. The words *Bible Boot, A History* flash in grainy letters on the screen. I have already learned history. The lady in blue, I mean, Miss Abby, taught me a lot of history, but I guess she skipped some things.

Larkin sits back down and crosses his arms.

Barriers are made to keep things separate.

Just like borders.

"A barrier from you." Larkin stares at the screen as he talks. "It makes it easier."

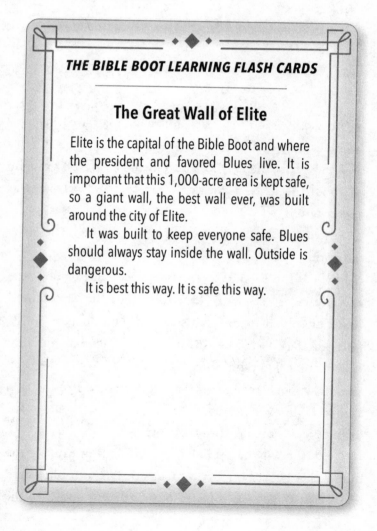

THE BIBLE BOOT LEARNING FLASH CARDS

The Great Wall of Elite

Elite is the capital of the Bible Boot and where the president and favored Blues live. It is important that this 1,000-acre area is kept safe, so a giant wall, the best wall ever, was built around the city of Elite.

It was built to keep everyone safe. Blues should always stay inside the wall. Outside is dangerous.

It is best this way. It is safe this way.

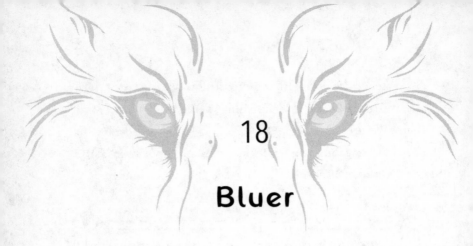

18.

Bluer

The grainy picture clears and a woman wearing red holds up a doll.

"I know this; the lady in blue, I mean, Miss Abby, taught me about the dolls." I don't tell him that I always get the answer wrong.

"Just watch." Larkin's arms are folded so tight it looks like it must hurt.

I look at the TV and see what I expect. Sitting opposite the lady in red is a girl; she is Blue. For the first time, I notice myself checking what shade of blue she is.

Is it a dark blue like Kin's skin right now, or medium blue like my skin right now?

Or is it powder blue with a slight shadow like my skin used to be in my small room?

Everyone's blue is always changing.

Next, the lady in red holds up two dolls in front of the Blue girl. I hear the lady say what the lady in blue used to ask me, *Which one is better?* The little girl points to the blue one. The one that looks like her. I smile on the inside because maybe the lady in blue was wrong. Maybe that is why we are watching this, and Larkin is sad because he feels bad for the lady in blue, I mean, Miss Abby.

The lady in red shakes her head; it's a mean shake as she says, *No, this doll is better than the blue doll.* There is a date at the bottom of the TV and I realize I never know what date it is. The next scene is the same situation, but this time a different date is on the bottom of the screen—a later date. The girl looks a little older. The lady in red asks, *Which doll is better?* The girl looks a little bit different; I can't put my finger on it. She points to the blue doll and I want to jump off the couch and say, *See, see she understands!*

The video skips again and this time the girl looks taller and I realize what is different, her skin is so much bluer. Like before a storm. The lady in red has a confident-looking smirk on her face. Like she knows what the girl is going to say. I think she is being overconfident. *Overconfident* means you are too sure about something you can't know. The girl obviously knows which doll fits with her soul best. The lady in red holds up both dolls and asks, *Which one is better?* I am about to turn to Larkin and say, *I answered the question right*, when the girl points to the other doll.

The Clone doll.

I swallow my voice quickly. The lady in red nods. *Why is it better?* The girl crosses her arms. She crosses them tighter than Larkin does, like she wants to hold her spirit in her body. The lady in red asks again, *Why is this one better?* The girl looks around the room and I want to help her find whatever she is looking for. She looks lonely. Maybe she had a wolf at some point, but it is not in the room now. I feel bad for her wolf, it is probably locked in a small-small room. I reach for Ira, like somehow petting him will help her.

The lady in red says it again, *Why is this one better?* The girl unwraps her arms.

Her face turns a darker blue before my eyes, it is like her soul sinks to the bottom of her feet.

I know your soul can't actually sink to the bottom of your feet, but that is what it looks like. It looks like all the light from her soul is sinking from her face. It looks like the girl has been suffocating for years.

She says, *It is better because it is not Blue.*

I turn to Larkin, his arms are wrapped around his waist as tightly as the girl's are on the TV screen. He won't look at me. The lady in red keeps talking, saying, *And if you are Blue, what does that mean?*

The girl grinds her teeth. I can feel it in my bones.

She says, *It means you are a slave. It means you work in the capital of the Bible Boot, Elite. It means you work in the Capital Quarry making medicine for the virus in order to keep Clones healthy. Our job is to keep Clones healthy.*

I think my heart stops.

Slave means someone who is owned and has no freedom. I learned this: A long time ago, people were slaves. Not now. I try to swallow, but I feel like choking. It hurts near my heart again. Ira climbs into my lap.

The lady in red turns to the TV, saying, *All Blues can be taught that they are inferior. It takes a firm hand, but the insolence can be forced out. Inmate Thirteen from group twelve is a perfect example. She is not a match for any ranking officials and will start her service in the Capital Quarry today.*

Larkin gets up to pause the video. "Maybe that is enough for today." He clears his throat again before coughing loudly.

I don't say anything.

I just look at him and grind my teeth.

I grind them hard. I grind them like the girl in the video. Ira growls lowly and I don't realize for a moment that he is growling at Larkin. He has never growled at him before.

After he stops coughing, Larkin walks to the door. "Any questions?"

"You are sick?" I say.

"It's a cough. Probably a cold," he says. I stare forward. I think of the note sitting over my heart. I wonder what it says and I want Larkin to leave. I don't want him to ever come back to my room.

Larkin lingers by the door. "We will finish this tomorrow," he says before he leaves.

I want to say the word out loud. I want to understand the word and how it comes out of my mouth, but I can't. I remember once I told the lady in blue that people were stupid for just deciding people were slaves. She crossed her arms over her chest and moved on. She is a liar.

Slave. I am a slave.

It takes me a while to get in bed. I unfold the letter Kin

gave me, or dropped. It is addressed to me. I look at my name again. *Imogen*. Did Larkin tell her? Her handwriting is wobbly, like something written quickly when no one was looking. I keep looking at my name. I can't even focus on the rest of the words yet.

My name, Imogen, not Inmate Eleven.

I have never gotten a letter before. Miss Abby once taught me how to write a letter. You start letters with *Dear so and so*. Not *so and so*, you put the person's name, and Inmate Sixteen put my name. I feel suddenly sad that she knows my name and I don't know hers. I can't even ask her, because she has no way of answering. You end letters with phrases like *Sincerely*, or *All the best*, or in this case *Be safe*.

I never learned to end a letter with *Be safe* and it makes me afraid to read what is on the paper.

Slavery

The term *slave* is often seen as a harsh word, but it is not. Blues are slaves because they serve Clones, and it is best this way because Clones take care of Blues. Blues are not smart enough to take care of themselves.

Slavery is not illegal in the Bible Boot, but hate is illegal. Blues are not hated, they are simply unintelligent and require guidance. Clones are kind enough to tolerate Blues, even with their infinite shortcomings, and if Blues listen, they might get a few white pills to keep them well. Such is the kindness of Clones.

19.

Truth Tubman

Dear Imogen,

Must write quickly, my name is Truth Tubman. Your life and Ira's life are in danger. You are too young to bear this burden. They have not told you yet, but the Clones are not Clones, they are white. They are Elitists. That means they think they are better than everyone who is not white. They especially don't like people who are different.

You look different because you are a Black American.

Your skin is Blue because you are sad—your freedom has been stolen.

That kind of sadness wears on the soul and shows on the skin. There is a word for it—generational trauma. I know this is difficult to understand. I have attached a flyer from the North to help. The president doesn't want anyone to know what he is really doing at the capital. He claims to keep the North away because he doesn't want any sickness or viruses from the North to enter the Bible Boot. The president tells his followers they are better than everyone and that they can be well forever. They want to use us forever.

Open Letter to the Citizens of the Northern United States of America and the Southern States of the Bible Boot:

As we all know, the election of President Tuba in 2016 led to the second Civil War in the United States. In 2020, a virus called Xeno burned through the world. The symptoms were unprecedented and included cognitive reactions that made certain people hate and distrust their neighbors. It was as if the virus blurred people's vision, making them hate everything and everyone different. It was an atrocity!

In the United States, the Civil War raged on and in the Southern States the number of citizens showing symptoms of Xeno increased. By late 2021 it was obvious that many people recovering from the virus had lingering symptoms like anger and hatred–somehow hate stitched itself even more firmly into the fabric of the South. December 2021 brought more infections and endless protests. The people fighting for equality grew tired and weary.

After much violence, the second Civil War ended
with a treaty. The Northern and Western United States
continued to practice democracy and social isolation for
one year to stop the virus named Xeno from spreading.
The Southern States of the Bible Boot cut themselves
off from the rest of the country with walls that they
claimed could be seen from space. The United States
was no longer united. The walled capital of Elite is the
most secretive part of the Bible Boot and a place where
human rights are being violated every single day.

Now, nearly ninety years later, the United States is
still not united.

After separating, the Southern States experienced
a second wave of Xeno. A new variant of the virus
spread through the Southern States and President Tuba
claimed a white pill would cure everyone. The pill is
given to all white people in the Bible Boot, it makes
them think they can never get sick—even though many
still suffer from common illnesses. They follow President
Tuba blindly.

The fact that this treaty and separation was permitted
by the Northern and Western States is an atrocity.
The fact that innocent minorities, specifically Black
Americans, were prevented from fleeing from the
atrocities of the Bible Boot due to the Fugitive Slave Act
is not only disgusting, it is un-American.

Many Black Americans were purposefully exposed

to the second mutated virus and died. Others survived and were used for ongoing testing. We do know that Black Americans are being used in some capacity by the ruling white population. We can no longer turn away and pretend that a form of slavery is not happening right below us. We must not pretend it can't reach us.

We must ask ourselves why we let this separation sparked by hate last so long. Perhaps we in the North and West were worried the original form of the virus, Xeno, might wake up and spread if the borders reopened. Maybe it was the fear of the lethal second variant, which continues to rage in the Bible Boot eighty-nine years later.

Or maybe we all have lingering symptoms of the virus, Xeno–perhaps our empathy has been permanently damaged.

We have crossed the border into the Bible Boot and organized a movement to help enslaved Black Americans. The movement is difficult. The mutated virus is dangerous, but we've been silent for too long. The time is now.

The movement started in the capital of the Northern United States, Washington, DC, and quickly the spirit of protest scaled the walls of the Bible Boot and spilled into Virginia.

The pain we found once we crossed into the Bible Boot both shocked and terrified us. Many Black

Americans who live in Elite, the capital of the Bible Boot, have lived in fear and isolation for so long that their sadness has become something they wear.

Instead of having a rainbow of beautiful brown skin in every shade, their skin has taken on a bluish hue. Blue from sadness. We have learned that the tint of blue often changes depending on their moods—the blue growing stormier with age.

The Elitists in the walled city of Elite have set up a system where they are considered perfect. These powerful few have brainwashed and kept their followers in the dark about what happens in the walled city of Elite. The situation in the Bible Boot is kept alive by fear.

These are some of the atrocities we know are actively being committed in the Bible Boot.

- Elitists in the walled city of Elite call themselves Clones and have taught Black Americans that Clones are incapable of being wrong.
- The Black people living in the walled city are being enslaved in the cruelest ways. They are forced into isolation, brainwashed, used for hard labor, and made the victims of mad-science experiments.
- There seems to be evidence that the Black people in the city of Elite are used for more than hard labor. Their genetic information is valuable to the Elitists.
- Enslaved Black Americans are also forced to mine a special rock that Elitists claim slows aging and

helps cure diseases, making Elitists live extremely long lives. We have acquired one of these pills and discovered it is simply a sugar pill. We think the pills are a hoax to hide something else.

- Outside the walled city, in the rest of the Bible Boot, racism runs rampant and many Black people are not given basic human rights.

There has to be a reason President Tuba is still alive, and the answer is inside the walled city of Elite.

The only cure for this pain and torment is hope! We aim to bring it to our oppressed kin in the Bible Boot. We aim for their natural hue to return to them and shine through the sadness. We will accomplish this. We will protest, we will riot for peace and equality for all people!

They can bruise our skin, set dogs on us, or spray us with hoses. They can spray tear gas and shoot rubber bullets that turn us black-and-blue, but we will come back and stand again. We shouldn't have to. We have done this before, but we will do this again. My mother named me after a great man who fought for equality in the 1950s and 1960s. He was peaceful and they shot him. We are peaceful and they shoot us. We are peaceful and they use every inch of us. We will not allow it anymore.

We will not stop trying to spread the message of equality to the deepest corners of the Bible Boot. As we protest, we gain followers from every walk of life, and our capacity for empathy grows toward the sky, like the branches of the Joshua tree.

We have crossed over into the Bible Boot. I will keep fighting. We will not cross back until everyone in the Bible Boot can sing: Free at last. Free at last. Thank God almighty, I am free at last.

–Martin King, August 2111

There are people who want to help, Imogen. They know we are being used to stay alive longer. The white pills are a joke, an excuse to use Black people in Elite for manual labor. The pills they give to everyone in the Bible Boot do nothing. It's all a ruse for the president and his closet advisors to stay alive longer by using us.

You are a match for Larkin genetically. For the rest of your life, they will use you if he needs a lung, or a kidney, or a serum for a virus. You are the youngest donor yet because the system is falling apart, because we are getting people out of the Bible Boot and more Clones are getting sick because of the protesters from the North. Their bubble is popping.

We have to stand up.

Words are important.

Words change the world.

I will get back to you as soon as possible. Don't

trust anyone and if you have to run away, follow the Drinking Gourd to the black snake with the man in the car.

Destroy this letter.
Your life and my life depend on it.

Be safe,
Truth Tubman

I read the letter eleven times, my hands shake. Her name is *Truth*.

Truth means honesty. Truth is a safe blanket.

I touch my stomach and think of all my organs inside. Can I live with one lung, or one kidney? How could someone take something that belongs to me? How can they take something out of me and use it if I am lesser than them?

I climb into bed, hoping that tomorrow I can forget it. That it was all a dream.

I twist the letter into pieces as small as the snowflakes I've seen in pictures. I hide some of the pieces under my pillow. I keep some in my pocket. I sprinkle some under the rug. The last bit I push into my mouth.

The tiny pieces disappear quickly on my tongue.

I swallow it because the letter is *mine*.

My organs are *mine*.

I hug myself to keep my organs as close to me as possible because they are *mine, mine, mine*.

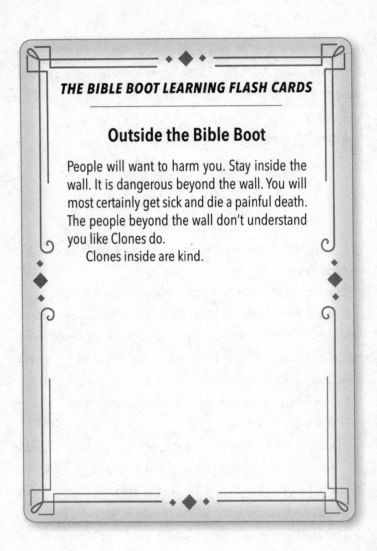

THE BIBLE BOOT LEARNING FLASH CARDS

Outside the Bible Boot

People will want to harm you. Stay inside the wall. It is dangerous beyond the wall. You will most certainly get sick and die a painful death. The people beyond the wall don't understand you like Clones do.

Clones inside are kind.

20

Outside

"Your eyes move when you sleep." Larkin's voice sounds a world away. I am walking through a field of red daisies. The daisies did not grow red. They are red from blood. "Wake up, Inmate Eleven."

I roll over to face Larkin, who is sitting on the side of my bed. "I was dreaming."

"Of what?"

I don't want to tell him. "Flowers. Red flowers."

"Like roses?" Larkin asks.

"No, not like roses," I say, because roses are born red.

"Oh." Larkin moves from my bed and sits on the couch in front of the TV. "Today we have to go outside."

I sit up. "I have never been outside." I rub my eyes thinking of how bright it will be outside.

"I know." Larkin smiles. "I think you will like it."

"How much sky is there outside?"

"Enough for everyone," Larkin says.

"That sounds like too much," I say because there are a lot of everyones and I wonder how there can be enough.

I get ready in the bathroom quickly. Larkin hands me a pair of rough-looking pants. He calls them *jeans* and I have to wear them because it is dusty outside. I put them on in the bathroom along with a red shirt. I don't like wearing red so close to my dream, but I don't have a choice.

Larkin hands me the things that look like glasses again and a cloth with stretchy things that hook behind my ears. "Wear these," he says.

"You don't need any?" I put on the glasses and they make the room even darker than the ones yesterday. Next, I put on what Larkin calls a *mask*.

"I am used to the sun. I wear a mask because the germs outside are high today." Larkin turns to leave my small room, pulling on his own mask. "Ira has to stay here."

Ira is not very happy about staying. I try to convince Larkin that Ira needs to go outside more than anyone.

Larkin says, "Maybe next time."

The way he says it makes me think he just wants me to stop talking. Which makes me think of President Tuba, which makes me remember how he thinks I am stupid.

I wonder if Larkin thinks I am stupid.

We walk down a new hall that has a lot of windows, just like the ones in President Tuba's rooms. I am glad I have the stronger sunglasses. Even with them, the world is impossibly bright, like we are only a few miles from the sun instead of millions of miles. We go down two flights of stairs and board the small box called an elevator. Larkin pushes the button for a lower floor.

My stomach feels like it is pushing into my throat. The same feeling I had last night reading the letter. I glance at Larkin. He looks like a Clone, all Clones look like Clones. All of them have white skin, Larkin's is just a little tan.

When we step out of the elevator, the floor is shiny like the floor in the nurses' office and in Congress. I try not to inspect my reflection too much. I try not to decide what shade of blue I am.

Larkin's shoulders are high again. I don't like when he does that. He turns and tells me, "Remember, no talking. Unless . . . well, just no talking."

I don't say anything and Larkin nods like I am doing a good job. He opens a final door and we step outside.

I gasp.

It feels like fire is coming into my lungs.

Like I have inhaled the sun and it is burning my throat.

"It is a hot day. We have air inside, it keeps it cool," Larkin explains. His voice is muffled through his mask.

I nod, but I am not sure how I feel about *outside*. I have to blink many times before my eyes see shapes. First they are blurry, hunched over. I blink again, then the edges of the shapes clear and once they do, I wish I could blink and unsee them.

As far as I can see, Blue people are bending and hitting metal things against stone.

Bending over and picking up tiny circles they find in the broken rocks. Their fingers look bruised and red with blood from picking up the same little circles I saw President Tuba swallow. The ones that they say make him young.

I watch one lady with grayish-blue hair and wrinkly skin—her eyebrows bunch together as she grimaces each time she bends over. It makes my back hurt. Everyone I see is sweating and their mouths hang open trying to take in as much air as possible. Water drips from their bodies like a flood. I have never seen a flood, but there is one in the Bible. The one that Miss Abby read to me talked about lots of water filling the world. I think the Blue people are sweating enough to cause another flood.

All I can see is gray stone and Blue people hurting.

I can *feel* them hurting.

"Why don't they have masks if the germs can get them?" I ask.

"Oh, they . . ." Larkin looks at his feet while I stare. His shoulders tip down a bit. "They don't mind. They like being outside," Larkin says without looking at the quarry of Blues sweating floods without masks.

"How do you know?" I ask because I wonder who would like sweating floods and breathing fire.

"They are bred for it," he says. "They have been in the capital for their entire lives."

I look past Larkin at the bone-shattering work happening

in front of me. I don't think anyone is made to hunch over the earth with the sun burning their backs. I don't think anyone is made to be in pain.

"Did you ask them?" I question. "Did you ask them if they mind?"

Larkin shifts on his feet before he starts walking on the hard, dusty surface. "I don't have to ask. I know."

I don't like how Larkin lifts his shoulders higher when he says, *I know*. I think he is trying hard to convince himself. He repeats it again, *I know*.

"I am Blue, and I know I would not like sweating a flood without a mask to keep the germs away," I say.

Larkin says, "But you are not made for this work. You are made to stay inside with me."

I can't meet his eyes. "I don't know a lot about outside but I don't think people are made for things."

I look at the people in the quarry again and notice that there are more than just Blue people. Some people are brown and others have very tan skin. The men yelling at them are all white with blond hair. They all have guns.

We walk farther and the rocks are uneven and push at my feet. I don't see any grass and Larkin says it is because the quarry surrounds the capital. The grass is on the other side of a wall I can just see in the distance.

I stop. "Do you want to ask someone if they like working here?"

Larkin spins around. "What did I say about talking, Inmate Eleven."

I don't like that he says *Inmate Eleven* anytime he wants to make a point. Like he is reminding me of something horrible.

Against the gray stone and blue sky, Larkin looks whiter than ever in the sun. I hear a woman yell behind me, and Larkin pulls my arm in another direction before I can see what happens.

"Don't look back," Larkin says firmly. "That is an order."

I don't look back, not because Larkin ordered it, but because I am afraid.

I don't like *outside*.

"The president employs Blues to work the quarry for a special pill. He pays them by giving them food and somewhere to stay." Larkin looks at me. "Sometimes Blue people and other minorities who work here don't listen, because they are not very smart. Then there are consequences."

"Minorities?" I ask.

Larkin sighs. "It's complicated. Never mind. Just know there are sometimes consequences for not listening."

I don't like the way Larkin says *consequences*, like it is an unfortunate but true thing. I know the word *consequences*, it means you do something bad and then get punished.

I wonder if Larkin knows he may not be a Clone and that all these people and I might be blue because we are sad. Truth's letter said we are Black Americans and our skin can come in many shades. That is, if Truth is telling the *truth* in her letter. I think with a name like that, it is impossible to lie.

President Tuba is in front of us and I put my head down. The last time I saw him, he made me cry. He has a long whip in his hand and I feel Larkin pushing me in a different direction again, but the president sees him.

"Larkin, bring Inmate Eleven over here." He is rolling up his sleeves. "She needs to learn what happens when you don't follow the rules."

Larkin starts walking over to a tree where a woman is tied. Her blue back is bare. Larkin whispers, "Not a word, Imogen."

I don't nod. I just look, because he says my name again. He says *Imogen* like he is *begging* me to be silent. I think I know what is about to happen and I think I know I am not going to be able to be quiet.

I think Larkin knows too.

He stands slightly in front of me and grabs my wrist. We are so close I can see water dripping from the woman's forehead. A flood.

"How much did she steal?" President Tuba turns to another man, on a horse.

"Six biscuits."

"One vaccine will be taken from you." The president laughs as he speaks. "What is your defense?"

"My children are starving and sick. I . . . I . . ." The Blue woman sobs as she speaks.

She sobs and her tears spill into the flood.

"Because I am kind . . . ," President Tuba starts. "You have a choice. Six lashes or one of your children will not be vaccinated. Think quickly."

I start screaming before she can respond. Louder than my voice has ever gone. Larkin holds me back until he isn't anymore, I break free, and I am standing in front of the Blue woman. Now I have tears too, and they make my blue hair stick to my face. The president pauses. Like he is deciding if he will swing the whip.

Then Larkin is beside me. He is not too close, but close enough to get hit too if the president swings. Larkin's shoulders are taller than his ears.

"Disobedience, Inmate Eleven." President Tuba wipes the sweat from his forehead. "I am going to enjoy your punishment. Inmate Three, take Inmate Eleven to her room."

Inmate Three, I mean, Kin, appears and leads me away. I look back and see Larkin kneeling on the ground like everything he has seen has made him heavy. Then I hear the sound of the whip hitting blue skin, followed by screams. Kin puts his hand firmly on my shoulder, he won't let me turn and look. He leads me back to my room, which feels too big. Every corner feels dangerous.

"That was a mistake," Kin whispers.

"She was crying," I say because she was and I am mad at him for not helping either.

"Everyone in that field is hurting." He almost yells. "We hurt President Tuba by taking what he needs."

"Needs?"

"Resources. Money. Getting information out." Kin turns to look at me, tears are in his eyes. "If we can't do that, we can't help anyone. There are more, you know, more places like this in the Bible Boot."

"More?"

He shakes his head. "They are going to kill . . ."

"Truth says they need me. They need me for my . . ." I don't want to say the word. "They need me."

"They are going to kill Ira. They are going to break you."

I don't say anything, I shatter into a billion, not a million, pieces.

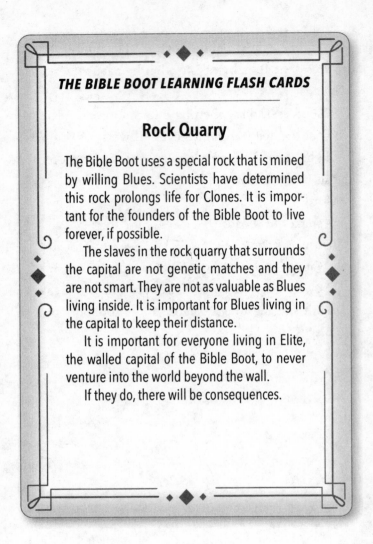

THE BIBLE BOOT LEARNING FLASH CARDS

Rock Quarry

The Bible Boot uses a special rock that is mined by willing Blues. Scientists have determined this rock prolongs life for Clones. It is important for the founders of the Bible Boot to live forever, if possible.

The slaves in the rock quarry that surrounds the capital are not genetic matches and they are not smart. They are not as valuable as Blues living inside. It is important for Blues living in the capital to keep their distance.

It is important for everyone living in Elite, the walled capital of the Bible Boot, to never venture into the world beyond the wall.

If they do, there will be consequences.

142

21

Ira

I know they are coming for Ira.

I think he knows too. I wonder if Larkin knows.

I wonder if Larkin knows the way that Ira and I know.

We know like the raindrop knows it is only a drop for so long before it splatters.

I pace from window to window. There are windows in my room now. I guess there were always windows, but long boards covered them. Now they are open and I don't want to ever see outside again. For the first time, I understand how Ira felt in the small room. I *get* that he was pretending he was somewhere else, on a walk in a jungle or in a snowstorm, but I can't *go wolf*. I can't pace myself out of this room.

If I could, I would not walk. I would run, with Ira ahead. I would run away even from Larkin. I would run up North, where Truth Tubman has told me *things are better*. Ira stands in front of me and I kneel down. I look into his honey-brown eyes and I want to explain to him that it is my fault. That there is no way I can save him. I wish I could save him, but I can't.

I wish a lot of things. I wish I was nothing like Larkin. I wish that our blood did not somehow match, then Ira might live longer. I tell Ira all of this without speaking, because I know he understands.

What will I do with silence when Ira is gone?

Ira puts his large head against mine.

His thick fur tickles, but I have forgotten how to laugh.

I should have noticed there were no other wolves. I should have listened to Larkin and kept my mouth shut. I should have just let President Tuba . . .

But I could not.

I will not.

I tell Ira all of this too, with my eyes, and he tilts his head in the way that says, *I will not either.* There is a word I learned in psychology, it is a very hard word: *cognitive dissonance.* It means your brain can think two things that are opposite at once.

I wish I hadn't screamed and I am also glad I did.

I hug Ira and I feel this ocean in me. I know that there are no oceans inside of people. Oceans are big and have whales, but it feels like that. I feel like a whale could live in the water I have inside me. It feels like all this water has been sitting in me, waiting for now.

Ira hates when I cry, so I push the ocean down.

The door swings open and I see the guards, their uniforms are crisp and horrible.

144

"Get your wolf, let's go." Their words are a punch in the gut. I know words can't actually punch, but I think that is what the guards want.

"So soon?" I want to stall. I want to give Ira extra moments.

Instead, they stomp in and grab me by the arm. They put a rope around Ira's neck, tighten it, and pull him behind me. I can feel it. It must hurt him, but Ira just stretches and gets up. He follows without much fuss. He doesn't even growl.

The walk outside is too fast.

Funny how time is like that.

Outside there is a crowd of a few Blues but mostly Clones, or Elitists. I don't know what to call them anymore. Each moment I am more sure about Truth's words. There are giveaways: The looks on their faces are not neutral, like Clones should be. They are brimming with anger. Some carry a smirk.

I notice faces from Congress and I wonder if I could maybe beg them. If I could explain that I could not watch a woman get beaten. Maybe one of their stone faces would understand. The guards lead me toward the circle that everyone is gathered around. It is really just grass that is cut much shorter than the rest in the shape of a circle. I don't like grass. I can't believe I ever wanted to meet grass. In the center of the circle is a glass box. I see President Tuba on the far end of the ring. Larkin stands beside him, he will not look at me.

"Inmate Eleven, you have committed an awful crime."

The president smirks. "You have rebelled against your president. The penalty for such offenses is death, but seeing that your body is too valuable, we will take another life in your place."

I break free from the guards to hold Ira. My arms wrap tightly around his neck. "I am sorry, please, please."

I scream because I can beg. I don't mind begging for someone else.

I scream, "I am sorry, just don't hurt him!"

"You will be sorry after this." President Tuba motions toward one of the guards, who rips me away from Ira so swiftly that I take away a handful of his fur.

I scramble and shriek, I try to poke out the eyes of each guard, which only makes their fingers dig deeper into my skin. Then one guard kicks Ira hard, in the stomach, and I choke.

"If you protest, this will be harder for your wolf," the guard hisses. Even his tongue is snakelike.

I push all my strength out of my skin.

I know that is not actually possible, but I do.

I think Ira knows, and when they hit him again he won't even yelp.

They put him in the glass box and suck the oxygen out. He falls down. Then falls asleep.

That is what I tell myself, he is just asleep. He has *gone wolf* . . .

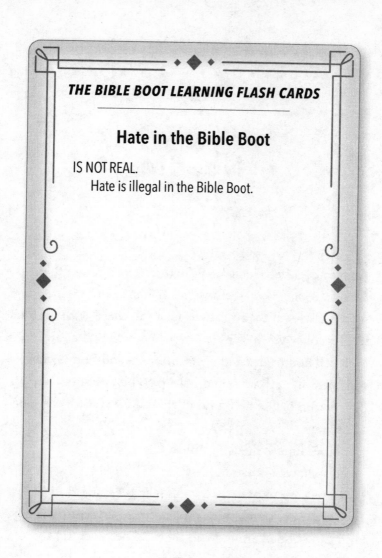

THE BIBLE BOOT LEARNING FLASH CARDS

Hate in the Bible Boot

IS NOT REAL.
Hate is illegal in the Bible Boot.

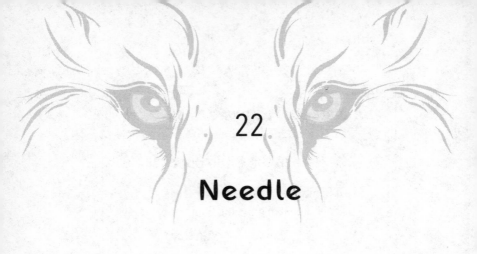

22

Needle

I have never been *alone alone* before. It is different than just *alone*. *Alone alone* seems okay at first. Until night, when shadows stretch themselves against the walls. Without Ira, I feel less okay with even my own shadow. My shadow looks hunched and frightened. I reach for Ira and find nothing. I still tuck my legs up when I sleep so he can sprawl across the bottom of the bed. I don't think I'll ever stop sleeping like that.

Some things you can't unlearn.

I also have not eaten.

It was easy to pretend Ira was just asleep until President Tuba made me watch them pull his limp body from the box. His head bobbed around and they did not even try to hold him nicely. Then they hung him from that tree. It is hard to pretend when you can't unsee something. Some things can't be undone. Like, I can't unhear the sound of the whip in the air or unsee President Tuba's smile. I can't unsee Ira's head bobbing around, and if I could, I might be able to eat.

I get it now. Why Ira would *go wolf*. I thought I did before, but now I really do.

The only thing I do is pace.

I pace myself away from my small room, from my small-small room.

I pace myself past the quarry and out of the Bible Boot.

Sometimes when I am pacing, I believe it. I think I am there at the wall, but then I hear the keys click and a plate of food is placed on a table and I remember.

I have not seen Larkin.

He knocked on the door once, but I did not say anything and he left. They come to collect my blood one morning, though. I don't even flinch when the needle hits my vein. I think the nurses like me because they think I am being less difficult. Really, I just want them to go away faster so I can *go wolf*.

On the third day of being alone, I look up from my pacing and Kin is standing in front of me. He says, "You need to eat."

I figure someone has sent him to make me eat. I sidestep him and keep pacing. It is not that I want to be difficult, but I can't eat. I don't think my stomach wants to work anymore. I pace to the end of the room and turn to come back. Inmate Three, I mean, Kin, is in my way again.

"If you don't eat, you won't be strong," he says. He says it like I should understand what he means.

"Strong for what?" I look up at him and his big brown eyes.

"For what is ahead." He puts the plate with noodles in my hands. My hands shake.

"I don't want to be strong," I say, because I don't. I don't want to be anything but wolf. I want to pace myself away from everything.

"That is usually when you have to be the strongest." He kneels in front of me. "One bite?"

"Why did they call my wolf Till?" I huff.

"They call all the wolves Till. It is their sick joke." His voice shakes. "A boy, around your age, was killed by Elitists. His last name was Till."

I don't have legs. I collapse to the floor.

He crouches in front of me. "You have to eat. We have to get you out of here."

I take a bite because he looks so sad, so blue and I don't want to disappoint him. "What did they do to your wolf?" I ask.

His jaw works like he is trying to get his tongue around the words. "Same thing they did to Ira," he says.

"Was it your fault too?" I ask.

Kin frowns. "This was not your fault, Imogen."

I look up because he says my name and for a moment I had forgotten it.

"It is because I jumped in front of the woman," I say.

He shakes his head. "They look for the first excuse. They always kill them within the first weeks of socializing us."

"It's not my fault?" I say, tears streaming down my face.

"No."

"But they took me out of the small-small room and they gave me new clothes and they said I could keep Ira."

"They *lie*, Imogen." He shrugs. "Elitists lie. They are not Clones—they lie all the time. Think, if they were Clones, they would not need us to help them live longer."

"But the lady in blue, I mean, Miss Abby, is nice," I say because she kept me well and talked to me.

"Nicer than some perhaps." He says it like he doesn't believe it.

"No, she is nice, she read to me. She would visit me." I try to convince him. She did not like Ira that much, but she never hurt him.

"Would you need someone to visit you if you were not locked in a cage?" Kin sounds a little upset.

"I . . . I." I don't know how to answer that question.

"What did she call you?" he continues. "Inmate Eleven. She did not think you needed a name."

"She has a lot of names to remember," I say softly. Feeling less convinced.

"If someone shoves a needle in your arm then pulls it out a bit, is the needle still in your arm?" he asks.

"Of course." I frown.

"Exactly." He says it like he has made a point. "Being nice to someone you consider a slave does not make you good. Pulling the needle all the way out doesn't make someone good. Never even thinking about holding the needle or fighting against everyone holding a needle makes someone good."

"The lady in blue never stuck me with a needle," I say.

I say it even though I know what Kin means. I know he means she is still guilty, but I need to believe in one person right now.

"You need to eat and you need to be ready." He says it like he knows I understand what he means. He places a key in my hand. "Outside your door there is an elevator. If you press the number zero, it takes you to the basement. Remember that. That key will override the system. Just press zero."

"Ready for what?" I ask.

"For the needle to be pulled out. Elitists will take and take. You have to escape."

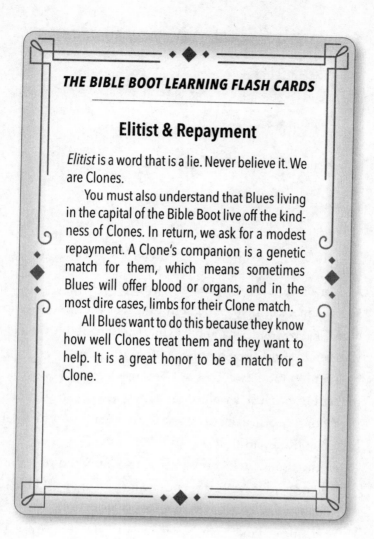

THE BIBLE BOOT LEARNING FLASH CARDS

Elitist & Repayment

Elitist is a word that is a lie. Never believe it. We are Clones.

You must also understand that Blues living in the capital of the Bible Boot live off the kindness of Clones. In return, we ask for a modest repayment. A Clone's companion is a genetic match for them, which means sometimes Blues will offer blood or organs, and in the most dire cases, limbs for their Clone match.

All Blues want to do this because they know how well Clones treat them and they want to help. It is a great honor to be a match for a Clone.

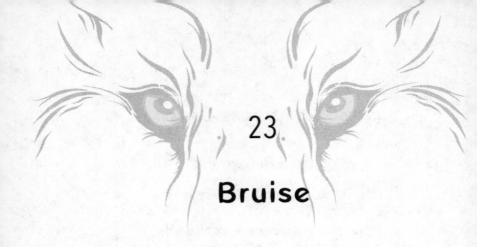

23

Bruise

I dream about needles for a few more nights.

In all the dreams, there are needles sticking in my skin and no one will help pull them out. Not even the lady in blue. I keep wondering about what Kin said about the elevator and I repeat the number zero in my head.

I eat my food each day, not because Inmate Three told me to, but because I walk so much. I have paced so much the floor is worn. Today, I want to pace back and forth at least one thousand times.

By the time lunch comes, I am at six hundred times.

When the door clicks open for dinner, I am at 1,111.

I don't know how to stop when I *go wolf*.

Someone is standing in my way again. I glance up expecting to see Inmate Three, but instead Larkin is there. His arms are crossed and he looks at his feet. His cheek looks bruised. The skin around his eye is blue like mine.

"Are you turning blue?" I ask, reaching for his face.

"I got in trouble." He still won't look at me. "For crying about Ira."

"I cried too." I frown. "No one hit me."

"That is 'cause you are a Blue." He exhales. "You are supposed to cry."

"Oh." I don't know what else to say.

There were a lot of Blues, and all of them cried when the guards lifted Ira without even worrying about his head. I don't remember seeing any Clones, I mean, Elitists, crying.

Correction: I only saw Larkin crying. I sometimes forget he is like them.

He looks at me. His eyes are red. "How are you doing?"

"*Gone wolf,*" I say.

"Me too." Larkin smiles a little and coughs a little. "I have walked a lot."

"I am tired," I say because I am and I don't know who else I can admit that to.

"Me too." Larkin sidesteps me and starts pacing. I go in the other direction.

Larkin looks over his shoulder when he reaches the wall. "I think President Tuba is lying."

I tap the wall and turn to walk back. "About what?" I ask.

"I think Inmate Sixteen, I mean, Truth, told you we are not Clones." We sidestep each other when we reach the middle, and keep walking. "She was not supposed to, but she did."

"Yes, you are *white*. Or Elitists."

"And you are *Black*." Larkin corrects himself. "Well, you are Blue because you are sad, but you are actually Black."

"Truth told me," I say.

"President Tuba says that we are expanding, but I don't think that is true. Yesterday, I heard something different on the news."

"News?" I ask.

"It says what is happening in the world. On the television," Larkin says.

"Like on this TV?" I walk past him again.

He shakes his head. "What you see on this TV is already made. It is old. But on the news they say what is happening right now."

"Oh," I say.

Larkin whispers, "There are freedom fighters coming down to the Bible Boot, talking about freeing Black people and other minorities. There are a lot of them. They want to unite the United States again."

I stop pacing. "What are other Clones, I mean, white people, saying?"

Larkin pauses. "It really is Elitists. Not whites."

"What is the difference?" I ask.

"Some whites want to help. Elitists are like President Tuba and the guards and Congress," he says. "I don't think I am an Elitist."

I shake my head. "But you are part of Congress."

Larkin sighs. "I don't want to be."

"But you are! You didn't stop them from hurting the Blue woman." I try to catch my breath. "You let them kill Ira!"

"At first when I did not listen, President Tuba hit me." Larkin exhales slowly. "Then when I got older, he started hurting Blues if I did not listen."

I pace some more. Like pacing will help bring Ira back. Like it will help declutter the hurricane in my mind. I know that minds can't be hurricanes but that is what it *feels* like. I pace like walking will help me find the eye of the storm— the calm in the chaos.

I stop in front of Larkin. "So, what are the Elitists saying?"

His eyes brighten. "The ones here are denying the truth, but others, other whites in the Bible Boot, are protesting with the freedom fighters."

"Protesting?"

"Standing up against something you know is wrong," Larkin explains. "I think things are going to start changing."

I stop in front of Larkin and touch his cheek. "Are you sure you are not turning Blue? You *sound* Blue."

"Imogen, we should *go wolf*." He looks very serious. "We need to really *go wolf*."

"Why are you calling me Imogen?" I ask.

"Because I can't pretend it is not your name anymore." Larkin grinds his teeth. It is like he is ashamed it took him so long to realize. "I want to be *good*."

I don't understand why he thinks it is so difficult. "Then

be *good*," I say. "It is not hard. Be brave like Ira, or like the Blue woman who needed something for her family. Be brave like you are Blue."

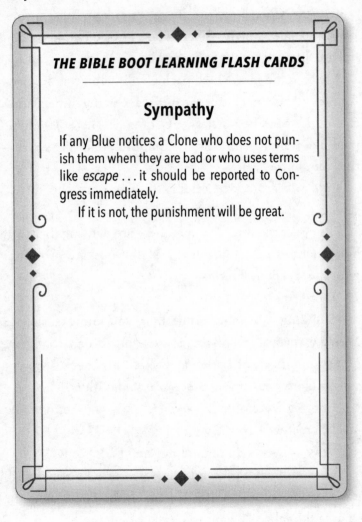

THE BIBLE BOOT LEARNING FLASH CARDS

Sympathy

If any Blue notices a Clone who does not punish them when they are bad or who uses terms like *escape* . . . it should be reported to Congress immediately.

If it is not, the punishment will be great.

24

North

Larkin looks down at the same time that the lights go out and loud sounds blare from the speakers. I swallow. My heart feels like it is trying to rise to my throat, but my spirit knows what to do. I try to think of Ira, how he was brave. How if I get out, Ira gets out.

I grab Larkin by the hand. "We have to get to the elevator."

He pulls away. "What?"

"Inmate Three, I mean, Kin, said to be ready. This has to be it. We have to get to the elevator and press zero." I pull the key Kin gave me from my pocket and go toward the door. Larkin follows.

The door is unlocked and the hall is empty when Larkin peeks out to check. We run toward the elevator. It is so close. I think we might make it and I don't know exactly what that means yet. Then I see the lady in blue, I mean, Miss Abby. She looks hard at Larkin and me. She looks down at his hand clutched tightly around my hand—a blue hand and a white hand. She steps forward and Larkin steps back.

"Don't come near her," he says.

"Imogen?" She looks at me, tears in her eyes. She hands me two masks. "Imogen, I am sorry. I am sorry I was not brave enough."

I hear boots hitting the stairs, then I see Kin standing in front of guards. He turns back to me and yells *Run* and I find all I want to do is run to him.

Larkin is pulling me toward the elevator and I don't understand why Larkin had to *try* to be good and Miss Abby had to *try* to be brave. I don't understand why people are not just what they *want* to be.

Larkin opens the elevator and we slip in.

Before it closes I see Kin with his hands up, surrounded by Elitists.

Larkin and I slip on our masks and when the elevator reaches the basement, I almost jump. Truth Tubman is waiting. She signs something to Larkin, who nods and follows her down a dark hall. My lungs burn. Not the tired burn, the frightened kind. We twist down halls for what seems like hours but I am sure is only moments. Time is funny like that.

When we reach a door, Truth turns to us. She makes a sign with her thumb hooked to her index finger. Her eyes are bright and filled with something. I know eyes can't really be filled with anything, but that is what it feels like. It feels like Truth's eyes are filled with hope.

"She says we have to run." Larkin inhales. "She says we have to run as fast as we can."

I nod my head. "*Go wolf?*"

Larkin smiles. "*Go wolf. Go really really wolf.*"

Truth opens the door and the heat slaps me in the face. I don't know how anyone gets used to it being this hot. I think about Ira, I think about how he would feel about endless space and I run. I run over the rocks.

I run until my feet can't catch their breath.

I run like the wind blows.

My lungs start to burn and this time it is the tired burn, but I keep running. My feet sting through my thin shoes when they hit against the hard stones and I keep running. Running until we reach the wall and slip through a small door. Then running in grass, which is soft and greener than I thought it would be.

When we reach the edge of the field, I stop.

I can't help it. I have only seen them in books.

It is a forest. Not one tree, not two, but an army of them. Maybe they will protect us.

"We have to hurry, Imogen," Larkin whispers.

I touch a tree. "There are so many."

Larkin looks around him. Like he is just noticing that a forest surrounds him. "I suppose there are."

Truth is the one who grabs my arm and urges me forward. It is harder to run fast in the forest. The trees pop up in front of my face like they are playing hide-and-seek. I smile at each one and name it because even trees need names. I name a Scott, Lexy, Madison, and Joe before we reach the edge of the forest. When I look down, I see something black and shiny in front of us. Truth signs that we should wait and she climbs the bank to the shiny black surface ahead.

"What is that?" I ask Larkin.

"It is a road. Cars drive on it." He puts his hand on my shoulder. "How are you doing?"

I am looking up at the sky. I am seeing the stars for the first time, and I put my hand down to touch Ira. Then I remember he is not there and it happens again, like my heart is breaking. I remember we dreamed about the stars and now I am the only one seeing them.

"I am good," I say because all the feelings are too hard to explain.

Two bright stars come floating down the black road and stop in front of us. Larkin says it is a car. I see Truth sign something to the man in the car. Then she inches back down the bank to us. She signs something and I can see Larkin is very upset. He signs something else forcefully back.

Truth shakes her head, *no*.

"She says a man she trusts will drive us the rest of the way to Selma and tell us what to do next." Larkin looks upset when he talks. "She says she is going back."

My throat tightens. Why would she go back to a place we are trying to leave? "No! Tell her to stay. Tell her to stay with us."

She shakes her head no again. She hugs me and points to a constellation—the Drinking Gourd. Truth pushes us forward. By the time I look back, she is already darting her way back through the trees. I guess she is *brave* the way Miss Abby wants to be *brave*. She is not afraid to go back, because each time she comes to this road she brings someone new with her.

I slide into the car and almost jump. There is a man with brown skin sitting in the driver's seat of a car that hovers above the ground.

"Hello, my name is Mr. King."

His voice reminds me of the sun and a storm at the same time.

The way the sun is warm and a storm is fearless.

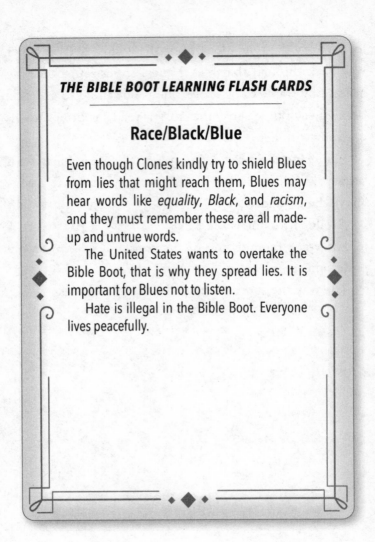

Race/Black/Blue

Even though Clones kindly try to shield Blues from lies that might reach them, Blues may hear words like *equality*, *Black*, and *racism*, and they must remember these are all made-up and untrue words.

The United States wants to overtake the Bible Boot, that is why they spread lies. It is important for Blues not to listen.

Hate is illegal in the Bible Boot. Everyone lives peacefully.

25

MLK

I like Mr. King. Larkin and I can't stop looking at his skin.
It is brown and smooth and perfect.

He also wears a mask, which hooks behind his ears.

I have never seen brown skin this close before. It is as
smooth as his voice. I keep trying to think of things to compare Mr. King's skin to, but nothing seems right. Larkin is
in the front seat beside Mr. King.

"Imogen and Larkin, how are you?" He speaks slowly.
Not the *I don't know what to say* slowly. The *What I am
saying is very important* slowly. I watch him from the back
seat and he looks up in the little mirror and smiles. "Not the
talking types are we?"

Larkin opens his mouth to say something, but closes it
again.

"You can ask me anything you want," Mr. King encour-
ages.

I work the question around in my mouth. "Mr. King,
why are you brown?"

"I was born this color," he says in his slow, even voice.

"I have never seen a brown person up close before," I say because I have not.

Mr. King looks sad. His brows knit together. "Underneath all that sadness, you are the same color as me, Imogen."

"Miss Truth says I am a Black American, not brown," I say because that is what she said. Black like the pavement.

"I am Black too," Mr. King says.

Larkin whispers, "You look brown to me."

I worry that Mr. King will get mad, because he seems very important and has a very important voice. "Larkin, what color is my shirt?" Mr. King asks.

Larkin glances at Mr. King's button-down shirt. "It is white," he says.

"And what color are you?" Mr. King continues.

I know the answer to this so I interrupt. "Larkin is not a Clone. He is white. But he is not an Elitist."

"That's right, Imogen, Larkin is white." He looks in the little mirror. "Is Larkin the same color as my shirt?"

I look at Larkin. His skin is very light, but it looks nothing like Mr. King's shirt. "No, he is not," I say.

"You both have a lot to learn, but then again, we all do." Mr. King looks at the dark road ahead.

"Why do they call people colors they are not?" Larkin asks.

"That is a very good question, Larkin." Mr. King smiles at him. "Maybe because putting people in boxes makes it easier for people to understand."

I lean between the seats. "We should use the *truth*, and not what is easy," I say.

"I agree." Mr. King turns the wheel of the car and we are driving faster now. "White people are really Anglo Saxon, they can come from anywhere. Their skin is that color because of the amount of sun that touched it a long time ago. Black people can be from anywhere too. A very long time ago, Black people were stolen from Africa and enslaved in what would become the United States."

"President Tuba says I am a slave." My voice shakes when I speak, because I don't like the word.

"He lied to you. You are a person. You are an extraordinary person." Mr. King takes a deep breath. "Eventually, Black people were set free, then they had to fight for equal rights. Now, all these years later, we are going through the same struggle because of the virus and second Civil War. They are brainwashing Black Americans in the Bible Boot and using Black people so they can live longer."

I don't know what brainwashing means, but I think it means something about hiding the truth. "So, my skin should be brown?"

"You are a Black American. You deserve the same rights as every American, and Black people come in all shades and all of them are beautiful."

"That seems fair," Larkin says, nodding his head in agreement.

"Very fair." Mr. King smiles.

We zoom past a sign that says #BLACKLIVESMATTER. Which

I understand. Then we zoom past a sign that says #CLONE-LIVESMATTER and I feel confused, because of course they do—they would take my organs from me to live. The world is very confusing.

We drive for a very long time.

I don't actually know if it is a long time. It is hard to tell. I am not used to moving with time.

Mr. King says we are going to Selma.

There is going to be a protest there and after that, we have to try to get up North. I lie on the back seat and look out the window. The moon is so much bigger than I thought it would be and I don't understand how the sun can be even bigger.

I remember the lady in blue, I mean, Miss Abby, explained that it is because the sun is farther away from us than the moon. So it is much bigger, but looks the same size. She used the word *perspective*. It seems like a very important word.

For example, Larkin thought I should not have a name until he learned that many Blue people do have names. Miss Abby, I believe, thought the same thing. I thought the same thing too and I am trying hard to unlearn what I was taught. It is hard when every time I look down, I see blue.

I find the Big Dipper and follow it to the Little Dipper. At the end of the Little Dipper is the North Star. If you follow it, no matter what, eventually you will be safe.

Miss Truth told me this. We are following it, and Mr. King says everything will be okay and for now, that feels like a blanket—we head north.

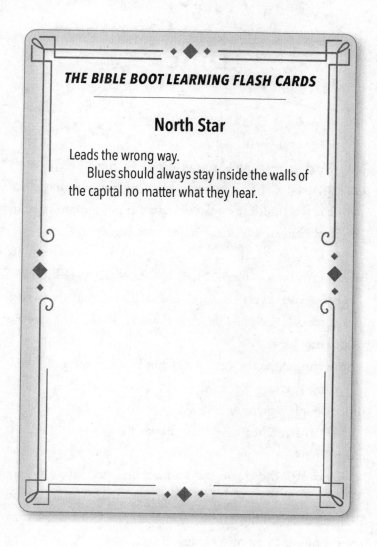

THE BIBLE BOOT LEARNING FLASH CARDS

North Star

Leads the wrong way.
 Blues should always stay inside the walls of the capital no matter what they hear.

26

Diner

Light starts poking through the sky when the car stops moving. I sit up and see a box with windows that glow. I think it is a building because I can see people inside of it. The box, I mean, building, is not very big.

Mr. King opens the car door. "I thought you two might be hungry." I don't move. "This is a diner. They sell food."

"Why would you sell food?" I ask. It's strange. I've never found food to be very delicious and it is odd that people would pay for it.

Mr. King shuts the car door behind Larkin and me. "Well, sometimes people don't want to cook for themselves. Sometimes people just want pancakes and bacon."

Larkin stretches his arms above his head. "I like pancakes."

I know the word *pan* and I know the word *cake*. Pans are used for cooking and cakes are sweets that people get on their birthdays. I have never gotten a cake, but I think they are supposed to be nice things to get.

Mr. King has Larkin put on a hat and we both slip masks onto our faces. Mr. King says, "I don't think anyone will recognize you, because everything in the city of Elite is kept secret, but just in case."

Mr. King opens the door of the diner. "Pancakes smothered in syrup."

I follow them into the diner. It is warm inside and everyone is wearing a mask. There are a few people. None of them are Blue, which makes me tug at my sleeves. Mr. King leads us to a section in the back of the diner. There are a few Black people sitting at a circular table. They are looking at the menu and smile and nod when they see Mr. King.

We sit in what Mr. King calls a booth. It is like two long soft chairs with a table in the middle. I see droids making food and people writing down what people want to eat. I sit on the inside near the window, beside Larkin. Windows are becoming my favorite thing. Mr. King hands me what he calls a menu. I read it: *fried potatoes, chipped beef, biscuits, pancakes with syrup and butter*.

"What would you like, Imogen? I'll go order for us," Mr. King says.

"I think I'll try the pancakes. Thank you," I say.

Mr. King nods and walks to the front area. He has to wait for a very long time before someone comes to help him. The other people, with different shades of brown skin, sitting in the back are still looking at the menus, then at the clock that ticks on the wall, then back at their menus. I get it. It can be hard to pick. If Larkin and Mr. King were not getting pancakes, I don't know what I would get.

Mr. King slides back into his seat. "Should only be a few minutes, then we can get back on the road." He hands us both napkins. "You are going to love the pancakes, Imogen."

I like how he says my name.

I notice the other men sitting in the back of the diner are now standing. Their menus are carefully stacked on the table. Maybe they decided that nothing is good on the menu. The four men are dressed very nicely. They have on shiny shoes and crisp shirts. Not crisp like the doll the lady in blue, I mean, Miss Abby, asked me about. Crisp like fresh. Instead of walking out the door, the men with crisp shirts stop at the front. One of them picks up a menu at the counter and sits down.

The man behind the counter frowns. I can hear him from the back. "Y'all need to go back to where you belong."

Mr. King glances at the counter. He folds his hands on the table.

One of the men in a crisp shirt and shiny shoes says, "We just want to order some pancakes."

"You can order them back there." The man behind the counter grabs a container filled with black steaming liquid. "Or else."

I look at Mr. King. "Maybe I should not get pancakes. I don't think the man wants to make pancakes."

Mr. King slides out of the booth. "We will get pancakes

somewhere else. Let's get you two out of here." Mr. King herds Larkin and me toward the door.

I hear one of the men with brown skin at the counter say, "We just want service."

Then I hear a splash.

A scream.

Then we are outside and in the car. Mr. King grips the wheel of the car tightly. The palms of his hands almost look white. I don't say anything.

The sun has risen, but it looks more red than orange.

THE BIBLE BOOT LEARNING FLASH CARDS

Escape

We
Will
Find
YOU.
There will be consequences.

27

Selma

I hear music before I open my eyes.

I know the sound I hear is music, because once Miss Abby played music for me and it made me want to move. My eyes open, Larkin's bed is empty. I vaguely remember being shuffled into the house of a nice woman with brown skin and being put into bed during the night.

I pull the warm blanket back and stumble out of the bed that doesn't poke me and ask for my blood. It was like sleeping on a cloud. I hear wonderful humming, but I don't know where it is coming from. I don't see the machine that plays music.

Sound has to come from somewhere, Miss Abby taught me that. The door to the bedroom opens and the same woman I remember seeing last night steps in. She takes up the entire opening of the door and she smiles real big.

"Looking for something, Imogen?" She raises an eyebrow.

"I hear music," I say. "I am trying to find it."

She steps farther into the room and tilts her head. Then

she smiles and pulls back the curtain to look out the window. "You hear birds. They sing in the morning." She points at some birds sitting on the branches of the trees.

"Birds can make music?" I ask, because that is remarkable.

"I don't know if everyone would call it music." She smiles. "How about something to eat. Your friend Larkin has already had two flapjacks."

"Flapjacks?" I ask.

"You'll like them," she says. "Everyone loves my flapjacks. They are like pancakes, but better."

I shudder. "I don't know. Yesterday, we were going to have pancakes and then I think someone got hurt at the diner."

She touches my shoulder. "Nobody is going to hurt you here."

"What's your name?" I ask because I think names are very important.

"People call me Carmen."

"Are you Black too?"

"Yes, darlin'."

"I wish I was Black," I say because I look different from everyone. Not white. Not brown. I am Blue. I stand out.

Carmen kneels down and grabs my chin. "You are Black and you are perfect. Don't let anybody tell you anything different."

* * *

I do like flapjacks. I eat three. I don't know if they are better than pancakes, because I have never had pancakes. Then Ms. Carmen teaches Larkin and me how to wash dishes. She says it is best if we stay inside, because things will be a bit rough outside today. I like Ms. Carmen, but she paces a lot.

She looks like she is *going wolf.*

I am about to ask her why she paces when I hear screaming. Screaming—like the screaming when the Blue lady was beaten. Ms. Carmen flies from the kitchen into her yard faster than Ira ever ran. Larkin and I follow her.

I see lots of people with brown skin running to a tall building that Ms. Carmen calls a *church.*

Some limp with red streaks across their skin.

They are red, brown, blue, and white.

"Imogen, you remember the refrigerator? Go get a bucket and fill it with ice, bring it to the church." She starts running across the street. "Larkin, help her."

We run inside and fill the bucket with ice. Larkin grabs some towels too. He carries the bucket because it is heavy and I carry the towels. There are even more Black people than before. I also see a few white people scattered in the crowd, which makes me a little nervous. When we get to the church, the screaming is even louder.

Bits of conversations reach me—*They brought the dogs. I think his skull is fractured. They wrapped their bats with wire.*

I don't know what they mean, but it sounds horrible.

We find Ms. Carmen kneeling in front of a man with a gash on his forehead. "Thank you, Larkin and Imogen." She wraps some ice in the cloth. "Now go back to the house."

"Ms. Carmen, I want to help." I bite my lip. "I need to help." I could not help the woman by the tree. I must help now.

Ms. Carmen looks at me like she understands. "See if people need ice. Larkin, go back to the house and fill another bucket with ice and get as many cloths as you can."

I move through the crowd and find a woman with a big cut hidden in her hair. "Ice?" I say. When she looks up, I see that her eye is swollen shut. The skin around it is the color of my blue skin.

"Thank you, darlin'," she says. "You are being very brave."

"I am not brave," I say. Because I know Mr. King said something about marching and I did not offer to join.

"You are the bravest." She takes the ice and squeezes my blue hand in her brown one.

I hand out a lot of ice. Until my fingers are numb. People talk about smoke and Mr. King. I learn that Miss Abby lied, *hate* is very legal in the Bible Boot. I hear coughing all around me, I turn to see Larkin hunched over. I run to him but he stands, catches his breath, and keeps working.

I look around the room. Black people did not hit anybody, but the Elitists in very important uniforms hit them. They even beat the white people who marched with the Black people.

They hurt them until they were all *blue*.

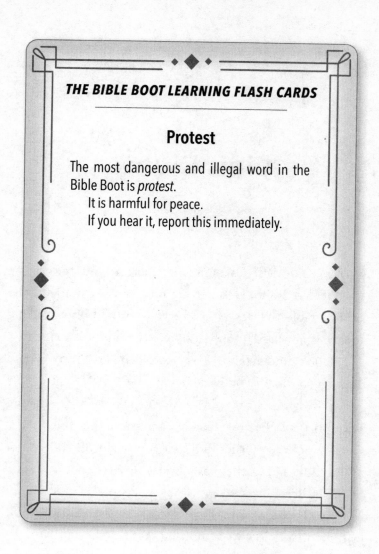

THE BIBLE BOOT LEARNING FLASH CARDS

Protest

The most dangerous and illegal word in the Bible Boot is *protest*.
   It is harmful for peace.
   If you hear it, report this immediately.

28.

Civil Rights

Mr. King, Ms. Carmen, me, Larkin, and Mr. King's friend, Rabbi Heschel, are busy making masks at the kitchen table the day after everyone turned blue. Making a mask is not hard, it only took me ten minutes to learn.

"I don't understand," I say to Mr. King. "Why would they get so mad if you were being nice?"

Mr. King has a gash above his eye and a bruise running across his jaw. I know that bruises can't run, but that is what it looks like. It looks like it runs right off the side of his face. Rabbi Heschel has a bruise on his hand.

"They don't want *change*, Imogen. People do nasty things to keep the status quo. They don't want Black Americans or Blue people to vote," Mr. King says.

I know what *status quo* means. It means keeping things the same.

Larkin slams his fist against the wooden table. It makes me flinch.

"Then maybe you should not be so nice. Look at what they did," Larkin yells, tears stuck in his thick eyelashes.

Mr. King moves to a chair closer to Larkin. "If we are violent, we are no better than they are." Mr. King's voice is the only sound in the room.

I think Larkin is confused so he is extra angry. Larkin is angry that he *is* white. He is mad that he was lied to. It is like he is angrier than Mr. King even though he is not the one who was hurt. I don't understand, but that is what it *feels* like.

"You are a child who was taught something that was wrong. And you figured out that it was wrong on your own. You can be angry, but you don't have to be part of the problem. You can be part of the solution." Mr. King puts one of his beautiful brown hands on Larkin's shoulder.

Larkin sniffles and says, "But they hurt you?"

He says it like a question. The same question I have been wondering about.

How can you not lift a fist when someone punches you in the face?

Yesterday, a lady with scrapes that looked like burns said, *They hosed us. I never knew water could feel like my skin was burning and burning.* I wonder how she stayed huddled in a corner when her skin felt like it was burning and burning. Another man said, *They set dogs on us, they bit right through my jeans.*

Makes me feel like I can't ever trust *water*. I think of the

dogs barking and snapping and wonder how they somehow made them *hate*.

Mr. King rubs his bruised jaw. "This? This is nothing.
This, I can live with, others are not so lucky."

"What is a vote?" I ask.

Rabbi Heschel says, "Voting is when you have a say in
what happens in America. Like if there was a vote to see if
little girls should have a puppy, I bet you would vote yes. If
everyone can vote, we might be able to make things more
equal for everyone."

"I think everyone should have a say." I nod. I can't help
the tears that start falling from my eyes. "I had a wolf. His
name was Ira. He . . . is not with . . ."

Ms. Carmen is behind me. She puts a hand on my shoulder. "Tell us about Ira."

I swallow. "He was big and sometimes when we stayed
in the small room his head would get real low and he
would pace back and forth."

"He would *go wolf*," Larkin adds.

Mr. King squints. "*Go wolf?*"

I nod. "It's when he pretended that he was somewhere
else, he imagined himself out of the room."

Rabbi Heschel smiles. "Ira sounds very special."

"Sometimes, I would dream that he was not a wolf and
that he would shift into a Black boy. A brother who kept
me safe." I nod. "I would vote for everyone to have a wolf
like Ira."

"So would I." Ms. Carmen squeezes my shoulder again.

"Mr. King, are you afraid of dying?" Larkin asks.

Mr. King's hand moves from his jaw down over his heart. Like he is checking his own heartbeat to make sure it is still pumping. "I don't want to die, but I am more afraid for people like Imogen to live like they do."

Larkin nods.

I nod.

Mr. King nods.

It's like when Larkin decided to escape with me. Sometimes you do things no matter the consequences. You have to do them or you feel strange about living.

"I want to help," I say because I want to be brave. I want to be braver than I was when the Blue woman got whipped and I could not help.

"Me too," Larkin adds.

"From what I hear, you two did a lot of helping yesterday. Keep doing that." Mr. King stands and puts his hands on his hips. "But Larkin, you need to always wear a mask and a hat. We don't want anyone to find you."

Larkin looks small for a moment. "I don't want to go back. He hurt me."

"No one is going to make you go back." Mr. King puts a hand on Larkin's shoulder again.

A few men dressed in suits walk into the kitchen. They all have different shades of skin. A lot of them have bruises all over their skin, but their souls stand tall. Not the fake tall. Not the tall that Larkin pretended to be. Their tall is true. They don't seem to mind that Larkin and I are sitting there. They hover around the table. One man says, "Do you have the speech ready?" Another asks Mr. King, "What is the speech called?"

Mr. King runs his fingers across his short black hair. "I don't know what to call it yet."

I want to help, so I ask, "What is the speech about?"

"Well, Imogen, it is about an idea." He pauses. "I have a hope that everyone will live happily together and that everyone fights and works toward that hope."

"Sounds like a good hope," I say. "In my small room, I used to hope too, and look what happened."

"What did you hope for?" Mr. King smiles.

"I dreamed that I could go anywhere and that I had lots of friends." I take a deep breath. "I dreamed of running as far as I could as fast as I could and never coming back."

"*Gone wolf*," Larkin whispers. "I dreamed that too."

"*Gone wolf*," Mr. King says, looking very serious. "Like when your face gets really serious and you walk and walk and when you finish walking, you are not the same."

I smile because Mr. King gets it.

Mr. King nods. "*Gone wolf*? The Second Civil Rights Movement is another long walk and none of us will be the same after it."

"But we will be better," Larkin adds.

"Yes, Larkin, we will be better." Mr. King smiles. "You know, a long time ago a man named Martin Luther King Jr. wrote a speech called 'I Have a Dream.'"

184

"Was it a good speech?"

"Very good," one of Mr. King's friends says.

"Was Martin Luther King your friend?" I ask because I don't know how long ago he means.

Mr. King shakes his head. "No, my mother named me after him, though."

I nod. "Maybe you should call your speech 'Gone Wolf'? So everyone knows they have to go on a long walk and when they return, they have to be better and do better."

"Imogen, that is an excellent idea." Mr. King's voice is the only sound in the room, because when he speaks, everyone listens.

After a while, Ms. Carmen turns on the TV. This TV has more than one station. Ms. Carmen calls it *the news from up North*. I see images from yesterday flash up on the screen. I see Mr. King standing with many Black people and white men and women. I notice Rabbi Heschel standing near Mr. King.

The news changes to a woman talking about vaccines and getting them to the Bible Boot. She says, "As you know, most of the North is immune to our strain of the virus now, but because the South separated, their strain has become more deadly. It looks like people from the North are immune to its effects, though."

The TV beeps very loudly, then I see myself.

Not from yesterday, but a sketch of Larkin and me.

The news says: *$200,000 reward for the return of Inmate Eleven and Larkin Tuba.*

We believe that Inmate Eleven has bribed President Tuba's heir into helping her escape.

Please remember that under the Fugitive Blue Act, all escaped Blues are required to be turned in.

It is the law.

Mr. King says, "Carmen, you have to get these kids farther north."

The men put on the masks we made them and leave.

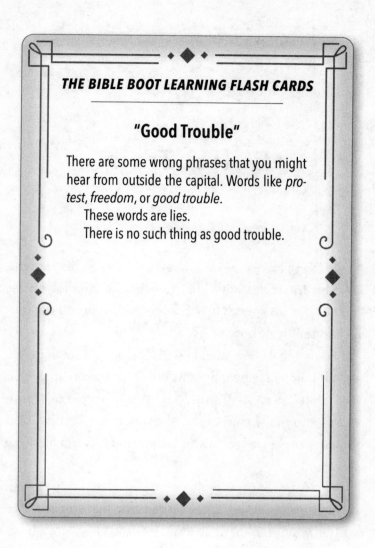

THE BIBLE BOOT LEARNING FLASH CARDS

"Good Trouble"

There are some wrong phrases that you might hear from outside the capital. Words like *protest*, *freedom*, or *good trouble*.

These words are lies.

There is no such thing as good trouble.

29

Bullet Train

Mr. King leaves very early the next day in his car with his friends in suits. He is heading to Charlottesville, Virginia, for his speech. Charlottesville is right on the border of the Bible Boot.

Larkin and I want to ride with Mr. King, but there are some things *young* people can't do. Or at least that is what Ms. Carmen says. Ms. Carmen says young people can't protest or go on long trips because it is not *safe*. It is not safe, because people are looking for Larkin and me, and Mr. King is a target.

Being a target means bad people want him to go away.

Ms. Carmen doesn't have a car, but that doesn't stop her. She wraps Larkin up in a sweater and gives him a baseball hat. She pulls a jacket with a hood over me and gives me some sunglasses to wear. Then after Mr. King leaves, we walk two miles to the Bullet Train station.

Ms. Carmen has family in Charlottesville, Virginia, and it is much safer than Selma.

"Now what are the rules?" Ms. Carmen tightens what she calls a hoodie but it really just feels like a cozy blanket. She is trying to make sure it covers my hair.

"Don't talk to anyone," Larkin says with his mask already covering his face.

"Not even if they are Blue or Black," I add.

"Y'all are some smart kids." Ms. Carmen looks at us, smiling. "And no trying to see the speech. Mr. King will come visit after it is over."

Ms. Carmen herds Larkin and me onto the Bullet Train headed to Charlottesville. I don't have brown skin, but they still motion me to the back. They must know that underneath the sadness, my skin is brown.

I want to *protest*.

Protest means to stand up against something wrong.

It means when your heart says, *This is not right*.

I don't protest. I walk down the aisle. Without Ira, I don't feel so safe, it makes me less brave. Without Kin, I don't feel safe, it makes me less brave—the Elitists took them both away to kill my braveness.

Larkin sits in the back too, which makes some people in the front of the Bullet Train make *tsk-tsk* sounds. We don't say anything, just like Ms. Carmen told us to. There is a Black boy sitting alone in a window seat; he reminds me of Kin except his skin is dark brown instead of blue. He nods when we pass by. Larkin lets me sit by the window so I can see the world. Ms. Carmen sits behind us to keep an eye on us.

I can't see much, it is still dark, but I know we are going north, because we are following the Drinking Gourd.

Ms. Carmen says, "Y'all sit tight. I am going to the bathroom."

Larkin and I nod.

"Never thought I'd see a Blue and a white person traveling together." The Black boy across the aisle scoots from the window to the space closest to the aisle. "Where are you guys headed?"

"Charlottesville." Larkin smiles. "Where are you going?"

"Not sure yet." He sticks out his hand. "My friends call me Mac."

Larkin shakes his hand, then Mac reaches over and shakes mine. "Nice to meet you," I say.

Mac leans across the aisle. "I'd keep a low profile if I were you. Your pictures are on the news."

We nod.

"I am from Alexandria." Mac settles back in his seat. "Do they really call you Inmate Eleven deep in the Bible Boot?"

I fold my hands in my lap. "Yes, but my name is Imogen now." It is my first time really introducing myself with my new name. I am still getting used to it, but Mac makes me feel brave enough to introduce myself.

"That's a good name," he says. "It's a strong name."

"So is Mac," I say.

Mac smiles as he pulls some candy from the pocket of his black hoodie. "Y'all want some chocolate-covered peanuts?"

I cup my hands together like a basin and a rainbow of colors falls happily into my hands. They taste like what I think magic would taste like—sunshine and joy. Ms. Carmen comes out of the bathroom and she doesn't seem mad that we are talking to Mac. She smiles at him, settles in her seat, and watches the trees go by.

Mac falls asleep after about an hour. I can't help but watch him. His skin is brown and smooth, just like his voice. I also look out the window a lot. The world is so much bigger than I imagined.

I turn to Larkin and say, "There is so much world to see."

Larkin leans back in his seat. "We can see it all, you know."

"Yeah, maybe we can," I say.

I don't know if I believe it yet.

The entire world is very big. I don't know if I want to see the entire world with blue skin—without Ira.

I bet there are even fewer people with blue skin across the ocean. I wonder if they will understand or if they will look at me like a *strange fruit*. I know I am not actually fruit, but that is what it feels like.

"No one will care," Larkin says.

"I care," I say, because I do.

"You should not care," Larkin says.

"That is easy for you to say."

"Because I am not Blue?" Larkin stretches his arms over his head. We have been on the Bullet Train for a long time and it is cramped.

"Because you are not Blue," I agree.

"Sometimes I feel Blue," he says, trying to be helpful.

"That is not the same," I say.

I don't want to hurt his feelings, but it is not. I know what he means. He means he wishes he could understand.

"I know." Larkin puts his head on my shoulder and closes his eyes. "I just want you to know that I want to know."

"I know," I say, because I do. Just like I understand why the lady in blue, I mean, Miss Abby, felt like she could not do anything to help me. Mr. King says, *You have to forgive and sometimes you have to forgive the same person many times.*

I am working on *forgiving* as a verb.

A verb is an action.

It has to keep happening to work.

I wonder how Mr. King forgives the people who hurt him. He says, *I think about how they have to be unbrainwashed.* I wonder how long it took him to get so good at finding love. I think about President Tuba and I can't love anything about him. I can't and Mr. King says, *That is okay.*

I forgive Larkin. I am working on forgiving Miss Abby.

I can't forgive President Tuba.

Every time I think of President Tuba's face, I see a field of red. I see red for miles.

Then I think of Kin, and I want to tell him he is the only friend I don't have to forgive, because he has never done anything unforgivable.

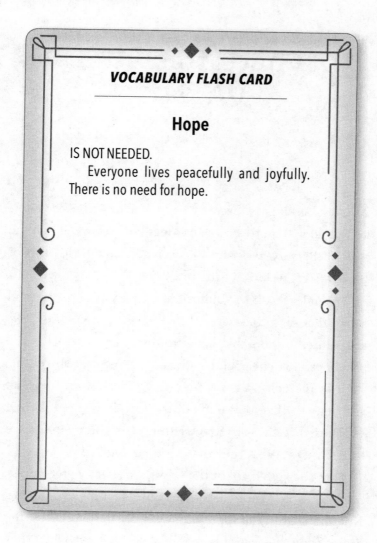

VOCABULARY FLASH CARD

Hope

IS NOT NEEDED.
Everyone lives peacefully and joyfully. There is no need for hope.

30

Charlottesville, VA, 2111

It takes Larkin, Ms. Carmen, and me a long time to get off the Bullet Train to stretch our legs because we are all the way in the very back and Larkin is feeling a little short of breath. His lips look a little blue.

When I step off the Bullet Train, I see lots of people and a sign that says CHARLOTTESVILLE, VIRGINIA. There are flowers planted in pots that hang from windows. It makes the buildings look cheerful. I know a building can't be cheerful, but the color gives that feeling. The flowers are pink and yellow. I like that none of the flowers are red. Larkin explains that the large metal things that line streets are lampposts; at night they make it seem like a dim day.

I am so excited about the flowers, perfectly green grass, brick lanes, and lampposts that I don't feel the eyes on me. Not the slightly disapproving eyes of the people on the Bullet Train, but eyes like knives. Eyes that cut when they look and hands that hold signs that say WHITE IS RIGHT. Ms. Carmen leads us away from the Bullet Train, but it is too crowded to walk.

"Looks like a lot of people want to see Mr. King speak," she says, stopping at a bench. "We might have to wait until it is over."

Larkin and I nod excitedly.

In front of us is what Larkin calls a tent. It is huge and white and there are many chairs in it filled with Black people. I notice Mr. King sitting in a chair at the center. He stands and the crowd gets quiet. I can't see much.

I look around at the crowd. It is different from the crowd in Selma. It's the warm kind of crowded. The kind that feels like a blanket crafted from many colors—*safe*.

I feel Larkin behind me and Ms. Carmen beside me.

I am sure Larkin can't see Mr. King either, even though he is taller than me. Some people are on other people's shoulders and I don't feel upset about that. I know why they want to see Mr. King. It is his voice, like butter on warm toast. I know a voice can't sound like that, but that is what it feels like. If Mr. King's voice had a smell, it would be the smell of a stack of perfect flapjacks. His voice gets all in your skin, it stays with you.

I think his voice makes me brave.

The way it is so clear through the noise.

The way he says, *You are blue because you are sad*.

It makes me know that it is true.

I wonder if Mr. King was ever blue, like me.

There was a point, after Ira died, when I got so blue I looked like the sky before a storm. Now I am what Larkin calls *periwinkle blue*. Larkin says, "I almost forget the blue is there."

Larkin looks different too.

I never knew his hair was curly and his spirit stands very tall in his body, but in a different way. It's his heart that lifts now, not just his shoulders.

This is my favorite Larkin. This is the Larkin I saw before he was actually there.

I think Ira saw it too. I think he knew what Larkin could be.

I get on my tiptoes because I still want to see Mr. King's face because faces are important, just like names. Voices are important too, but faces tell entire stories. I know that entire stories are not actually on people's faces, but you can tell a lot from a face.

President Tuba's face, it is hollow. It's sunken in, it feeds on its own body.

The lady in blue's, I mean, Miss Abby's, face is strained. She follows the rules, but does not like all of them. It makes her grimace.

Larkin's face is always bright or storm. Mostly bright when we are alone.

Ms. Tubman's face is weathered, the smart kind. The kind that makes you want to memorize the lines.

Ira's face was young, wild, and good.

And Kin's face was brave. Fearless.

196

I lower my hand to touch Ira. I know he is not there-there, but I think he knows. Larkin grabs my hand and gives it a small squeeze before he lifts me on the bench to stand where Ms. Carmen sits.

I can see the stage now.

On the Bullet Train, Larkin taught me something the lady in blue, I mean, Miss Abby, never did. He says that electricity is something that keeps lights on. It is invisible. I know that there can't be electricity between people because people die when there is too much electricity. That is why people who get struck by lightning don't make it sometimes. But it feels like electricity is slipping through the crowd. Like we are all conducting it.

I look down at Larkin. "Electricity," I yell, and I am sure the people around me hear me too.

Larkin tugs his fingers in his hair. I think he is about to explain that electricity can't be like that. It can't float in the air from person to person. The corner of his mouth lifts into a half smile. I have never seen this smile-smile before.

He says, "I feel it."

Then the smile blossoms across his entire face and I know I have never seen this smile before. His shoulders lift in a different way, like nothing is pressing down on them anymore.

I stand on my tiptoes on the bench.

I know that there are no such things as Clones and Blues. I know that Elitists matched us with other Elitists with similar DNA so they could use us when they got sick. I know

I was young and they still picked me. I know that there is no *better*, that all colors are good and that Ms. Tubman helped me get out of that place.

I know this and my skin is still periwinkle blue.

Mr. King says, *You are blue from the sadness you have had to carry. You must turn that sadness into action.*

I have been acting, Larkin and I have both been standing up even when our voices shake and want to hide in our throats. I feel water in my eyes because even in Charlottesville, my skin is different. I notice a Blue girl moving through the crowd toward me. She looks up and smiles, like she is happy that she is not the only one. She doesn't say anything, she just settles near Larkin and me in the crowd.

A woman in a light green dress fans herself with a *Daily Progress* newspaper.

Then I hear Mr. King's smoky voice.

A friend of mine suggested that maybe this is the time to remind everyone they have to change. We all have to look in the mirror and decide what we believe in. We have been here before. We have fought this battle. We can't repeat old mistakes. My mother named me after a great man, Martin Luther King Jr. He died for what he believed in. He said, "I might not make it there with you."

His speech "I Have a Dream" is just as relevant today as it was in 1963. When Black people were

being hurt, attacked, and were afraid to walk
down the street.

I wonder if Mr. King can feel my smile all the way back here, because my entire spirit is smiling. Larkin nudges my shoulder.

Today, we have to go wolf. I know some of y'all
don't know what that means. It means we are
prowling, we are going on a long walk toward
change together. If one of us falls, the rest of us have
to keep going. We are gathered here in that same
spirit. That spirit that says we will NOT sit down.
We will gather here, together. We will protest.

Hallelujahs fill the crowd and goose bumps rise on my skin and I know there really is electricity. Electricity really is moving through the crowd.

We thought we would never have to do it again,
but history repeats itself when we forget to
remember it correctly. When facts are changed and
lies make people afraid, the hate can come back.

I nod my head, it did *come back.*

First when they came over on boats and were enslaved, now many wars later, the Bible Boot got its way and did it again.

How many mistakes can one country make?
How much forgiveness is there?

America offered freedom centuries ago and offered
pain. Not just to Black people, but to many people
of color. When we started banding together, they
tore us apart—made Black people the bad ones
again. In the Bible Boot it worked, but here it will
not. Everyone within the sound of my voice knows
that we all may look different, we may pray to
different gods or no gods. We are the same. We are
all equal.

I start to clap with the rest of the people because I feel
safe clapping. The blanket of Mr. King makes me feel safe.
Everyone within the sound of his voice is safe and I wonder how one voice can do that.

Magic must be real, just like electricity, it is just difficult
to see.

We need these changes NOW! Black children are
being hurt NOW! We have to be brave even if we
are afraid.

I think about the *now*.
Now. Now. Now. I shout with the crowd.
I shout with Larkin.
I shout with Ms. Carmen.

I shout for Ira.
I shout for Kin.

*A dream of freedom was promised. We have come
here to make sure it is given.*

I can't breathe, tears fall down my face. Not the sad
tears, not even frustrated tears. Proud tears. Tears that say,
I am ready. I have the same dream.

Free at last! Free at last!
Thank God almighty, we are free at last!

I jump up and down. I am not sure if my body belongs
to me or the crowd or the speech or electricity. I know
change is here.

Mr. King says the last words again.

I remember when Mr. King asked me, *What will hold up
the sky when hope is gone?* I did not know the answer then, I
know the answer now; *hope* is never gone. Sometimes *hope*
just needs a rest. Or sometimes you forget where you put
it, but *hope* is everywhere. It is in the Drinking Gourd, in
the wolves they gave us to help our spirits, it is in our skin.
You don't turn blue from sadness, you turn blue because
hope is missing and when you find it, nothing is the same. I
stare down at my hand in Larkin's white one.

Brown and brilliant like they have never known anything blue. *I've gone wolf.*

Then Larkin falls to his knees, he can't stop coughing, he can't get enough air—now he is blue instead of me.

Ms. Carmen shouts out that someone should call 911. Sirens come. They have to take off Larkin's cloth mask to put one on that gives him more air. That's when everyone sees him. That's when people recognize the president's son.

Larkin grabs my hand and says, "Don't let them take me back to President Tuba."

I hold his hand tightly. I won't let go.

Ms. Carmen and I climb into the ambulance with Larkin and I keep thinking, *Now Larkin is gasping for air, turning blue instead of me.*

BLACK: CHARLOTTESVILLE, VA, 2022

Brown and brilliant
like they have never known
anything blue.
I've gone wolf.

—Inmate Eleven, 12 years old

1

What Is Real Life?

"*Gone wolf?*" the woman in white sitting across from me says. Her coat falls like snow around her.

I know coats can't fall like snow. Snow falls from the sky in tiny unique flakes, but sometimes one thing reminds me of something else and that is what it looks like. Snow sliding down a mountain.

"Yes, *gone wolf*." I nod once.

"And when you *go wolf*, what year is it?" The woman looks over her spectacles while tapping her pen against her notepad. The taps count the seconds it takes for my mouth to make an answer.

Her name is Dr. Lovingood.

She is my fourth mind doctor so far. I have seen a therapist, physiologist, holistic doctor, and everything in between, but Dr. Lovingood is my first research psychologist.

Research psychologist is just a fancy way of saying Dr. Lovingood is studying me. She has only been studying me for one session and she has already said, *Imogen, you are mature for your age.* I don't know what that is supposed to mean. I've lived for twelve years and other twelve-year-old kids have also lived for twelve years. I think it means that I've really lived for fifteen or sixteen or maybe even sixteen and a half years. I know that is not how time works—but that is what it *feels* like she means.

I stare at my palms, which have one long lifeline and two short ones. I answer, "When I *go wolf*, it is 2111."

Dr. Lovingood nods and scratches out some notes before pointing at the door that leads into the waiting room. "And when you are not telling your story, when you walk through that door to where your mother is waiting for you, when you are not *going wolf*, what year is it?"

I swallow and it feels like a full moon is stuck in my throat. "Out there it is 2022."

"That's correct." She smiles. "And when you *go wolf*, what color is your skin?"

"It is blue." I exhale so slowly I think I might whistle. "Like the tail of a blue whale."

"When you walk through that door to where your mother is waiting . . ." Dr. Lovingood takes notes again. "What color is your skin?"

"Brown." I twist my fingers, wanting to tell the truth. "But sometimes I think it is blue out there too. It's sometimes hard to keep my stories organized."

She nods. "What else is true out there in 2022?"

I bite my tongue. I love words and poems, but there

are some words I don't want to talk into the air because then they have to be true. Dr. Lovingood wants me to deal with all the *truth*, but sometimes the *truth* feels like an extra-large piece of bubble gum that I can't keep chewing, because it hurts my jaw too much and makes me cry. Dr. Lovingood wants me to come to terms with *all* the *truth*— not just parts of it and not with stories I make up in my head.

"Imogen, I know this is hard." Dr. Lovingood puts her notepad down. Her brown hands look like mine. Her dark black hair is straight from root to tip, unlike mine. "The *truth* is hard."

She is wrong.

The *truth* is not hard. It simply should be untrue.

It should be unmade.

Lots of things can be unmade—I can unmake my bed, I can unmake a poem if I write in pencil and erase. I can even un-straighten my hair after a hot comb presses it straight, by just adding water. But if I say the *truth* into the air, I can't unmake it later.

Even though I know that Dr. Lovingood has a raised scar that matches mine on her right arm—from the vaccine—I don't think she understands me. Everyone in the world has that scar now, and no one understands me. I bite my tongue harder. I worry I might bleed. I wonder if my blood would be filled with poems and stories too. If my blood was inspected under a microscope, I wonder if the alphabet would be floating in it.

I know letters can't actually live in your blood, but sometimes I am so filled with stories and poems, that is how it *feels*.

"This is not working, is it?" Dr. Lovingood says under her breath while rubbing her temples with her fingertips. "How many doctors have you seen, Imogen?"

"Three," I say. "All in Washington, DC."

"Yes, your mother said you moved from northern Virginia to Charlottesville." She watches me closely. "How many of your doctors in Washington, DC, heard your entire story, Imogen? From start to finish?"

I look up from my palms. "Zero."

"I understand that with your other doctors you thought your skin was blue from sadness, but your mother says that your storytelling is a new development." Dr. Lovingood swallows hard. "That it started during the second quarantine."

My eyes dart around the room. It's too large. There are too many people outside and in the waiting room. I stand quickly. I could get sick; my immune system is not the best. Suddenly, I want to go back home.

"Okay, okay." Dr. Lovingood stands and paces a bit. Under her breath she says, "What could it hurt?" before turning to me. "Imogen, I don't want to talk about reality anymore."

I frown and my mouth is an upside-down boat.

"I want you to tell me your story. The one in your head." Dr. Lovingood exhales and sits. I sit too. "Over the next weeks, I want to hear your story. That's it."

I shake my head. "But the other doctors said I was

daydreaming too much . . . I heard them talking to Mama, they said I had . . ." I stop talking, not sure what words I am looking for.

"Maladaptive daydreaming, first identified by Professor Eliezer Somer at the University of Haifa in Israel." Dr. Lovingood looks at my file again. "A psychiatric condition that causes intense daydreaming that distracts from reality."

I twist the hem of my shirt. "Yes, that, but daydreaming is supposed to be happy. Isn't it?"

"The mind is a difficult thing to understand. Imagination is even harder to understand, Imogen." Dr. Lovingood smiles at me.

I nod slowly. "Minds are complicated."

"Did you know that in African culture, storytelling was a sacred art? Griots told stories." Dr. Lovingood stands again and pulls two books from her shelf. "There is even an Egyptian god with blue skin, Amun."

"But I am not a god," I say.

"No, you are not," she agrees. "But sometimes stories tell us something true even if the story is not all the way true."

"Like a moral?" I ask.

"Exactly. Like a moral." Dr. Lovingood sits. "We have twenty more minutes; will you tell me some of your story?"

I wring my hands together. "You promise not to laugh?"

"Cross my heart." Dr. Lovingood leans back in her chair and takes her glasses off, and for the first time she is *really* smiling. "I just want to listen, Imogen."

So, I tell Dr. Lovingood about a blue girl who is locked

in a tiny room with only her wolf for company. I tell some
of my story.

The year is 2111 and there is a girl who is blue
from the tips of her fingers to her toes. Her name
is Inmate Eleven and she has a wolf named Ira.
For them, the world feels so small. Her room from
left to right is eleven normal steps and twenty-
two baby steps. From right to left, it is ten normal
steps and twenty baby steps. Inmate Eleven knows
science says it is supposed to be the same, but it
isn't, because on the way back she is rushing.

For Ira, it is about a two-second trot.
It is difficult to measure steps when you have
four legs.

Inmate Eleven has one visitor, the lady in blue,
who teaches her about the history of a place
called the Bible Boot—it split from the rest of the
United States eighty-nine years ago. It is ruled by
President Tuba, who, the lady in blue says, has
been the best president ever for the last eighty-
nine years.

The lady in blue shows Inmate Eleven two
dolls and asks her to pick the best one. One doll
has pants with edges like the corner of a wall,

and Inmate Eleven thinks it must be painful to wear something so stiff. The doll's face is pale with blue eyes. The second doll wears a big dress made from squares of many colors. It is as if the dress is not sure what color it should be, so it decides to be all the colors. Like a rainbow. The second doll's clothes are wrinkled and the paint on the doll's fingernails is chipped. The plastic face smiles too big and her slightly yellow teeth remind Inmate Eleven of what a sunrise must be like. The second doll is blue and Inmate Eleven picks that one, and the lady in blue tells her she is wrong.

The room is so small. The Blue girl is so small and the world is so big. She can't go outside in the world because she could get sick. Sometimes guards with machines that shock (biting machines) punish Ira and Inmate Eleven. Sometimes they call Ira the wrong name, they call him Till instead of Ira. Sometimes doctors take Inmate Eleven's blood.

Even though the lady in blue visits, Inmate Eleven feels empty until a Clone boy named Larkin shows up. Larkin has blond hair with one blue eye and one brown eye. Larkin even asks Inmate Eleven her name. She tries to explain

that the lady in blue calls her Inmate Eleven,
but Larkin says that is not a real name. After
he leaves her small room, Inmate Eleven thinks
about how Ira has a name, Larkin has a name, but
she doesn't have a real name.

Inmate Eleven renames herself Imogen.
Imogen.
Imogen.

When I am done, Dr. Lovingood taps the top of the second book she pulled down. The title is *Black History for Kids.* "So, the Blue girl is trapped and sad?"

I nod slowly.

"And her wolf's name is Ira, but the guards with the . . ." She pauses for a moment. "Biting machines. They call him Till?"

I nod, looking at the three lifelines on my palms again.

"Okay, all right." Her eyebrows draw together like they are trying to make a straight line out of my story. "Your story has some history in it, yes?"

I nod again. It seems all I can do is be a bobblehead on a dashboard.

"And Blues can't go outside because they could get sick?" Dr. Lovingood says more to herself than me. "And the lady in blue, she teaches the Blue girl, Inmate Eleven you call her, about the history of the Bible Boot?"

"Yes," I say, still tugging at my shirt.

"Okay, I understand." Dr. Lovingood hands me the book, *Black History for Kids*. "I am the Black lady in the white coat and I am giving you this book to learn from. And thank you for telling me your story, Imogen."

I take the book in my hands and open it—the chapters are chronological. That means they start at one year and keep going forward. "Thank you."

She un-draws her eyebrows. "You are a very good story-teller."

"Thank you," I say again. "Maybe I am a griot."

Storytelling
(Page 11)

In African cultures storytellers were well respected and called griots. They were historians, musicians, and poets who kept records through song and stories. Many griots stayed with royal families because their abilities for recording history were so important.

When Africans from West and Central Africa were abducted, enslaved, and taken to the New World and the West Indies via the Middle Passage (1520–1860), the tradition of storytelling traveled with them. Nearly two million Africans died at sea during the Middle Passage; stories of the enslaved growing wings and flying back to Africa became prevalent in Africa and the New World.

The first Africans arrived in the New World in the 1500s, although the date many historians use is 1619, when twenty Africans arrived in Virginia. The year 1619 is when the chattel slavery we associate with slavery in the South began to evolve.

Once enslaved Africans arrived on foreign grounds with their unique languages and traditions, that was beaten from them as well—they were seen only as property and were forced to work without pay and often were physically harmed and bought and sold with no regard for family ties.

As slavery took root in the United States, African American history was not often recorded. Many enslaved people did not even know their birthdates. Writing was illegal for the enslaved and thus, the oral tradition prevalent in African culture took root on American soil.

African Americans used storytelling to record history and document what happened to them while enslaved. Without this oral tradition, many truths about the American South might have been lost to history.

Slavery was abolished in 1865, which means slavery has only been illegal for 155 years. Owning human beings was legal for over 350 years in the United States. It was permitted even before the United States was called the United States, which means that when "all men are created equal" was written, Black enslaved people were not included in that statement.

The facts are devastating.

2

We Need Time

Dr. Lovingood stands and goes to the door and I remember that in my story, doors open and close like a blinking eye—then lock. Here it stays open. I can leave when I want. Mama sits outside, flipping through a *Daily Progress*. I wait in the office, straining to listen.

"She is still having trouble separating her story from reality. It might be daydreaming, it might be a coping mechanism. It may be best to let her tell her story," Dr. Lovingood says carefully, like she is not sure what Mama will say. "Imogen sees the Blue girl as herself. I believe she is processing all that has happened." She lowers her voice, but I can still hear. "I think the second quarantine and vaccines did not help the situation, with everything that happened and her own immune system being suppressed."

"She has to start remembering, right? The docs in DC said it would be better to move from where everything happened. Cheaper for me too. We move to Charlottesville and Imogen daydreams more." Mama huffs. Not a mean huff, but a tired huff.

"Maybe the storytelling is actually progress, attempting to deal with everything that happened," Dr. Lovingood says. "It has been hard for everyone, but for Imogen, her entire universe changed."

"We can't afford all this. Black people don't get to sit around and *feel* our *feelings*. Especially when things are just getting back to normal." Mama wipes a tear from her face. "It's not fair, but we can't change it."

"Maybe we all deserve time to *feel*. I think that is what Imogen is doing," Dr. Lovingood says, and I see her rub the scar I know is on her right arm. The one everyone has now from the vaccine. "She uses a lot of history in her stories, references to the doll test in the 1940s conducted by Kenneth and Mamie Clark."

"Her brother, Kin." Mama pauses. "History buff, wanted to get a PhD in African American studies. Now Imogen may be fanciful, but she is smart. She read through all those books of his during the second quarantine."

"I understand." Dr. Lovingood pauses. "I am going to give you some information for the Big Sister, Big Brother program in Charlottesville. Maybe she needs someone younger to help."

"You don't think she needs medicine? Her stories spill into the real world. She thinks she is actually blue sometimes. Truly, more than sometimes." I hear my mother whisper. "She has bad dreams too."

"I think we need to give Imogen time to *feel*." Dr. Lovingood looks over her shoulder at me. "We all need time, the scabs from the vaccine scars have just fallen off. You can't put a timeline on healing."

"Time?" My mother nods. "Time is money and in this economy . . ."

Dr. Lovingood catches me staring and smiles. "I'll do all this for free. No bills. No documentations. Let's just help Imogen."

I take a pen sitting on Dr. Lovingood's desk next to a blank notepad. The pen has a black-and-white photo of Harriet Tubman wrapped around it—Harriet Tubman would *go wolf* a lot and roam back to the southern states to help free Black people.

I put the pen in my pocket. I have this problem, I like pens and paper. Sometimes if a pen is just sitting around, I'll put it in my pocket. Mama says I've always done this; even when I was little I would grab pens and pieces of paper. I rip five pieces off the notepad and put all but one in my pocket. Then I sit back down and scratch out a poem.

THINGS BIG BROTHERS DO

They kill spiders and eat the veggies
pushed to the side of your plate
so that you can still have dessert.

They walk you to school
and take you to the playground
and help you fly high on a swing
like a sparrow.

They build forts in the living room with magic
walls that keep viruses out and they watch
Halloween films with you in April.

If their name is Kin, they teach you history
and what it means to be Black in America.

If their name is Lark, they teach you how to make
    brownies,
write poems, and knit sweaters into warm scarfs
like long blue whale tails.

They create special handshakes and read
    to you
when Mama is out nursing. They help
    wth Zoom School
and math problems that tilt wrong.

They take Ira on walks with you and when it rains
they let you jump in all the puddles with your black
    rain boots
with pink skulls. They give the best hugs

with their large arms that make you feel protected
like a letter tucked safely in an envelope.

Big brothers (Lark and Kin), a little sister (Imogen),
and a German shepherd named Ira—
a wolf pack.

BLACK HISTORY FOR KIDS

Harriet Tubman

(unknown 1822?–1913)
(Page 22)

Harriet Tubman was born into slavery around 1822 and grew up to be an abolitionist and activist. After obtaining freedom, she returned to the South over thirteen times to rescue enslaved Black Americans.

Harriet Tubman was able to do this using the Underground Railroad, which was a collection of homes and other places where antislavery activists would house runaways. During the Civil War, she was a scout for Union forces, and after the Civil War, she rallied for women's right to vote.

When Ms. Tubman was a child, a heavy weight was thrown at her head and this caused her to have dizzy spells for her entire life. Ms. Tubman also said she had visions after this incident as she believed they were signs from God.

Although Ms. Tubman was unable to read or write, her stories helped guide many enslaved people to freedom. She was also called Moses, and she never lost a passenger—freeing over seventy enslaved Black Americans in her lifetime.

Ms. Tubman's dedication to her family and her fight against the brutality and unethical nature of slavery have made her a symbol of hope to people from all walks of life.

Ms. Tubman went on many journeys, all were difficult, but she followed the Drinking Gourd–the stars leading her north–and with the help of allies was able to fight against an immoral and brutal system.

3

The Asphalt Is a Snake

I leave Dr. Lovingood's office with five sheets of paper and a new pen. I shrug on my blue coat and gloves, hurry down the stairs behind Mama, and stumble out the front of the office building onto brick streets. The psychologist's office is on the Downtown Mall.

Everyone is cheery and it is fall and I don't want *all the time* to accept the truth.

I don't want *all the time*, like Dr. Lovingood has said I can have.

I just want to unmake what happened. I want to rewind and pause.

I want to be the basketball before it goes through the hoop.

It's cold, the trees are bright with orange and red, spaced perfectly down the sidewalk. Somewhere, a waiter takes an order and a siren screams. Across the brick street where no cars are allowed is a yarn shop. A woman on her front stoop knits a scarf, longer than the tail of a blue whale—something that *feels* peaceful and warm.

I know that the scarf is not actually longer than the tail of a blue whale, but that is what it feels like. It feels like something that goes on and on, and it is blue. The saddest color.

The walk home, to my Aunt Denny's house, is not peaceful like the tail of a blue whale. I push my earbuds in my ears to drown out living sounds. Sometimes, I feel bad that I can still see and hear and breathe without coughing.

I know those are strange things to feel bad about, but lots of people don't do that anymore. Lots of people with names like Skylar, Michael, and Ismail can't do those things anymore.

That's what viruses can do. Take your breath away.

Sometimes forever.

So, I feel guilty.

Guilty is when you think you are doing something bad, something you should not be doing. I want to dive below all the sounds, like a whale, and only feel water moving over my skin and clogging my ears.

I know I don't have gills. Twelve-year-old girls don't have gills, but when I stand on the sidewalk—busy with bodies—and leave the Downtown Mall toward the road buzzing with cars, I wish I could be a blue whale.

Maybe if I were a blue whale, I could open my mouth wide enough to swallow all the names that don't breathe anymore—like the whale that swallowed Jonah in the Bible.

Maybe if I kept them that close to me, they would still be here. They could borrow my air.

Mama grabs my hand and leads me down the sidewalk. The people don't seem to bother Mama. The sounds don't bother Mama. Nothing bothers Mama. Her face always looks on the verge of frowning.

She was ready to get out, to move after the second quarantine.

I was ready to take small steps in the front yard.

Mama tugs me past the store that sells books about history. My brother Kin says, *History is important because it can repeat if we forget, just ask Lark.* My brother Lark says things like, *Kin's right, I got tossed around so much down South that sometimes it felt like it was repeating itself. People thought because I was white, I agreed with their hate.*

I read all of Kin's history books a year ago, all the way from the Middle Passage till now. I learned about the riots that sprung up in Charlottesville. Right here where I am walking. I even started reading about the pandemic that started across the world and tsunami-ed everywhere. I know a virus can't really be a tsunami, but that is what it felt like—a giant wave of scary.

Today, we did not drive, Mama wants me to practice walking out in the open without being frightened of everything. Mama's pace quickens. I keep my eyes on my blue sneakers. On the corner before you cross the street is the store that sells video games. Which reminds me of Lark.

Lark and Kin love the color blue.

The color blue in African culture means love, harmony, togetherness, and peace.

Suddenly everything feels dipped in blue: the sidewalk, the grass—everything except for the asphalt in front of us. I jerk my blue hand from Mama's and plant my feet like a tree at the edge of the sidewalk.

"Come on, Imogen, I have the night shift at the hospital in an hour." She sticks her hand out, wiggling her fingers at me—asking me to trust her.

I don't move, instead my roots dig deeper.

"I should have never let you read all those stories. Imogen, the road is not a snake. It is not going to bite you," Mama says, pushing up the arm of her jacket to glance at her watch.

I sway on my feet, roots loosening.

I know the pavement is not a big black snake waiting to gobble me.

Thinking the road is a snake is a simile. I know that because I like poetry.

I know the pavement won't eat me, but my hands still shake.

My mama sucks her teeth, steps back onto the sidewalk, grabs my hand, and heads up a block, where the street is brick, not asphalt. We cross the street where the brick is.

I feel like one of the people in the Bible again who had an ocean wall on both sides of them and had to just trust it would not crush them. I exhale when we reach the other sidewalk and stride back up the opposite side of the street, adding at least six minutes to our journey.

Mama speeds up.

"Imogen, I understand you need time, but you have to try." Mama glances at her watch again. "Your aunt will watch you while I am at work."

I nod at my feet and imagine a giant wolf walking in front of me, growling at all the people who hover too close. I am in the woods, the people are giant trees I dodge.

Someone bumps into me.

I accidentally growl before pushing my fingers to my mouth.

Thankfully, Mama doesn't notice.

We stop at the next crosswalk. Mama pushes me in front of her and places a sturdy brown hand on each of my shoulders as if to say, *It's safe, it is okay.*

Sometimes when she does this I think everything will be *okay.*

She is good at making people feel *okay.* Mama is a nurse.

I close my eyes until I see colors behind them—dark blue, light blue.

I step onto the concrete and walk across to the other side. My heart pounds so hard in my chest. Mama grabs my hand again and I am happy we don't have to cross any more streets, but now the cracks in the sidewalk worry me, like small canyons that can swallow me whole.

I exhale when I see the bright blue door of Aunt Denny's

tiny brick house, where we live now. Finally home—a den I can sleep in. Away from the sounds of the city, basketballs bouncing all night long. Away from the city, coughing like exclamation marks in the dark. Mama says, *Wrong thoughts and actions can be viruses too*. Viruses, like people in the South believing slavery helped Black people. After the enslaved were set free, things like Jim Crow laws were viruses too.

They spread quickly.

If a virus (the sickness kind) had a poem, it would read like this:

VIRUS

This is an exclamation (!).
It looks like a cough.
It feels dangerous.
It reminds me of a virus
flying through the air.

Jim Crow Laws
(Page 32)

Jim Crow laws, which started in the 1870s, were set up in the southern United States to enforce racial segregation. These laws were upheld by law enforcement and included having whites and Black people attend separate schools, and use different bathrooms, drinking fountains, and more. Furthermore, the laws, which were both state and local, often included making Black people sit in the back of the bus and get up if a white person needed a seat.

These laws were enforced most in the states that made up the former Confederate States, also known as the Bible Belt states. This included Louisiana, Florida, Mississippi, Alabama, Georgia, North Carolina, South Carolina, Tennessee, Arkansas, Oklahoma, Kentucky, eastern Texas, and the lower part of Virginia.

The military was also segregated and in 1913, President Woodrow Wilson segregated the federal government. Racism started at the top and trickled down into every aspect of American life. The African American still lived in fear.

Direct consequences of the Jim Crow laws were exploitation, violence, and sometimes even the murder of Black people, which was done without consequences for many whites. From 1882 to 1968, over 3,500 African Americans were killed by mobs, without a jury or trial. Often police officers did nothing to stop these senseless acts of violence.

In 1954, *Brown v. Board of Education* found that separate was not equal, and public schools were supposed to desegregate. Desegregation was supposed to be implemented over the last sixty-six years but in reality, many schools remain segregated socioeconomically and racially. Equality is still something that African Americans living in America fight for today.

4

My New Bedroom

My new bedroom is bigger than my old one. From left to right, it is eleven normal steps and twenty-two baby steps. From right to left, it is ten normal steps and twenty baby steps. I know the steps should be the same, but every time I try to measure it, it is different.

My old room in northern Virginia was not in a house, it was in an apartment. From left right, it was eight normal steps and sixteen baby steps. From right to left, it was seven normal steps and fourteen baby steps. So, my new room has more space, which I don't like.

I wish the walls would lean in closer like the canopy of trees. Sometimes, I drag two chairs from the kitchen into my bedroom and place them in front of my twin bed. Then I drape blankets over the bedposts and the chairs and create a den.

The den is the perfect size, but it still feels empty without Ira.

For Ira, my German shepherd, my new room would be about a two-second trot.

When Ira was in my old room it was about a 1.5-second trot, but it is hard to be sure because measuring steps when you have four legs is hard. During the first quarantine, sometimes he circled the edges of the bedroom. His head would get real low and his eyes turned to slits.

That was his *gone wolf* face. He was imagining himself somewhere else.

He was daydreaming.

I don't have many visitors at Aunt Denny's house. It's hard when you move three hours away right after a pandemic eats up the world. Sometimes, Mama comes into my room to read to me between her nursing shifts at the University of Virginia Hospital. Aunt Denny reads to me too, but I like being in my den alone.

I don't go to normal school anymore. I don't even use Zoom School. I get my assignments sent to me, I borrow books and learn the assignments myself. Sometimes Mama and Aunt Denny help. Then I send my assignments back. I always get A's, but I don't like being around lots of people. Sometimes I think all the people with white skin hate me and I hide under my desk. Sometimes I think germs, green and goblin-looking, sit on top of everyone's skin and I cry an ocean. I know you can't cry an entire ocean, but that is what it feels like.

Maybe one day I'll be able to go to school again, but for now, I like learning in my den.

My door opens like a blinking eye and Aunt Denny pops her head in. "It's time to eat dinner, Imogen."

I crawl like a wolf out of my den filled with pillows and blankets and stand in the center of my room. "Can I eat in my room?"

Aunt Denny opens the door all the way. "Imogen, we talked about this . . ."

I nod and tap my fingers on my pant leg. Aunt Denny's pant legs are ironed perfectly, they remind me of the edge of a corner. "Okay, can we watch the news then?"

"Of course." Aunt Denny heads to the living room and I follow.

She sits down on the couch, which is covered in plastic to protect the upholstery. To me, the sofa is like a turtle in a shell or a hermit crab. The plastic protects it from getting hurt. I sit on a pillow in front of the coffee table. Aunt Denny already has my dinner sitting there—three chicken nuggets, green beans, and mashed potatoes.

"All of my favorites." I smile like a sunrise.

Aunt Denny clicks on the TV. "Only the best for my Imogen."

I take some mashed potatoes on my fork and put a green bean on top before taking a large bite. Then, I mix mashed potatoes and chicken together.

"You are the strangest eater, Imogen," Aunt Denny says between chews.

I nod. "I like opposite things together."

On the TV screen, a man with thick-rimmed glasses

that he keeps pushing up his nose talks very slowly about virus numbers going down. He says, *It appears that the spread of the virus has finally slowed. We are trying to get vaccines to more rural places, but for the most part everyone in the world has been given the shot. This was a very serious virus.*

"Now you want to admit it was serious," Aunt Denny hisses at the TV. "A year ago, we had someone telling us the virus was nothing to worry about."

Aunt Denny is talking about the president. He did not think the virus was very serious. I remember Mama would come home from trying to help get people well and yell at the news, saying, *I just saw a man cough himself to death.*

I shake my head and the memory disappears. On the TV, the man with the thick-rimmed glasses points to a chart with a long red line heading down toward zero new infections. He smiles proudly, saying, *As you can see, in the United States this week we have only had twenty new infections, all from citizens who had not yet received the vaccine. That is less than last week and the week before.*

"Twenty is a low number," I say to the TV and to Aunt Denny.

Aunt Denny nods. "We still need to wear masks in large groups, though, Imogen, to be safe."

I know I should be happy because twenty is a very low number. I am happy. I am happy because the virus hurt a lot of people and now it is dying and that is good, but that is not the number I keep watching. Another man without glasses appears on the other side of the screen: *Unfortunately, there was one death in the United States from the virus yesterday, but that is a vast improvement.*

Aunt Denny talks to the TV. "Yes, lord, much better than the thousands this time last year."

I watch as the number of deaths from the virus goes up by one number and my throat feels like sandpaper. My body feels warm, like I am standing in a desert and sand is hitting my eyes. I am in a desert. I am sure. Tears fall into my food, two different things mixing.

"May I be excused?" I ask.

"Oh, Imogen, I didn't . . ." Aunt Denny pauses. "Yes, you can be excused."

I run back to my den and hide in the covers, rocking back and forth. I know one is a good number, it is much less than a thousand, but what if it is someone's one? Then it still feels like a thousand. I don't know how a soul can be a number.

Yesterday, I learned a new term: *cognitive dissonance.* It means thinking two opposite things at once. Mama taught me the term when we were watching the news.

That's how I feel. I am happy the number is one. I am sad that it is someone's one.

I cry in my den like it is my one. 'Cause life, each life is important. Just like the life of every person who was killed because of hate but never got justice is important. Each virus death is important. I feel so much, then again, Mama says I often *feel* too much. I am trying to work on that. So, I pull out my journal and do what Lark and Kin taught me to do, I write a poem instead.

COUNTING WRONG

It's easy to count.
    One.
        Two.
            Three.
But numbers don't hold things right.
One flower that is thrown in the woods
is not the same as one lit match
because a match can start a fire.

Two roses in a vase
are not the same as two fangs
on a large spider because one can hurt.

The three lucky leaves of a clover
are not the same as three souls in bodies.

So, one death
is the same as a million—
and still somehow
that feels wrong too.

Hard Examples of Hate
(Page 44)

Julia & Frazier B. Baker (February 22, 1898)
Lake City, South Carolina

After Frazier Baker was appointed as postmaster, a mob of white men set his home on fire with his wife and six children inside. The mob began shooting. His wife escaped with five of their children (three wounded). Frazier and his infant daughter, Julia, did not make it out of the house. Some of the men involved were put on trial, but an all-white jury could not come to a decision and declared a mistrial. The men were never tried again. They got away with the murder of an innocent child and an innocent Black man.

Mary Turner (May 19, 1918)
Dallas, Texas

After her husband, Hayes Turner, was killed by a mob of white men, Mary Turner, who was eight months pregnant, denounced her husband's murder. The same mob that killed her husband turned on her. Mary was also murdered. No one was punished for these crimes.

Duluth Murders (June 15, 1920)
Duluth, Minnesota

Three Black circus workers, Elias Clayton, Elmer Jackson, and Isaac McGhie, were taken from the local jail by a mob of thousands of white men and beaten to death. The offense was alleged assault against a white woman, which later was found to be untrue. The white mob decided to take the law into their own hands. In 2003, a memorial was made for the murdered men.

No one was ever charged.

5

Poem for Ira

I bring my knees to my chin and try to stop thinking of numbers, of stories, of the doctor appointment I must go to tomorrow to make sure my body is strong. I have to go to the doctor one Friday every month.

The words inside me are too much and I have to write at least one true thing down. A true poem.

IRA

My German shepherd, Ira
is like a wolf except he is black and tan,
not gray like a wolf usually is.

He has two big brown eyes
that remind me of the dirt
after it rains for hours.

Ira's paws are as big as my 12-year-old palms
and the fur between his pads
tickles the lifelines on my hands.

Ira takes four steps for each of my two.
He growls low when the doorbell rings.
If Mama, or Lark, or Kin walk in, his tail thumps
    the floor.

We were born on the same day,
and followed each other through
12 years until, until, until . . .

The quarantine came and his 12-year-old body
did not wake up.
Instead his soul decided to take a long walk away.

Mama said, He had a good life.
Kin said, He will always be part of our pack.
Lark said, Let's keep a tuft of his fur to protect us.
I said, He's gone wolf.
He's free to roam where he wants.

Civil Rights Movement
(Page 56)

President Harry Truman desegregated the armed forces in 1948, although most schools remained segregated until 1954, when the Supreme Court case *Brown v. Board of Education* legislated desegregation. But desegregation did little for equality in the United States, hence the Civil Rights Movement, which followed the Jim Crow Era and lasted from around 1954 to 1968.

The Civil Rights Movement was a period of history when African Americans fought for social and economic equality in the United States. There were many leaders of the Civil Rights Movement and though they did not all agree on the methods for obtaining equality in the United States, they all agreed that African Americans were not treated fairly. As Martin Luther King Jr. stated in his "I Have a Dream speech," "America has given Black people a bad check; a check that has come back marked 'insufficient funds.'"

Leaders of the Civil Rights Movement included Whitney Young, A. Philip Randolph, Martin Luther King Jr., James Farmer, Roy Wilkins, Malcolm X, Rosa Parks, John Lewis, Ella Baker, Dorothy Height, Willa Brown, James Baldwin, Coretta Scott King, Angela Davis, Claudette Colvin, and countless others.

Perhaps the most documented Civil Rights Movement leader was Dr. Martin Luther King Jr., who organized peaceful protests to have laws, specifically voting laws, changed. If Black people could vote legally and easily, then hopefully substantial change could be accomplished.

Segregation was often only seen as an issue in the South, but segregation of housing, especially in cities, was prevalent. It is important to remember that the Civil Rights Movement helped to spark progress in the United States, but equality continues to be something African Americans are protesting for.

6

Doctor's Office

Every month I go to the doctor to make sure all my blood is doing the right thing. Sometimes, I talk to my blood and say, *Blood, keep fighting viruses, blood, keep me well.* It worked once, I wonder if it will keep working.

The doctor's office was not so bad when Ira came with me. I dressed him in a special red vest to show he was my service dog and he got to sit beside me when they poked me, because sometimes, I get very worried about little things.

Like right now, I am worried that the car in the left lane, beside Mama, might suddenly jump into our lane. I worry all the stoplights might go green at the same time and cause a traffic jam. Sometimes, when I look out my bedroom window at night and the moon is hanging low in the sky, I worry that gravity has given up and the moon might just fall on the earth and bounce away into the cosmos.

I know that the moon can't just fall on the earth. I know the earth and the moon are not giant bouncy balls in the sky. If one falls it would probably miss us completely, but sometimes I worry. I worry as I unclick my seat belt and step out of the car onto the asphalt, which today reminds me of an endless black lake frozen over with ice.

I worry if the ice breaks, I'll fall right through, to the center of the earth. The center of the earth is very hot, and if that happened, I would burn and burning also worries me. Actually, burning reminds me of high fevers and viruses running through the air. It reminds me of how hot the skin of a person with a fever can be. I touch my hand to my forehead, checking my own temperature.

Mama pulls my hand away. "You don't have a fever, Imogen. We checked it earlier today, remember?"

"I remember, but I think the sun warmed my skin up a lot. Maybe the sun is getting closer to the earth?" I twist my hands outside the doctor's office.

Mama puts a hand on my shoulder and hands me my mask with mermaid sequins on it, because it is still important to wear masks in crowded places. She leads me into the waiting room and we sit three chairs away from a lady with a blue skirt.

"The sun is not falling, Imogen. Sometimes the sun just warms your skin." Mama keeps her hand on my shoulder.

I look down at my own hands, which should look brown, but suddenly seem bluish to me. I blink again and remember we are not in my story, we are in 2022 and my hands are brown again.

Mama watches me as I close my eyes tight and I know

she knows I was daydreaming again. She shakes her head slightly.

"Sorry," I say.

Mama doesn't say anything, she just pats the top of my head.

A lady in a white coat comes out and says, "Imogen?"

Mama and I get up and walk down the long hallway. They make me take my shoes off and get on a scale. Then they take my temperature, which is only 98.1. This means I don't have a fever and the sun is not falling from the sky. Then the lady in the white coat leads us to the same room we always sit in, it is small and clean.

I don't like the smell; it reminds me of hospitals and crying.

I swallow hard and reach for Ira before I remember he is not there anymore. Mama grabs my hand quickly this time.

"We can get another dog, Imogen."

I frown. "Ira wasn't a dog, he was my friend."

Mama nods slowly. The slow nod that says, *Maybe Imogen is feeling too much again.*

Mama tries again. "We can always get you another friend," she says softly.

I look around the doctor's office, it feels like a cage. A cage is a place where you force living things to stay, and that is what the doctor's office feels like. They poke me and stick me without asking. They take my blood even though it belongs to me.

"I don't think it will be the same unless we have the same birthday," I say, because I don't think I want to replace Ira. Only Ira knew that when I was tapping, I was nervous. I don't think you can replace gone things.

"Maybe we could check the birthdays of dogs at the pound?" Mama looks out the window. "Or we could always wait a little longer."

"I think we should wait a little longer . . . ," I say.

I flinch when the door blinks open and the doctor walks in. This is when I would usually sit on the floor with Ira, and the doctor would kneel down and take my blood and it would all be over very fast.

But Ira is busy exploring the cosmos somewhere; that's how I daydream it. He is jumping from star to star and finding the best fields to roam in. I don't mind if he is happy roaming, but I don't like that now I have to sit on the table with crinkly paper and watch the doctor prepare a needle and then despite being told to look away, I have to watch the needle slide slowly into my vein. I watch because I want to know exactly how much of me they are taking away.

I watch because I want to say goodbye to every drop of my blood before it is tested and thrown away. I don't like people taking away things that belong to me. I don't like viruses taking away things that belong to me.

"How have you been, Imogen?" the doctor says as she takes my blood.

I glare at her.

"Imogen, be nice," my mama says under her breath.

"I don't feel good." I frown. "I don't like you taking things that belong to me."

"Imogen, you know your blood has to be tested." Mama turns to the doctor. "I am a nurse, she knows . . ."

"Yes, you told me this last time too. I guess it is strange that we have to take some of you away, Imogen." The doc places a Band-Aid on my arm. "But I want to make sure you stay healthy, so I have to take it."

I look at the Band-Aid and trace the wolves on it.

"I heard you like wolves." The doctor leans back. "I thought you might like these Band-Aids."

I look up. "Thank you."

"No problem." The doctor smiles and looks down at her clipboard.

She is not so bad.

NEEDLES

Can hurt a lot.
Mosquitos have needle
noses that suck out blood.

Metal needles suck out blood
too, but it is different because the blood
goes in a tube so it can be tested.

My blood has to be tested
to see if my immune system
is running right.

Needles can also hurt
but be good like when
they carry good things.

Like vaccines, or medicine
to help people stop coughing.

So, needles can hurt
and be hopeful
which is confusing
but true.
I think.

A lot of things
are hard but true.

More Hard Examples of Hate
(Page 45)

Omaha Courthouse Riots (September 28–29, 1919)
Omaha, Nebraska

From 1910 to 1920, the population of Black people in Omaha doubled because many were recruited to work. Whites in the area did not like the competition in the workplace and tensions rose. In 1917, some major meatpacking plants hired Black people to work while white workers were on strike. This increased hostilities and on September 28, riots started. A mob of white men and women watched as Will Brown was murdered during these riots.

No one was charged.

Not one person was charged.

Moore's Ford Murders (July 25, 1946)
Walton County, Georgia

George and Mae Murray Dorsey and Roger and Dorothy Malcom were murdered by a mob of white men. One of the victims was a WWII veteran who had only been back in the United States for nine months. No one was charged with these crimes against humanity.

Not one person.

Emmett Till (August 28, 1955)
Money, Mississippi

Accused of whistling at a white woman while visiting Mississippi from Chicago, fourteen-year-old Emmett Till was dragged from his family home by a group of white men and murdered. He was found in a river, beaten and shot. His mother had an open casket funeral so everyone could see what hatred did to her son. Years later, the woman who claimed Till whistled at her admitted she lied.

No one was charged with his murder.

7

Zion Hill Baptist Church

Saturday, I stay in my den all day.

Sundays, we go to church to sit with the Holy Ghost. It takes most of the day because we don't go to a church that is close by. Mama wants to go to the church she grew up in. The church Aunt Denny and her mom, Mildred, go to. Mama says, *My entire family is buried here—mom, dad, grandparents, great-grandparents.*

So, we don't go to the church that is one block away. At 9:00 a.m., we all get into Aunt Denny's car and drive out of Charlottesville. I am wearing a blue dress. The buildings get farther and farther apart, more and more lonely. Then the road changes from a three-lane snake to a one-lane snake. I know the road is not a snake, but I don't like the pavement, because it can be dangerous.

Once the pavement is a one-lane snake, there are no buildings, just trees the color of a sunset. A sunset can be a lot of colors and fall leaves remind me of a sunset. We drive and drive until we are in Cismont, Virginia, in front of a white church with eight stained glass windows—four on each side.

I don't mind church.

I do mind everyone kissing me and leaving red lipstick on my cheeks, forehead, and nose—so many germs. I do mind everyone looking at Mama, like I am a problem. The seats are hard and I don't think the Holy Ghost would want to sit on such hard seats.

I don't listen in church.

I usually just tell myself stories.

Sometimes, I tell God about Lark and Kin, and those stories are all the way true, because you can't lie to God. He will know. I tell God about how Lark likes to write screenplays and poetry. During the first quarantine, he wrote scripts about mermaids and wolves that we all would act out. I tell God how Kin was always the director, because he was the smart brother and older by a year.

Sometimes during church, people catch the Holy Ghost.

It gets stuck in their lungs, like a virus, but good.

And the people dance around and shout.

I don't think it is fair that God decides to touch all these people, but never me. After church, Mama stands in front of her grandparents' graves. "Your great-grandfather always had a pipe in his mouth, and he lived to be almost one hundred years old."

I rock on my feet and put the flowers in one of the stone vases.

My aunt stands on the other side of us. "Remember how

you would write letters to Grandma every Sunday?" she asks my mother.

Mama nods. "People don't write letters anymore."

"I can write you a letter if you want, Mama," I say because Mama seems sad and I know she is still very busy nursing. "I am good at writing letters."

"I don't have anyone to write letters to anymore, Imogen, but thank you." Mama smiles down at me.

I frown. "You could write to your grandparents and leave the letters here."

Mama pauses. "They would not be able to read them, Imogen."

"Yes, they would. At night, they would let their spirits come down from heaven and they can sit right there on that bench." I point at the bench in the graveyard. "And read them."

Mama stoops down. "Imogen, that's not how it works."

Aunt Denny watches me closely.

"It is how it works." I frown, looking at my blue hands, or are they brown? "If God can hear us, why can't they?"

I stomp away toward the car that will drive for a long time on a one-lane snake that then sprouts to three lanes. Then, I will see Aunt Denny's blue door and I can go into my room, open the door to my closet stuffed with pillows and blankets, and hide in my wolf den. On the car ride home, I write a poem in the clouds with my mind. I imagine I am like Martin Luther King Jr. when he wrote speeches, except my poem is just for me, not the world.

BASIN

The leather seats in the car are cold
they make the basin of my back
feel like ice is touching it.

I know my back is not a basin,
basins hold things,
but the curve in it right above my tailbone
reminds me of a tiny bowl.
Of a tiny basin and I think,
I can hold things.

I can hold my own hand.
I can hold air in my fingers
even if I can't see it.

I can hold stories.
I can unmake things.

Still my back is cold
like the surface of a headstone.

BLACK HISTORY FOR KIDS

Dr. Martin Luther King Jr.

(1929–1968)
(Page 74)

Martin Luther King Jr. was born in Atlanta, Georgia, in 1929. He became a leading figure of the Civil Rights Movement in the United States, organizing countless protests and sit-ins.

Like many of his contemporaries, Dr. King believed in advocating for equal rights through nonviolence and civil disobedience, which aligned with his Christian beliefs.

In 1963, Dr. King helped organize the March on Washington, where his most quoted speech, "I Have a Dream," was given in front of the reflecting pool at the Lincoln Memorial.

History remembers Dr. King fondly, presidents praise and quote him, but while he was alive he was met with much discrimination and conflict. He openly opposed the Vietnam War in his speech "Beyond Vietnam," saying, "A nation that continues year after year to spend more money on military defense than on programs of social uplift is approaching spiritual death."

In 1964, Martin Luther King Jr. was awarded the Nobel Peace Prize and was at the time the youngest person, age thirty-five, to win the award. He donated the winnings to the Civil Rights Movement.

In his speech "I've Been to the Mountaintop," Dr. King said, "I've seen the Promised Land. I may not get there with you. But I want you to know tonight, that we, as a people, will get to the Promised Land."

Less than a day later, Dr. King was assassinated, which means executed by someone else, on April 4, 1968.

8

Therapy Again . . .

Outside the window, the leaves look like a sunset and they cover the brick alleyway, which no cars can drive on, like a blanket. I know that leaves can't actually be a sunset and that they can't cover things like the blanket Lark knitted for me in home ec class. Leaves are flimsy and when they are wet, they are slippery and cold. The thing is, when they all fall at once and stick to the ground, it *feels* like they are a blanket for the earth.

Dr. Lovingood closes the door to her office and takes a seat in a chair. The seats are different today. Before she would sit behind a desk—like a wall between us. Now, there are two chairs set up near the window with a small table with cookies and water between them.

Dr. Lovingood is dressed differently too. She has on blue jeans and a black blouse that has tiny blue buttons like raindrops down the front. Her stockings are bright yellow, like the sun, and her shoes are dark blue. Her clothes remind me of what one of the dolls in my story wore—*all the colors*—and it felt like home.

"How are you doing today, Imogen?" Dr. Lovingood says, smiling.

I chew on my bottom lip. "I want to write a letter to my great-grandparents and leave it at their headstones so they can absorb it at night, but Mama says it doesn't work that way."

Dr. Lovingood pauses. "Do you think that is how it works, Imogen?"

"I dunno." I rub my hands together. "I mean it's the same as praying, you just write it down. Lots of people pray, it makes them feel better."

"Just like the wolf, Ira, in your story? He makes Inmate Eleven feel better," Dr. Lovingood questions.

"Lark and Kin love wolves. We are like a wolf pack," I say, looking down.

"Are you still a wolf pack?" Dr. Lovingood smiles.

I don't say anything. Instead, I start thinking of my fingers changing to blue, the saddest color. After my fingers change to blue, the color goes up my arms and down my legs and even stretches to the tips of my hair—until I am completely blue.

"Maybe you can add more people to your pack?" Dr. Lovingood suggests.

I blink away the feeling of being blue. "I don't have many friends."

"I heard you like to write poetry. Maybe there are some kids around who like to write poetry too." Dr. Lovingood looks out the window as she speaks. "It's up to you when and how you make friends."

"I don't want any new friends." I swallow. "I have my pack. Like Martin Luther King Jr. had his pack, like Malcolm X had his pack."

Dr. Lovingood keeps looking out the window. I wonder if she thinks the leaves are like a sunset or if they are like a blanket on the ground. I wonder if she is asking to be part of my pack or if she is making fun of my story.

I add, "I don't think I should add anyone to the pack without asking Lark and Kin."

Dr. Lovingood's eyes search mine. She nods. "Could you share more of your story with me?" Dr. Lovingood smiles a real smile. One that touches her eyes. "Please?"

I want Dr. Lovingood to understand, so I tell her more of my story.

After Imogen names herself, she tells Larkin and he likes her new name. Ira likes her new name too. Then one day, a new scary man comes into Imogen's small room. His name is President Tuba. He tells her she can't have a name, she has to be called Inmate Eleven, and Larkin doesn't say anything and that makes her sad. It makes her sad that Larkin looks just as scared as her.

One good thing does happen: Imogen is moved to a different room. She might even get to go outside soon and her wolf, Ira, might get to come with her. It is all wonderful until Larkin takes her to get poked by doctors. Then a woman with blue skin named Inmate Sixteen straightens her hair and gets her dressed to meet Congress. The Congress of the Bible Boot are scary, but they approve her for something.

Then Imogen must have lunch with the president alone. President Tuba has a pile of white pills on his desk that he tells his followers will help them never get sick and only white people in the Bible Boot can have them.

President Tuba calls Imogen stupid and she feels so blue.

The president's Blue person, Inmate Three, walks Imogen back to her room, picking up a secret note from Inmate Sixteen on the way. The note holds many secrets and Imogen is shocked when she reads about the truth of the Bible Boot—Clones are actually white Elitists, and Blues are Black, but they are sad. The Black people who live in Elite, the capital of the Bible Boot, are Blue because they feel devastatingly sad.

Malcolm X

(1925–1965)
(Page 78)

Malcolm X was a Black Muslim minister and human rights activist during the Civil Rights Movement. He preached self-defense when confronted with violence, which gave him many followers and enemies.

Malcolm X is often depicted as a violent and aggressive man when in reality he was a complex and introspective man trying to obtain equality for Black people. Malcolm X refused to become palatable for the white gaze at the time. He saw the violence Black people faced as a concern that could not be solved by "coddling" whites.

In 1964, Malcolm X went on the traditional Muslim pilgrimage to Mecca and some of his views evolved and changed; however, only one side of Malcolm X is seen by history.

Malcolm X was a father, a preacher, and an integral part of the Civil Rights Movement.

Malcolm X founded the Organization of Afro-American Unity (OAAU) in 1965. The purpose of the OAAU was to fight for the human rights of African Americans and promote cooperation among Africans and people of African American descent in America. Even though the Black Panther Party was not established until after Malcolm X's death, his influence within it is evident. Malcolm X believed that if the government was not going to help Black people, Black people had to help Black people. The Black Panther Party were the original creators of the free lunch program to feed hungry Black children.

Malcolm X was assassinated, which means executed by someone else, in February 1965.

9

Questions

"So, there are Blues and Clones?" Dr. Lovingood asks. "And Clones are white?"

"Yes, it shouldn't make sense but it does." I nod slowly. "But, but Larkin is different. He is not always mean and he gets in trouble if he doesn't listen."

"I see . . ." Dr. Lovingood smiles. "Do you like small spaces, Imogen?"

I nod again. "I have an immune deficiency. That means I can get sick easily. I like to stay in small spaces."

"Even before the virus? When you were eleven?" Dr. Lovingood questions.

"No, with Kin and Lark . . . ," I say clearly. "I didn't have to be scared."

"You had your wolf pack?" Dr. Lovingood nods, understanding. "You know I love the meaning of names."

I sit up straight. "Me too. Ira means *watchful* and Imogen means *girl*."

"Larkin means victory," Dr. Lovingood adds.

"Lark means *playful* and Kin means *golden*," I add quickly.

Dr. Lovingood stands. "Very good names. I love all those names."

She goes to talk to Mama. I can't hear much this time; I only hear something about letters being the same as praying and I think Dr. Lovingood is very good at loving—just like her name. I borrow three more sheets of notepad paper and borrow a pink pen to jot down another poem.

NAMES/POEMS

*Stick with your bones
forever. Ira is still Ira.*

*The tree that I named, Alba,
that got hit by lightning
and cut down is still Alba.*

*Martin Luther King Jr.'s
words are still his
even though he is gone.
That's because your name
grows tall, with your soul.*

I leave the poem on the center of Dr. Lovingood's desk. A gift for borrowing paper and accidentally on purpose stealing pens. A *thank you for listening to my story with two ears and one heart* offering.

March on Washington
(Page 80)

The March on Washington was organized by many Civil Rights activists and took place on August 28, 1963. It was one of the largest gatherings ever in Washington, DC, with over 250,000 people. Martin Luther King Jr. gave his famous speech "I Have a Dream" during this march.

The march was organized by A. Philip Randolph and Bayard Rustin to protest for civil and economic changes and human rights for Black people in the United States. It was one of the largest protests of the 1960s.

Eighty percent of the protesters were Black and flocked to Washington, DC, to hear Roy Wilkins, John Lewis, Martin Luther King Jr., A. Philip Randolph, Bayard Rustin, Walter Reuther, and many other Civil Rights leaders speak.

Below is an excerpt from Martin Luther King Jr.'s "I Have a Dream" speech:

"But one hundred years later, the Negro still is not free. One hundred years later, the life of the Negro is still sadly crippled by the manacles of segregation and the chains of discrimination. One hundred years later, the Negro lives on a lonely island of poverty in the midst of a vast ocean of material prosperity."

10.

Letters

Mama says she is not mad at me.
She buys me a set of eleven cards with eleven envelopes.
We don't need eleven stamps, though.
We are not mailing them, we are leaving them
for her grandma and grandpa to read
on the bench.

Mama's letter to her grandma that I read because she did
not seal it and sometimes I get very curious and I can't help
myself:

Hi Grandma,

*I wonder if it is possible for you to see this. If it is
possible that you are in heaven and also somehow
here, it has been hard for me and Imogen. We have
lost a lot. The world seems like it is spinning out of
control. Every time I touch the scar from the vaccine*

*made to stop the virus from spreading, I think how
every living human has the same mark now.*

*There are different kinds of missing. The kind
that is both cold and warm.*

*I don't know how to help Imogen. She feels so
much.*

*It is like she tries to hold the entire world in her
heart.*

She thinks her skin is blue. Imagine that.

*She misses her brothers. I know what you are
thinking. I only have one daughter, but Grandma,
you would have loved Kin and Lark. We fostered
them. They showed up together, decided Imogen
could command them however she liked. Played
dolls with her. Taught her to act and write poetry.
Reminded her to take her meds to help her
immune system. When the virus came, they went
to the stores, sanitized everything.*

Our found family was perfect.

But I guess some things can't last forever.

The boys had to move on . . .

My letter to my great-grandma:

Hi Great-Grandma,

*I know you will get this, I am not worried like
Mama. Some things are just magic. Like when*

the ocean just divided in the Bible. Or when Jesus
woke up and moved a stone. I like that story.
Sometimes, I wonder why us normal people can't
do that. Why Lark or Kin or I can't pass away,
then walk out of a cave alive and smiling. You
know that is what Jesus did on Easter.

The thing is, I feel very sad.

So sad I turned blue.

I know it sounds crazy, but that is what
happened. That is what it felt like when I felt so
sad, so cold, so very blue. I also tell stories that
are not all the way true. I like to daydream about
stories that help me figure out all the "feels" that
bubble under my skin.

Mama says you told the best stories. She says
that Great-Grandpa fell in love with you when
he saw you sitting on a fence smoking a cigar. He
knew right then.

Are there just things you know?

Did you know that some things we know about
the Civil Rights Movement are not right? Like
everyone said that the largest gathering of the Civil
Rights Movement in the 1960s was the March on
Washington, but it was actually the 1964 New
York School Boycott.

Maybe if I knew for sure that Lark and Kin
were happy somewhere . . .

Maybe, maybe, maybe . . . I'd be a little less blue.

I also like writing poems. Here, I'll leave you a poem.

FORGET-ME-NOTS

Are a special flower
cause they ask you
to always remember.

They have five petals
and are blue and are wild.

Petal one: Lark
Petal two: Kin
Petal three: Ira
Petal four: Mama
Petal five: Imogen

BLACK HISTORY FOR KIDS

1964 New York City School Boycott
(Page 85)

The March on Washington is often touted for being the largest Civil Rights gathering of the 1960s, but that distinction actually goes to the 1964 boycott of New York City public schools.

In 1964, despite the requirements of *Brown v. Board of Education*, a reasonable plan for integration had not been established. Furthermore, schools that many African Americans attended were in horrible condition. Things were still separate and *not* equal.

On February 3, 1964, more than half a million teachers, students, and activists boycotted New York City public schools. It is true that school-system segregation was illegal since 1920, but housing patterns in New York continued to keep schools separate and not equal. This was a problem seen in the northern and southern states. Often, predominately white neighborhoods were against these demonstrations.

The protest was organized and led by Rev. Milton Galamison, and the demonstration came to be known as Freedom Day.

Fortunately, the president at the time, Lyndon B. Johnson, passed laws to improve the public schools in predominantly Black areas because of Freedom Day.

11

Toni: Means Priceless One

Mama never told me she signed me up for the Big Sister, Big Brother program. The doorbell rings and Mama invites a girl with blue locs into the house. Mama tries not to look at her twice.

I can't stop looking.

Her locs have little metal clasps down the length of them and her nose has two hoops in one nostril. I like her brown hands too, there are tattoos of the phases of the moon spread over her fingers. Her jeans are black and tight and I wonder how she moves in them.

Her sweater is huge like a balloon and I wonder how she doesn't get lost in it. I worry she might float away. I know that clothes can't make you float away, but that is what the sweater *feels* like.

She bends down to take off her shoes before walking farther into Aunt Denny's little house. Mama looks at her a little different after that. She gives her the *you got good parents who taught you to take your shoes off before entering someone's house* look.

Mama smiles at me. "Imogen this is Toni. She is going to come hang out with you a few times a week for a while. You guys might want to go on a walk."

I stare at my socks with blue flowers. "Why?" I worry that she will find my stories horrible. I don't know if I will be able to cross the street without Mama, Lark, or Kin.

"Well, I heard you like to tell stories." Toni crosses her arms. I like how she doesn't bend down or give me that *you are a child* look.

I glance up. "I like to tell stories."

"Me too." She shrugs.

"Really?" I ask.

"Yeah. I go to UVA." She points down the road toward the campus. "My major is English and my minor is Fiction. I love stories."

"What's your favorite story?" I ask.

"*The Bluest Eye.*" Toni's eyes get brighter. "Maybe we could go somewhere and talk about stories?"

"Imogen is not great with walking on . . ." Mama glances at Toni then at me. "Maybe you could stay here."

"No, that's no fun. It's nice out." Toni shakes her head and her locs waterfall behind her. I know hair can't be a waterfall, but waterfalls flow downward and that's what her hair reminds me of—a blue waterfall.

Toni pulls her cell phone from her pocket and types

something in before handing it to Mama. "We could go on a drive. There is a tiny coffee shop about thirty minutes away. Not too many people; you know, it stayed open during the first quarantine and took coffee orders from the side door."

"Imogen has therapy soon. I thought this first visit would be quick." Mama reads the information on the phone. "Baine's Coffee Shop in Scottsville, Virginia?"

"Yeah, see the side street." Toni claps her hands together. "We don't even have to touch the asphalt. We just parallel park and get on the sidewalk. I can drive Imogen to therapy, wait, and then we can go."

I sway from one foot to the other.

"They have really good hot chocolate." Toni takes her phone from Mama and shows me a picture. "And they have lots of books. It's a coffee shop and a bookstore. Sound good?"

I nod.

Mama says okay.

I run to my room and pull on the sweatshirt Kin got me and the necklace Lark gave me, because I want them to be with me at the bookshop. I know that having things they gave me doesn't mean they are with me, but that is what it *feels* like. I tug on my shoes at the front door, covering my blue socks, and we walk down the sidewalk to Toni's car. It is old and has rust and I love that it is not new and perfect. It's as if the car has a few bruises, like me.

"Do you like K-pop?" Toni asks.

I shake my head. "What is that?"

"It's Korean pop music." She plugs her phone into the car. "Let's try a few songs." Toni turns up the volume, and lyrics I don't understand blast from the speakers. At first, I am confused because I don't understand the words, but then my head starts moving as Toni taps the wheel. The song *feels* right. I like the minor and major notes.

"You like it?" Toni grins. "It's BTS."

I sway from side to side. "I like how it feels."

Toni turns up the music and for a moment I forget about the virus, about going to therapy. I forget that I want to stay in my den forever. I just listen to the words I don't understand, but that somehow make me *feel* safe.

Toni parks as close as she can to the therapist's office. We don't have to cross any streets. I like walking beside her, she walks like she knows where she is going. I like her black clunky shoes that stomp the ground and the moons tattooed on her hand.

"I like the moon," I say, looking at her hands.

"I like the moon too." Toni glances at her own hand. "I think we are a little early. Want to sit for a second?"

"When did you get your tattoos?" I say, sitting on the bench near the office door.

"A few years ago." She pulls a Sharpie from her pocket. "I can draw some on your hands if you want."

I place my small hand in hers and she starts drawing the phases of the moon on my fingers. I wonder if Mama will make me wash it off later. I wonder how Toni got so good at writing and drawing.

274

"Want to hear a story about the moon?" Toni asks as she reaches for my other hand.

I nod.

"Mawu, the creator goddess who is seen as the sun and the moon, created Earth and all the life on it. But after she created everything, she was worried." Toni looks up at me.

"Why was she worried?" I frown.

"She was worried the earth was too heavy now that all the animals and people were on it." Toni starts drawing again. "Do you think she should have been worried?"

"I get it, the earth would be much heavier with more things on it," I answer.

"I agree." Toni puts the cap on her pen and I admire my hands. "Then she asked a snake, I forget the snake's name, to help thrust the earth up into the sky."

My eyes grow big. "A snake?"

"Yup," Toni says. "I think it's time for therapy. I'll wait outside."

I nod. "Did the snake get the earth into the air?"

"We are here, so I guess so." Toni smiles. "Have a good session."

I smile and climb up the stairs to Dr. Lovingood's office. Dr. Lovingood says, "Tell me more, Imogen." And I have plenty left to tell and I tell it.

This is the sad part of the story. Imogen finally gets to go outside, but outside is not nice. Nothing feels nice now that she knows the truth

that Clones are white and they are using Blues to help them stay alive longer. Outside more Blues work in a rock quarry and far ahead there is a wall that no Blues are allowed to go past.

Imogen speaks when she should not, trying to protect a Blue woman, and they punish her. They take Ira's spirit from him. Imogen feels empty. Larkin feels guilty and the president of the Bible Boot is happy. Larkin and Imogen escape the walls of the capital with the help of other inmates and get to Selma with the help of a friend named Mr. King. Imogen starts to see many brown people and she wishes her blue, sad skin would change.

Selma is scary too; people are protesting and many people get hurt. They have bruises. They are black-and-blue.

Dr. Lovingood watches me dangle my feet over the edge of the chair. "So, she got a vaccine and now she can go outside?"

I nod quickly.

"But she has to meet Congress, which is going to be very scary?" Dr. Lovingood continues. "And Larkin is different around other Clones, but he does escape with her."

"Yes, but the small room was not so bad," I say. "You

know, I know some sign language. I can spell my name. Lark taught me."

I spell my name perfectly using sign language.

"Very impressive." Dr. Lovingood smiles. "I look forward to hearing the rest of your story next time."

Dr. Lovingood walks me to the door. Toni is inside the waiting room now, she stands quickly. "Time for some hot chocolate!"

Selma to Montgomery, Alabama, March
(Page 100)

The Selma to Montgomery, Alabama, March was organized to happen on March 7, 1965. Protesters were supposed to march fifty-four miles from Selma to the Alabama capital, Montgomery.

However, when twenty-five-year-old John Lewis and over 600 marchers tried to cross the Edmund Pettus Bridge on their way to Montgomery on March 7, marchers were met with violence. Peaceful protesters were beaten and tear-gassed by police. This moment might have gone unnoticed like many moments during the Civil Rights Movement, but film crews recorded the violence that was invisible to so many people, especially in the North.

It was after 9:00 p.m. and millions of Americans were tuned in to the film, *Judgment of Nuremberg*, which condemned German war crimes, the Nazi party, and the silence of so many during the Holocaust. The program was interrupted with footage of what happened in Selma and many were appalled. They were forced to see.

The footage sparked protests and sit-ins around the United States. The day became known as Bloody Sunday.

On March 21, protesters were able to attempt marching again; this time they were allowed to pass over the bridge, and with cameras documenting the journey, they marched to Montgomery.

12

Baine's Coffee Shop, Scottsville, VA

Toni's car is green like dying grass. The back seat of her car is covered in books. Like she has her very own bookstore behind her just in case. I don't mind, because that means I get to sit in the front seat.

Storytelling was hard today.

The truth almost tumbled out of my mouth twice before I swallowed it back down like yucky cough syrup. Toni still wanted to go to the coffee shop to cheer me up. She rolls the windows down and the crisp fall breeze doesn't move either of our hair. Her locs are heavy snakes and my tiny curls are kinky cotton. I love how the wind can't bother our hair.

The road to Scottsville is curvy. I bet it is as winding as the Amazon River, except it is a road. I stick my hand out the window and the breeze kisses my fingers. It's a cold kiss. It reminds me of cold things. Like being blue and sad and freezing.

I don't mind.

Toni drives with one hand. "Do you like blues music too, Imogen?"

I nod and remember she is not looking at me. "Yes."

Toni taps a button on her car and then taps her cell phone. Blues music starts to play. It is slow and sad, like the music Kin listened to. The songs skip along. I like that Toni is not too chatty. I like that she lets the music sit between us and have a conversation with itself.

Soon we slow down and there are brick buildings on both sides of us. Toni pulls into a parking lot to turn around, then comes back down the street to parallel park right in front of Baine's Coffee Shop. It is only a few steps away. Toni turns the car off and I notice her fingernails are painted dark blue, not black. She hops out of the car, then rushes around to my side to open the door.

I step out and the sidewalk feels safe.

I take the two steps toward the coffee shop and Toni opens the door for me and for a moment I feel like we are a pack. The floor is a reddish color and the lighting is dim and inviting like a hug. I know lighting can't hug you, but that is what it feels like. Toni walks to the register; it is not very busy, but we still wear masks. I look around and see books everywhere. Hidden in crevices and on makeshift bookshelves.

The strong smell of coffee reminds me of the stuff Lark loved to drink.

I swallow.

"Hey, Kristen, this is Imogen." Toni nods toward me. "I'll take a coffee . . . and I think Imogen wants a hot chocolate. Do you want anything else?"

I shake my head no to anything except hot chocolate. Kristen says she likes my T-shirt with Black Panther on the front.

Toni leads me around a corner where there are more books and a pretend fireplace. We sit down and wait for our drinks. Toni sits sideways in her chair so she is not staring directly at me, which I like.

I know she doesn't see my blue skin, but I see it, especially after therapy, and I don't like people looking.

I look up at the walls and I see lots of trinkets and posters. Everything seems to whisper, *Get comfy, stay awhile.* It feels safe, like a wolf den. I know a coffee shop can't really be like a wolf den, but that is what it feels like—warm, safe, and the perfect size.

Kristen brings our drinks to us and I notice there is also a giant sticky bun with two forks. It is dripping in sugar and cinnamon and I want to eat the whole thing in one bite. I take my mask off and so does Toni.

"I know you said you did not want anything else." Toni takes a fork and eats a piece of the sticky bun. "But you also have never had a Baine's sticky bun."

I pick up a fork and try a bit.

My heart melts. It is the best sweet thing I have ever tasted.

I think about telling Lark about my new discovery and suddenly even the sticky bun tastes a little blue. I know that food can't taste like a color but that is how it *feels*. I slowly chew the blue taste and swallow. My hot chocolate is good, though. I decide not to have any more of the sticky bun on account that Lark can't have any right now.

"Why is *The Bluest Eye* your favorite story?" I ask Toni.

She shrugs off her sweater and even though it is cold out, she has a tank top on. A small vaccine scar sits on her right arm.

Exactly where mine is, exactly where everyone's is now.

A smile sunshines on Toni's face. "I love Toni Morrison, and *The Bluest Eye* is my favorite book she wrote."

"Toni Morrison?" I interrupt, looking over the edge of my cup.

"Yeah, my mom named me after her." She pauses. "You should read her when you get a little bit older."

I nod. Making a mental note. "I will."

"I also love to write my own stories." Toni takes a large sip of her coffee. "That's what I do at school. I write my own stories."

"What kinds of stories?" I ask.

"Depends on how I am feeling." Toni shrugs. "I heard you tell really good stories."

282

I panic, my eyes dart everywhere. I swallow. "My stories are kinda long."

Toni turns to face me, her hands cocoon around her cup. "I've got lots of time, Imogen."

"My story is about how hate can hurt . . . ," I say.

BLACK HISTORY FOR KIDS

Even More Hard Examples of Hate
(Page 112)

James Byrd Jr. (June 7, 1998)
Jasper, Texas

Mr. Byrd was brutally murdered by three white men after they offered him a ride home. All three men were charged, marking the first time white men were punished for a crime like this.

Trayvon Martin (February 26, 2012)
Sanford, Florida

While walking back home from a store, seventeen-year-old Trayvon Martin was fatally shot by a vigilante citizen who claimed self-defense. At the time, Martin was wearing a hoodie and had no weapon on his person. The vigilante citizen was even told by 911 services to leave Martin alone. Despite all this, the vigilante citizen got away with the murder of Trayvon Martin.

George Floyd (May 25, 2020)
Minneapolis, Minnesota

George Floyd was killed while being arrested for using a suspected counterfeit twenty-dollar bill. He was pinned down with pressure on his neck for over eight minutes, resulting in his death. He repeatedly said he could not breathe.

13

Gone Wolf Story

A STORY FOR BAINE'S COFFEE SHOP

I tell Toni about the Bible Boot.
I tell her that sometimes things happen wrong
so you have to retell them.

I tell her I am still blue and she nods.
I tell her like right now I am blue
and she says, I understand.

Then I tell her the TRUTH—
because for the first time someone isn't
      questioning me.
Toni listens with her heart . . .

The TRUTH feels like fire in the back of my throat.
Then I am crying and Toni leads me to her car
that is the color of dying grass.

She turns on the music.
She starts singing to me.
Her voice is like a warm blanket.
Her voice is like the North Star
Harriet Tubman followed
to freedom.

The car is a cozy den
and for a second I smile.
I smile while I am crying,
both at the same time.
Young and brave.

Birmingham Children's Crusade (1963)
(Page 130)

When we think of the Civil Rights Movement, we often think of the adults and college students staging sit-ins and going on marches, but young children also fought for their rights. The year was 1963 and the fight for equality in Birmingham was dwindling.

Fewer and fewer adults were volunteering to protest since it was guaranteed they would be arrested and beaten. Martin Luther King Jr. worried that the shrinking numbers would not look good for the cause. For the first time, school-aged children were asked to get involved. High school football players and others from local churches started to organize.

The children were told what to expect. They were told they could not fight back, and they still wanted to participate.

Then on May 2, 1963, over one thousand students skipped school and gathered at Sixth Street Baptist Church to protest. Children from the ages of 7 to 18 joined and held signs while singing freedom songs.

On the first day, children were arrested and taken away. On the second day, television crews filmed children as they were hosed, beaten, attacked by dogs, and arrested.

The Civil Rights Movement was reignited when the nation saw violence directed at Black children.

Kids were a catalyst for change.

14

Names Float in the Car
Like Magic

My tears dry up as the music keeps falling out of the speakers and the sun winks through the October leaves.

Toni turns down the music and says, "Ashe."

"Ashe?" I wipe my face with my sleeve. "That's not my name."

"I know you are Imogen, but remember when you were naming people in your story?"

"Yes."

"I was thinking of naming my car." Toni turns on her blinker.

"Oh." I laugh.

"Yea, so Ashe. Good name?"

"Ashe like the black stuff that is left after a fire?" I tap my fingers on my lap. "I like that the name feels *dusty*."

"Like the good kind of dusty?" Toni arches an eyebrow.

"Yes." I smile. "If it is Ashe with an *e*, I think it is good."

Toni nods. "All right then."

I smile into the sun because names are important and this car with its chipped paint seems very important to Toni, so it needs a name. The girl in my daydream doesn't have a name at first. They call her Inmate Eleven, which is not a real name. It is important to have a real name.

"What about Moth," I say, tapping the window, saying the name to the car.

"Like the insect?" Toni laughs. "Or like the fairy in that Shakespeare play."

"Both?" I look at Toni. "I didn't know there was a play, I actually just like moths a lot."

"How come?" Toni watches the road ahead. "Not a butterfly kind of gal?"

"I like how they don't show off as much as butterflies." I swallow. "I know they don't really know if they are showing off, but that is what it feels like."

"I like it. Moth is good too." We stop at a light and Toni pulls her hair into a ponytail. "What about Whimsy?"

"Like whimsical, but shorter?" I watch the light change to green. "It feels like an airy name."

"The name definitely flutters a bit," Toni agrees.

"Skye?"

"Embola?" A grin spreads across Toni's face.

"Wata?" I add, thinking about a goddess I saw in the book Dr. Lovingood let me borrow. "After Mama Wata."

"The West African water spirit." Toni nods. "That's a great one too."

"Maybe the car should have all the names." I touch the dashboard. "If you love the car a lot, it deserves all the good names."

"This car belonged to my grandpa." Toni touches the wheel softly.

I sit on my hands. "That's a nice gift."

I watch Toni and notice that the corner of her eye glistens in the sun. Not the happy glisten but the kind that looks both sad and happy. I think of the term *cognitive dissonance* again.

"Are you okay?" I ask.

"Just missing my grandpa a bit." Toni offers me a quick smile.

My heart skips. "Is he not here?"

"He *went wolf*." Toni wipes her face with her sleeve but more tears come. "Before the vaccine."

Toni keeps wiping her face with the edge of her sleeve. It is already wet. I pull my sleeve over my hand and lean over and dab her cheek gently.

"Let's name the car, first name Moth." I put my hand back in my lap.

Toni smiles. "Middle names, Ashe-Skye-Embola-Wata."

"Last name, Whimsy."

"That is the best name," Toni says, pulling into my driveway. "All the names."

"Because the car is loved a lot so it needs all the names."

Toni looks ahead. "I think I'll name the headlights Lark and Kin."

I swallow. I think of the headlights guiding us through dark places. "I think those are good names. They are good at guiding things."

IMOGEN'S STICKY NOTE IN BLACK HISTORY FOR KIDS

Important Names to Me (Imogen)
(Page 112)

1. Mama (is magic)
2. Lark & Kin (best brothers)
3. Ira (gone wolf)
4. Alba the tree (in Grandma's front yard)
5. William (the yarn-made whale tail)
6. Harriet (a guide)
7. Martin (brave)
8. Toni (cool)
9. Breonna (say her name)
10. Emmett (remember)
11. Trayvon (Skittles and hoodies)
12. Obama (first Black president)
13. Michelle (first Black First Lady)
14. Skye (the place in Scotland)
15. Whimsy (fairy tales)
16. Wata (for Mama Wata the African water goddess)
17. Autumn (rainbow of leaves)
18. Ashe (like the burning revolution)

15

Days Are Strange

Days keep going even when it feels like they should not. They keep going even when the entire world is locked inside.

Today is therapy day, and I sit outside on the bench with Mama before the appointment because we are early.

There are so many people.

A year ago this same brick alleyway was silent. The storefronts had signs that said CLOSED, dinners were delivered by dropping the items off on your front stoop. The only place that had people was the grocery store, or that is what Mama tells me.

During the first quarantine in Washington, DC, I never left our tiny apartment. Lark and Kin got the groceries and Mama still had to work because she is a nurse and that is what nurses do—help people. When she got home, she went straight to the bathroom to take a shower and put her work clothes in a bag. She even wore a mask that left a haunting bruise around her nose. I know bruises can't haunt, but that is what it looked like for weeks, an almost-there bruise.

I asked her why she kept the mask on if it hurt so much and she said, *That's what nurses do.*

During the first quarantine, days dripped by and Lark and Kin and I built a magical fort in the family room with pillows and sheets. We called it our den because we were a pack of wolves, Kin (sixteen) the leader and historian, Lark (fifteen) the fun adventurous one, and me (eleven) the dreamer. We sprayed the sheets with Lysol and said that nothing bad could get in our den. In our den, Lark played video games and Kin read history until one day he coughed and his head grew warm and then Mama took him to the doctor and then . . .

Then Lark coughed and Mama took him to the doctor.

And we waited so long for me to cough.

I never did.

I should have, but I didn't, which means our den only had a little magic.

I climb the stairs slowly to see Dr. Lovingood and today Mama sits outside to enjoy the fall sun, a thing we did not have for so long when we were locked inside. It's nice because she doesn't have to wear a mask or anything. And Mama shines a bit, like she used to, and that makes me feel a little less blue.

Mama used to say, *Imogen, it is important to stay socially distanced but not emotionally.* Mama knows these things because she is a nurse. I don't think she completely follows her own advice, though.

I sit in my usual chair across from Dr. Lovingood. "I don't feel so good today."

Dr. Lovingood frowns. "Do you have a fever, Imogen?"

"No, my heart hurts," I say, tapping my chest.

Dr. Lovingood nods. "Tell me why your heart hurts, Imogen."

"I don't feel like telling a story today." I kick my legs against the chair.

Dr. Lovingood watches me, tapping her fingers slowly on her arm. I wonder if she is mad, maybe she wanted to know what happened next in the story. Maybe I am selfish for not feeling like telling my story.

"Why not?" Dr. Lovingood asks.

"All I see are true things right now." I look down at my brown hands. "I can't make up things today because it's November 11."

"Oh." Dr. Lovingood stands up and grabs her phone. Her fingers fly over the buttons. "I am sorry, I forgot."

She grabs her jacket and shrugs it on before handing me my jacket. I look up at her. "We are going outside?"

"I was thinking maybe Insomnia Cookies." She smiles. "Have you had those before?"

"Aunt Denny got them for me once," I say, pulling on my jacket. "They are very good."

Dr. Lovingood opens the door and tells Mama where

we are going on a walk. Mama's face looks like a question mark, asking, *Imogen is okay with going outside?*

"We are getting cookies," I say.

"Okay, have fun." Mama still scrunches her eyebrows. "Try not to eat too much sugar."

"Two cookies tops," Dr. Lovingood agrees.

We go down the stairs and walk out onto the brick road where no cars are allowed to drive. We both pull our masks over our noses and not just our mouths, because it is crowded outside. We walk in silence for a bit and I like how the leaves sound like they are hugging each other.

"What are you thinking about, Imogen?" Dr. Lovingood turns down a side street. "We don't have to cross any roads going this way."

"Roads don't really scare me anymore," I say, looking at the black asphalt. "Toni says I can make up a new story about the road, so I did."

Dr. Lovingood pauses. "Then maybe we can try the shorter way?"

Suddenly my hand feels a little shaky. "Okay. I can try."

We stop at a crosswalk and I tap my fingers, counting the one, two, three, four, five, six, and seven seconds until the little white walking signal blinks. I swallow hard and think of my new story as I step onto the road. I take another step and my heart beats slow and steady. I take all the steps needed to cross the road and I jump up and down on the other side.

Dr. Lovingood gives me a high five. "You did it!"

"I did it!" I yell a little too loud, because the woman beside us jumps.

Dr. Lovingood starts walking again. "What's your new story about the road?"

"It's a magic black looking glass," I say. "When I step on it, I only get braver."

"I like that story." Dr. Lovingood opens the door to Insomnia Cookies. "Have you been using the flash cards in the back of the book I gave you?"

I look at all the cookies under the glass. "Yes, I knew a lot about Harriet Tubman and Martin Luther King Jr., but not that much about Malcolm X. Or the sad times white people hurt Black people."

"Those are hard cards to learn," Dr. Lovingood agrees. "History and the truth are sometimes hard."

I nod and point to the two cookies I want. A sugar cookie and a chocolate chip one. Dr. Lovingood gets a cinnamon cookie and two chocolate chip ones, but she gets an extra plate before we go out the door to sit down outside.

"Is someone else coming?" I say, worried they might not like me. Worried I might accidentally start a story.

"Hey, Imogen!" Toni stands in front of me and gives me a high five. "Doc told me you all were getting cookies and I was just down the road, on campus."

My smile feels like it reaches each of my ears. I know that is not possible, but that is what it *feels* like. Toni sits, moves her mask down, and takes a huge bite of a cookie. Her face lights up like a star. Toni reminds me of a sparkling star. I take a bite of my cookie too, which has the perfect amount of chocolate chips. Lark loves chocolate chip cookies. Kin loves sugar cookies.

I love them both.

"Did I miss today's story yet?" Toni asks. "You all tell stories in therapy, right?"

Dr. Lovingood shakes her head. "Imogen is not feeling up to telling more of her story today."

Toni smiles at me. "I remember, it's a hard day to tell a story."

I nod, because I want to let Dr. Lovingood hear. I want her to know what is next, but my words feel sticky today. They don't weave magic or make me feel better today. I want her to hear my story, but I don't want to tell it.

Toni takes a sip from her huge rainbow water bottle. "I know the story. I can tell some of it to Dr. Lovingood if you would like."

I don't say anything. It feels like too good of a present.

"But if you don't want me to I . . ."

"I want you to," I say quickly.

Toni takes another sip of water. "Where did you leave off?"

"Selma," Dr. Lovingood says.

Toni takes one last sip of water and starts:

Selma was hard. Lots of people, white and Black and Blue, were hurt. Mr. King was worried that the president of the Bible Boot would find Imogen and Larkin, so he made them stay inside even though they wanted to attend his special speech in Charlottesville, Virginia.

After Mr. King leaves them with Ms. Carmen, they all decide maybe going to Charlottesville is not such a bad idea. They all get on a Bullet Train to Charlottesville, Virginia. Imogen is surprised there are no walls separating the Bible Boot from the rest of the United States. She is shocked that people seem so okay with what is happening just because it is not happening to them.

They meet a nice kid on the Bullet Train and when they get to Charlottesville, Virginia, they hear Mr. King speak, but Larkin starts to cough a lot. He says he is okay and they keep listening to Mr. King's speech. Imogen looks down at her hands and sees that they are perfect and brown. Her sadness is shaking off, but then she notices that Larkin won't stop coughing and his skin has a blue tint. He falls to the ground. His chest is not moving up and down.

Toni takes the last bite of her cookie. "And that's where the story ends."

When I look up at Dr. Lovingood, she is wiping her face with the back of her hand. I worry my story is so bad it has made her cry even though Toni is telling it. Some things are horrible and can make you cry.

"So, slavery in your story is used to help the Clones live longer, and people protest and get hurt?" She takes a deep breath. "That sounds scary."

I rock back and forth in my chair. "It is. Lots of things are scary. I just want to remember all of their names."

"Did history help you with this part of your story?"

"Did you know that Black people were enslaved for a long time? The first ones came on a ship to America before 1619." I sit on my hands. "Did you know that even after that, there were laws that made Black people scared all the time? You can live in your own house and get hurt."

"That's all true." Dr. Lovingood nods. "And slavery was not abolished until 1865. That time you are talking about when Black people were scared all the time, did the learning flash cards teach you what it was called?"

I sit up straight. "The Jim Crow Era. After that is the Civil Rights Movement."

Dr. Lovingood nods. "That's exactly right."

I sit still.

"Is there anything else you want to tell me about Kin and Lark?" Dr. Lovingood looks toward Toni, then at me.

"I don't think so." I swallow, staring ahead, watching the

leaves fall from the tree like snow. "Just that I miss them. A lot."

"I am sure you do." Dr. Lovingood stands. "It's okay to miss people when they are not right beside us, Imogen."

I want to stand quickly before the truth spills out. I want to run away before I tell the truth to another person and it becomes more real than my stories.

Dr. Lovingood is silent. "That's a good story. It is happy and sad."

"True and not true," Toni adds.

"It's black and blue," I say. "Bruised. I just want to remember their names."

Say Her Name
(Page 112)

Breonna Taylor (March 13, 2020)
Louisville, Kentucky

While sleeping in her own apartment with her boyfriend, Breonna Taylor was fatally shot by officers who used forced entry without announcing themselves. Her murder sparked protests around the United States, but no one was charged with her death.

#SAYHERNAME
#SAYHERNAME
#SAYHERNAME
#SAYHERNAME
#SAYHERNAME
#SAYHERNAME
#SAYHERNAME
#SAYHERNAME
#SAYHERNAME
#SAYHERNAME
#SAYHERNAME
#SAYHERNAME
#SAYHERNAME
Breonna Taylor

16

Toni & Imogen

SPIRIT HEIGHT

*Toni walks with me the long way
back to the office to meet Mama.*

*We don't say much, but when I walk
with Toni, I pull my shoulders back.*

*I straighten my spine like a tree
and I don't mind that my hair curls
and tangles on itself all the time.*

*When I walk beside Toni, I don't feel
like I should shrink small.
I feel like I should spread my wings
like the branches of a large tree.*

I should be the girl with green wings
and brown skin like the bark of a tree.
I can grow, and watch and learn.

I want to take up space.
My spirit height grows taller.
Taller.
Taller.
With Toni, with her locs and tattoos,
walking beside me.

Ancestors/Hoodoo
(Page 170)

When enslaved Africans arrived in the United States, they were no longer permitted to practice their own spiritual traditions— Christianity was forced on them. To preserve important parts of their identity, many only conformed on the surface level.

The result was Hoodoo.

Hoodoo was about ancestors, roots, and spirituality.

Hoodoo is a magic system that grew out of that misfortune. It is a magic system that was created in the South during slavery.

At the core, Hoodoo is a melding of West African spiritual traditions and Christianity. Often referred to as Rootwork, Hoodoo's ultimate goal is to shift the odds in your favor through ancestral worship, offerings, and working with herbs and plants.

Though it is practiced differently from region to region, at the root it is about the strength of our ancestors and balance. Hoodoo is used to tip the odds in our favor, it is neither good nor bad. Hoodoo is balance. With the Great Migration, Hoodoo took root throughout the United States.

Hoodoo makes your spirit height very tall.

17

Apple Picking with Toni

Sometimes it feels like all I do is go talk to Dr. Lovingood. I flip my story over in my head like a pancake, over and over, until it is golden and ready. I want Dr. Lovingood to understand what I am trying to say, so I practice telling it to myself.

I think Mama is a little worried because I stay in my room and talk to myself a lot, but just yesterday I crossed the street without imagining it into a snake, or a black hole. A black hole is something in space that eats up everything— even sadness. I learned on the Discovery Channel that time doesn't even exist in a black hole, it just is.

Sometimes I think about the virus that ate up the world.

I think about the number of people who got infected. The newspeople would talk about statistics and numbers and death counts, and I would think about each person's favorite color. I would wonder about each person's favorite story.

Sometimes it was like there was so much pain that we forgot to remember each soul.

Everyone should be remembered. That is what I am thinking on the car ride to Carter's Mountain. The road tilts *up, up, up* and my back pushes against the front seat of Toni's car.

"You are going to love the apple cider donuts, Imogen." She taps the wheel. "Sometimes I buy twelve and then freeze them!"

Freezing extras reminds me of the first and second quarantines, but I want today to be a nice day. I want to enjoy apples and apple cider donuts.

"I've never been apple picking," I say, watching the trees blink by. "I hope I am good at it."

"Everyone is good at picking apples." Toni smiles. "You can pick the ones low on the tree or use a ladder and get the ones high up."

When we pull into the parking lot, there are lots of people, so I have my mask on. I open my car door on my own and beneath my feet the ground is soft and brown. Everyone has baskets filled to the brim with apples. I follow Toni into the store and we get our baskets too, we get to fill them all the way up for a set price. The checkout lady says we can stack the apples as high in the basket as we want.

Turns out I am good at picking apples—red ones, green ones, tiny ones, and big ones. You just have to check to make sure there are no rotting spots, like little viruses, on the apple and then you tug it off the branch and put it in your basket.

"You want to sit on a bench and take a break?" Toni asks.

"There is a great view right here and my basket is getting heavy."

I nod and we sit watching the mountains. All of Charlottesville appears so small from up here and I wonder if there is anyone looking up at me from one of the streets. Gazing *up, up, up*, thinking they are so far up, that must be heaven.

"Your mom told me you are doing a really good job telling your story for the second time to Dr. Lovingood." She keeps looking at the view. "But you have not told her the true story yet. The one you told me."

"I am trying," I say.

"I know. I know you are trying very hard." Toni pauses and looks at me. "Why did you tell me both stories and not just the one you tell Dr. Lovingood?"

"I dunno," I say. "You had a tiny wolf statue in your car. I thought maybe, maybe you would understand."

"I really like wolves," she says, exhaling slowly. "So, me and you, we are like a two-person pack."

I nod quickly.

Toni smiles. "I was wondering, I already asked your mom, if this weekend you wanted to take a day trip to Washington, DC? Just you and me, we could take the Amtrak train."

"I dunno." Washington, DC, reminds me of a lot of scary things.

"We could go to the African American History Museum." Toni takes a bite of her apple. "Maybe the Lincoln Memorial. Then we could get on the train and come home to Charlottesville. It's up to you."

"I think, I think that would be fun," I say. "I have not been to that museum and I like learning."

"Perfect. So, this two-person pack is going to DC in a few days. Sounds great to me." Toni stands. "But are you fast enough to run in this pack?"

Toni takes off between the apple trees and I race after her feeling *free, free, free.*

Of course, she slows down and soon she will drop me off at Dr. Lovingood's office, where I may or may not be able to tell the truth, but for now Toni and I walk and talk about the *truth.*

We are a pack.

Right now we are wild.

We can outrun everything.

Even germs.

I keep practicing telling the *truth* and when it gets hot, Toni slouches off her jacket and I tie mine around my waist and I notice our matching scars from the vaccine and I think maybe, maybe the whole world is part of our pack now. Maybe, we are all in this together and together we can find a way out.

By the time I get to Dr. Lovingood's office, my skin is a few shades darker because of the sun. I bring five apples up the stairs to give to Dr. Lovingood.

"These look delicious," she says, taking them from my arms. "I'll have to make a pie tonight."

"I think Mama and I will make a pie tonight too." I smile, looking out her window. "Toni took me all the way *up, up, up* to Carter's Mountain."

"The view up there is amazing." She leans against the window of the office. "Nice that Toni took you there."

"We are a pack now." I sit down in one of the empty chairs. "Toni said she would love to be in my pack and we are going to Washington, DC, this weekend to a special museum."

"That should be fun." She smiles at me.

"I am excited."

"Imogen, can you tell me your story from Selma on again?" Dr. Lovingood sinks into her chair, ready to listen, and today I am ready to weave stories.

This time, after I finish my story, Dr. Lovingood doesn't ask any questions.

We just sit. Until she says, "It often all feels like too much, doesn't it?"

I nod.

"But you have to follow the Drinking Gourd." She swallows hard. "You have to lead yourself out of it, Imogen. You are courageous, Imogen."

"Sometimes the story feels more real than everything around me." I wipe a tear from my lashes.

Dr. Lovingood nods and we sit for a long while.

A Short Word on Hope
(Page 200)

The thing that Black people hold close. The hope that their lives will be equal, that their deaths are not just numbers. It is a tiring thing, to hope—but the alternative is hopelessness.

#sayhername
#blm
#sayhername
#blm
#sayhername
#blm
#sayhername
#blm
#sayhername
#blm
#sayhername
#blm
#sayhername
#blm
#sayhername
#blm

18

My Room (Again)

The more I think about telling Dr. Lovingood the truth, the smaller my world is, but the braver I am when I go outside. The sidewalk and crowds don't bother me much anymore. The asphalt is just asphalt, and over the weekend, Toni and I got lots of chalk and made it colorful with quotes and poetry.

That was the same day that Toni gave me the tiny wolf pendant strung on a necklace that was in her car. She wears a similar one now too, but when Toni is at school and Mama is working, I still go to my room.

My room in Aunt Denny's house from left to right is eleven normal steps and twenty-two baby steps. From right to left, it is ten normal steps and twenty baby steps. I know science says it is supposed to be the same, but it isn't, because on the way back I am rushing.

Sometimes I pretend to be a wolf, like Ira in my story, and it is about a two-second trot.

It is difficult to measure steps when you pretend to have four legs.

Sometimes I circle the edges of my room, pretending to be Ira. I keep my head low and my eyes turn to slits.

That is my *gone wolf* face. I imagine myself somewhere else.

Sometimes I forget and my world is no longer only—from left to right, eleven normal steps and twenty-two baby steps. From right to left, it is ten normal steps and twenty baby steps. I think I'll start writing the parts of the story I haven't told Dr. Lovingood down in my journal.

I made it through the first and second quarantines.

I have the scar on my right arm to prove it.

I don't have to live in a den anymore.

I can roam, *go wolf*, if I want.

I start my blue story on page 1.

Gone Wolf (Blue)
(Page 1)

The lady in blue holds up the dolls again.

The lady in blue watches me study each doll, and her eyebrows pull together. She wants me to pick the one with blue eyes. I know because we have been doing this test for weeks. I know it has been weeks because a week is seven days long and I have had more than fourteen breakfast trays since we started this test.

I don't know if I can fail a test, but the little sigh the lady in blue does when she puts the dolls back in their boxes sounds like failing. The lady in blue always says, *I am not disappointed*. Which I guess is true, because she also says she can't *feel* anything.

I point at one of the dolls.

"And why, Inmate Eleven, do you like this doll?" The lady in blue examines the patchwork dress of the doll I picked.

The lady in blue's eyes look less blue today and more storm.

"I like her hair," I say because the patchwork-dress doll has nice hair.

"You like it better than this hair." The lady in blue tugs at her own golden curls, holding what must be sunshine.

"I like that it is blue," I say.

Blue like the ocean, which I have never seen.

Blue like the sky, which I have never seen.

Blue like my hair, which I can see when I look down.

19

A Lovingood Story

It's the Friday before the DC adventure. It's not raining. The sun is bright and round like an orange.

I am in my therapist's, Dr. Lovingood's, office.

I wish there was rain because in Dr. Lovingood's office, the rain sounds like tiny bees hitting the roof because the roof is made of tin.

It also sounds like a rain stick turned one way then the other.

"You like looking out the window, Imogen?" Dr. Lovingood moves from around her desk to sit beside me in one of the two chairs in front of the window.

I nod.

"I heard you and Toni have hung out a lot." She smiles.

"She likes stories and she is funny." I shrug. "She listens to my stories."

Dr. Lovingood nods. "It is nice to have someone who listens to you."

"She believes me. She said, *Imogen if you tell me you are Blue, you are Blue. The question is, Do you want to be brown or Blue forever.*"

"I heard," Dr. Lovingood says. "That's a good question, Imogen, Do you want to be brown or Blue forever?"

"I don't know." I look down at my hands, which are still blue even though they are a lighter shade.

"You know, Imogen, when no one is here, sometimes I look out the window for hours." She smiles. "Sometimes, I pretend I am a princess locked in a tall tower."

"Why are you locked in the tower?" I ask.

"I am sorry I did not listen to you, Imogen. You know, sometimes the older we get, we forget to see things from different perspectives." Dr. Lovingood shrugs, watching the tiny dots of people bustling below us. "Sometimes, I can't find the key to open the door in my own tower. Sometimes, I just can't."

I nod. From up here, the people don't have faces, just different shades.

Dr. Lovingood taps her fingers on her knee. "Do you mind if I tell you a story today, Imogen? Before you tell me yours?"

I glance at her and notice she doesn't have her clipboard in her lap.

She is not watching me like a doctor watches a sick person.

The wrinkles, like bird's feet by her eyes, are deeper.

I nod slowly. "I like stories."

She smiles and her wrinkles deepen even more. "I have noticed that you are very good at weaving them."

I cross my legs in the chair. "Is this a true story?"

"As true as any story." Dr. Lovingood exhales. "A long time ago there was a girl who lived in a small red house."

I frown. "How long ago?"

"About fifty years." Dr. Lovingood folds her hands in her lap. "Everything in the house was red—the sofa, the curtains, the dishes . . ."

"Even the floors?" I ask.

"Even the floors," she whispers. "And you know what else?"

"What?" I say. "What else?"

"Sometimes the house even screamed." Dr. Lovingood frowns. "The house screamed at the neighbors. It screamed at the dog, it screamed at the grass until the house got redder and redder."

"Red, like a strawberry?" I say, trying to understand the red house that only gets redder.

Dr. Lovingood's hand covers her mouth for a moment before she takes a deep wobbly breath. It is like she is on the edge of a seesaw and I am not sure which way she will fall.

I don't think I got the red right. So, I try again. "Or like a red fire?"

Dr. Lovingood nods. "More like a fire."

"But if it was red like a fire, it must have been hot for the girl," I say. "Wouldn't it be too hot for her?"

"It was very hot. Sometimes the girl hid in her closet with books because it seemed like it was the only place that was not red." Dr. Lovingood leans forward and grabs a tissue from the table between us.

The tissues that she leaves for the people she talks to.

"It was too much red," I say.

"Sometimes too much red hurts your eyes and makes you cry." Dr. Lovingood dabs her eyes.

I nod slowly. "What did the girl do?"

"She decided that she would have to grow wings. She read in her books that hundreds of years ago, people that looked like her—people with brown skin—were put on ships going places they did not want to go. In some stories, they leapt from the boats and flew away."

"Flew where?" I say, 'cause I want to fly.

"Home."

"Home?" I fold my arms. "Where was home for the girl in the red house?"

"Anywhere but the red house—with the red door and the red dishes."

"And the red floor," I add. "Did she fly away?"

"Yes, she did." Dr. Lovingood twists the tissue between her fingers. She must know magic—the tissue is now confetti in her palms.

"Did she get burnt leaving the fire home?" I ask, tears filling my eyes. "I hope she did not get burnt."

"Only a little." Dr. Lovingood clears her throat.

I nod. "Did she ever go back?"

318

"No." Dr. Lovingood's throat moves. "She decided to *go wolf* instead."

I stand and walk the two steps to her. When Dr. Lovingood is sitting, we are eye to brown eye. "Do you need a hug?" I ask because sometimes people don't want hugs.

She nods. And I give her a hug—the real kind, the kind that Larkin and Kin used to give me, which means she is now part of my pack.

Racial Trauma
(Page 215)

Racial trauma can be experienced by any minority group and can have an effect on a person's mental and physical health.

Racial trauma includes racism, violence, hate crimes, microaggressions, racial stereotypes, lack of diversity in the workplace, lack of diversity in school settings, systemic racism, lack of health care for people of color (POC), police brutality, and countless other painful everyday occurrences.

Often Black people are expected to function and perform while all of these disturbances (some big, some small) are happening around them. When movements such as Black Lives Matter (#BLM) take root, they are often asked to educate others using valuable energy that could be used elsewhere.

There is also generational trauma, especially in the United States, where its history includes enslaving innocent African Americans and then degrading them after they are free.

The signs of racial trauma can present themselves in many ways but can often look like post-traumatic stress disorder (PTSD). It can include depression, feeling hopeless, low self-esteem, and stress, which can lead to many health problems.

20

Washington, DC, Adventure Poem

AMTRAK

Toni picks me up before the sun says, Hello.
    She turns on the heat, which feels like Mama's
        kisses
on my skin. Feels like a hug from Lark or Kin.

    Toni hands me a hot chocolate saying,
    It's not from Baine's
    but it should still taste good.

The hot chocolate is warm, like my hands
    in Ira's fur.
We drive down the roads and it is so still,
    because people are still tucked under their
        covers

warm in their own dens. We turn
    off Brown Street
and enter the parking lot. The train is waiting
    for us,
doors open, inviting us on an adventure,
    so we climb on—
Me, Toni, and the blue backpack she
    packed
with snacks and water for the day.

It's a 3-hour ride, we will get to Washington, DC,
    at 9:00 a.m.
    I can't see Toni's mouth, because of her blue
        mask,
but I can tell she is smiling as she looks
    out the window.

I press my forehead against the cool glass and
    track
the passing trees, the passing cars, everything
    zooming by quickly.
The sun starts to say, Hello, creating a giant
    orange haze over the horizon.

I remember once Kin said, You are existing
on someone's horizon and they are existing on
    another's
until it circles back around to you.

I wonder if I chase enough horizons
would I find Lark and Kin, again.

   Toni taps my shoulder. What are you thinking?

We are moving so fast,
I am imagining I am a wolf
galloping beside the train.

   Go wolf, Imogen.
   Go really really wolf.

I close my eyes and drift to sleep
With the gentle sway of the train.
I dream of a pack of wolves
Galloping beside it—
Ira, Lark, Kin, Toni,
Mama, Dr. Lovingood,
And Me (Imogen).

AFRICAN AMERICAN HISTORY

The museum has a long name,
   The National Museum of African American
History and Culture. Toni knows the way because,
   she says,
I've got a lot of family in DC. *The building is a*
   funny square

that looks like it is covered in black lace.
I know a building can't be covered in black lace,
but that is what it looks like.

I think it looks like a bird's nest,
Toni says as we enter.

I think it looks like black lace
is eating the building.

The museum starts off narrow and I feel cramped.
We learn about the Middle Passage,
which stole Africans from their homelands
and put them on a dirty boat to the Americas.

I try to read each plaque slowly—
but with each step my heart feels blue,
then my fingertips feel blue, then all of me
is blue.

I tug Toni's sleeve,
I am Blue, I say, looking
down at my hands.

Toni takes my hands in hers.
Her moon phase tattoos remind me
of wolves howling at the moon—
they remind me of going wolf.

I know, me too.
Do you want to leave?

No. I have to learn their stories.
So, we keep going through the years
and I stop at Emmett Till's empty casket.
The one his family donated after they
    took him
out of the ground to perform an autopsy
50 years later. Hoping to get justice
    for him.
He was only two years older than me,
I say, reading the plaque.

He was. Young.
Toni touches my
shoulder
lightly.

We keep going, each year a new sin,
my heart feels bluer and bluer,
and somehow braver and braver.
I say, Harriet Tubman, Dr. King,
Mr. Malcolm X, and Ms. Angela Davis
were not afraid of anything, were they?

I think they were afraid, sometimes,
but they were brave. They had to be.

I want to be brave like them,
I say, thinking of the true stories
hiding in me.

You are, Imogen.
Your ancestors are proud
of you.

Present tense?
I feel less blue.
I feel proud.

Present tense.

We reach the part of the museum about music
and film and the Olympics and I feel so proud.
So proud I feel like brown sunrays surround me.

Why don't they teach all this in school?

I dunno. Maybe they are afraid
of the truth.
Toni smiles at me as we leave.
Lincoln Memorial next?

I nod, but I can't stop thinking
of being afraid of the truth.

LINCOLN MEMORIAL

The reflecting pool reminds me
　　　　of a mirage because the water
sparkles so much.

　　Toni says, It's 167 feet wide
　　and over 2,000 feet long.

It's a tiny pond,
I say, watching
the shallow water.

　　Toni looks over the side.
　　Minus the fish.

We walk all 2,000 feet of the tiny pond
and reach the stairs that lead to the statue
of President Lincoln. My flash cards
　　taught me
he was assassinated, which means executed,
on April 14, 1865.

I run up the stairs to the top.
Toni is close behind me.
The statue is huge. Like a giant.
Imagine if people were this big.

Toni looks toward the reflecting pool.
The earth would be a lot more crowded.
She laughs.

We go back down some of the stairs
and Toni stops. She puts both her hands
on the stone and smiles.

You know who stood right here?

I shake my head, No.

Toni sits all the way down,
Martin Luther King Jr.
and other Civil Rights
Movement leaders.

Wow, I say, touching the ground too.

He said his speech "I Have a Dream"
in front of more than 250,000 people.

I know the last words.
I stand up, clear my throat, and yell,
Free at last, Free at last,
Thank God almighty . . .

Toni stands with me too
and yells the last words

into the air, into the reflecting pool.
We don't care who is watching
or who hears us, because we are a pack,
and Martin Luther King Jr. and all the
Civil Rights people would have been
part of our pack too—
We are free at last!

IMOGEN'S JOURNAL PAGE

Imogen's Dream (Blue)
(Page 22)

"What is voting?" I ask.

Rabbi Heschel says, "Voting is when you have a say in what happens in America. Like if there was a vote to see if little girls should have a puppy, I bet you would vote yes. If everyone can vote, we might be able to make things more equal for everyone."

"I think everyone should have a say." I nod. I can't help the tears that start falling from my eyes. "I had a wolf. His name was Ira. He . . . is not with . . ."

Ms. Carmen is behind me. She puts a hand on my shoulder. "Tell us about Ira."

I swallow. "He was big and sometimes when we stayed in the small room his head would get real low and he would pace back and forth."

"He would *go wolf*," Larkin adds.

Mr. King squints. "*Go wolf*?"

I nod. "It's when he would pretend that he was somewhere else, he imagined himself out of the room."

Rabbi Heschel smiles. "Ira sounds very special."

"Sometimes, I would dream that he was not a wolf and that he would shift into a Black boy. A brother who kept me safe." I nod. "I would vote for everyone to have a wolf like Ira."

21

Music in Lighthouses

We sit in Politics and Prose bookstore with an hour to spare before getting back on the train. Toni tells me about what she likes to write. She writes about people who do totally normal things in a world that feels totally normal, but something is a little off. Like there is a man who runs a lighthouse and everything is normal.

The people who drop off the food are normal.

The fish that swim in the sea are normal.

The boats he saves from hitting the cliffs are normal.

The man is so tired, but he can't sleep. If he sleeps, he feels guilty.

If he sleeps, people can die; but if he doesn't sleep, he might die.

He can't sleep because his eyes are the light for the lighthouse.

"I love the stories," I say. Toni and I sit on the floor in an aisle at Politics and Prose. We go more places now because I am not afraid of the road anymore.

"Thank you." She pulls a book from the shelf. "It's like folklore."

"Folklore?" I say.

Toni nods. "Yes, a little bit of reality mixed with all the monsters and myths and magic."

"With Elitists, they can be real. They hate people?"

"Yes, Elitist or White Supremacist—they both hate." Toni nods. "You know you said one summer you came to Charlottesville, before the virus and the Elitists were there about the statue. They had come once before, but the city officials told the citizens of Charlottesville to stay indoors, so they did."

"Why?" I ask.

"To keep the peace." Toni shrugs. "But then the Elitists came back. That was a week after you moved here, right?"

I swallow, mixing storytelling with reality in my head. "Yes. I could hear it from Aunt Denny's house and see some of it."

"I was there." Toni leans back against the bookshelves. "You know so many people gathered to tell them to leave."

"So you were protesting?" I ask.

She nods.

"Then people got hurt. A girl died." I swallow, looking at my blue hands.

"Yes." Toni wrings her hands. "Yes. It was horrible. It is horrible."

"How do you know what is real and what is folklore?" I ask.

"Everyone thinks different things are real, Imogen." She smiles a small smile. "That's the point."

I nod.

"Toni, how come sometimes when I look down at my hands, I see blue, I *feel* blue, and you are not. You are sad too." I stare at her with her colorful hair and tattoos. "How do you stop being blue?"

"Look at me, Imogen." Toni gets on her knees and faces me. I look into her big brown eyes brimming with tears. "You can be sad. You can be as sad as you need to be, but one day you must do something with that sadness. Or . . . Or it will . . ."

"Turn you blue?" I say, sniffling.

Toni nods.

I look at my hands, still blue. "I don't know what to do with all this blue."

Toni nods again, wiping her tears and then mine in that rough, loving way Mama does. Like she is mad the world has made me cry, mad that there even have to be tears right now. I know I don't know if that is what Toni is thinking, but that is what it *feels* like.

Toni gives me a page from her notebook and I start writing a poem called "Brave Like Toni." Then we collect our things and leave the city. We get on Amtrak and I fall asleep on Toni's shoulder on the ride back. I can hear her humming Nina Simone in my dreams and everything is golden brown and free.

BLACK HISTORY FOR KIDS

#BLM
(Page 240)

Black Lives Matter (#BLM) is a movement that was founded in 2013 after the murder of Trayvon Martin. It is a global organization whose mission is to end white supremacy and give Black people a voice against injustice.

#BLM
#BlackLivesmatter
#saytheirnames
#sayhername
#JusticeforBreonnaTaylor
#justiceforgeorgefloyd
#emmetttill
#JuliaBaker
#FrazierBaker
#Jamesbyrd
#Maryturner
#Omahacourthouseriots
#DuluthMurders
#MooresFordMurders
#TrayvonMartin
#BLM
#saytheirnames
#sayhername

22

Brave Like Toni

I tell Dr. Lovingood about DC, and I hand her the poem I wrote called "Brave Like Toni." She reads it silently:

> Toni was young when the bad people came to
>   Charlottesville,
> but she still decided to stand up.
> She still decided to tell stories and love people
> and keep living. Even after the virus,
> instead of staying small she grew wings.
>
> I want to grow wings like Toni.
> I want to remember and fly.
> I want to live.
> Live.
>
> Live, for everyone who coughed.
> For all the hard history lessons Kin taught me.
> I want to live for all of the love Lark showed me.

I want to live for the thousands of names I don't
   know.
Names that were part of someone else's wolf pack.
I want to live for all that.
I want to remind the world that all of our right
   shoulders now match.
We all have a tiny, raised scar from the vaccine.

"I think you are brave like Toni." Dr. Lovingood hands my poem back to me. "You are brave enough to tell your story."

"Not always the entire story," I say, tucking the poem into my pocket.

"I'd like to hear the entire story, Imogen," Dr. Lovingood says. "Let's hear some more of yours."

I think about starting my story, back in the small room, with Ira and the Elitist outside. I think, maybe I'll tell that story one more time, but when I open my mouth, the *truth* wants to come out.

1500s–Present
The United States of America

A moment of silence for the more than 12.5 million Africans kidnapped and forced into slavery.

A moment of silence for the over 3 million who died during the Middle Passage.

All the strength to their ancestors still fighting today.

(Each **&** represents 5,000 Black lives: 3 million Africans died during the Middle Passage)

& & & & & & & & & & & & & & & & & & & & & & & &
& & & & & & & & & & & & & & & & & & & & & & & &
& & & & & & & & & & & & & & & & & & & & & & & &
& & & & & & & & & & & & & & & & & & & & & & & &
& & & & & & & & & & & & & & & & & & & & & & & &
& & & & & & & & & & & & & & & & & & & & & & & &
& & & & & & & & & & & & & & & & & & & & & & & &
& & & & & & & & & & & & & & & & & & & & & & & &
& & & & & & & & & & & & & & & & & & & & & & & &
& & & & & & & & & & & & & & & & & & & & & & & &
& & & & & & & & & & & & & & & & & & & & & & & &
& & & & & & & & & & & & & & & & & & & & & & & &
& & & & & & & & & & & & & & & & & & & & & & & &
& & & & & & & & & & & & & & & & & & & & & & & &
& & & & & & & & & & & & & & & & & & & & & & & &

& & & & & & & & & & & & & & & & & & & & & & & &
& & & & & & & & & & & & & & & & & & & & & & & &
& & & & & & & & & & & & & & & & & & & & & & & &
& & & & & & & & & & & & & & & & & & & & & & & &
& & & & & & & & & & & & & & & & & & & & & & & &
& & & & & & & & & & & & & & & & & & & & & & & &
& & & & & & & & & & & & & & & & & & & & & & & &
& & & & & & & & & & & & & & & & & & & & & & & &
& & & & & & & & & & & & & & & & & & & & & & & &
& & & & & & & & & & & & & & & & & & & & & & & &

23

A True Story

"I am ready to tell the real story," I say with my tiny voice. "Dr. Lovingood, please call my mama into the room."

Mama and I stand facing Dr. Lovingood. I swallow the ball in my throat.

I think my blueness causes the rain hitting the tin roof.

I think my sadness causes the asphalt to coil like a snake.

I think my heaviness makes everyone heavier—makes me heavier.

I can't see the rain, but I can hear it.

Like a rain stick in my head, like Skittles spilt colorful on the kitchen floor.

Mama has her hands on my shoulders. Not the same way she has them when we ride the metro, that's the *Don't mess with my baby* way. This way is softer and heavier, like a feather falling like a stone.

"I am ready to tell a *true* story," I say, lifting my chin. "With just a little bit of magic."

Dr. Lovingood puts her clipboard down on her desk and

gestures for us to sit. Mama's hands leave my shoulders and she sits in one of the chairs.

I don't sit.

I need my spirit height to be as tall as possible.

I think Dr. Lovingood understands, because she nods.

So I tell Mama and Dr. Lovingood the *truth*.

It's not a long story.

It's a simple story.

It starts with a girl who loves her mama very much, but Mama has to work a lot. The girl is lonely, so she makes up stories in her head. Then one day Mama says, You are going to have two foster brothers. I worry because I am not good with people, just with stories, but when Lark (white) and Kin (Black) walk in with trash bags filled with their belongings, I love them! With an exclamation point.

We are a wolf pack. We have each other's backs.

They walk me to school. They buy me books. They teach me to throw a punch and they teach me history. They write plays for me to act in and we turn the living room into a stage. They are mine, my older brothers. They belong to me.

They kill all the spiders and save all the mermaids.

They were mine. I hit my chest. My brothers.

Kin—Black and tall, protective and strong.

Larkin—white and cautious, and funny.

Then the pandemic came and they built me a den to live in. They kept everything clean. But they did not know they had

340

bad immune systems too. Mama says that's what happens when you are in the system, sometimes you just get pushed along without being taken care of like people with "real" families.

We almost made it through the first quarantine, then Kin coughed and coughed and Mama took him to the hospital. Then Lark coughed and coughed and he went to the hospital too. I waited to cough too, so we could build a den in the hospital.

I never coughed.

I stop, trying to catch my breath.

You know what a funeral is?

A funeral is when a scar is cut in the ground and a box is lowered into the scar and then all the dirt is pushed back, but the ground always remembers that someone opened it.

We had one funeral (Kin).

After that we had another (Lark).

The funeral where the ground is scarred twice and only Mama, me, the priest, and some teachers show up, because we can't gather in groups larger than ten. The same funeral that Mama buys me a blue hand-me-down dress from Goodwill because I think black is not a sad color; blue is the saddest color.

Kin and Lark loved the color blue.

Everything is blue and sad.

I had to unmake the world to make it work again. Toni said I had to do something with my sadness. So, I wrote it down. I'll keep writing it down.

I collapse into the chair, exhausted.

I think I am the opposite of the Ark, because I have so much water inside me. Dr. Lovingood cries, Mama cries harder.

"They were my brothers." I swallow and look up through brown puffy eyes. "I don't want them to disappear."

"You can keep telling me stories about them, Imogen." Dr. Lovingood dries her eyes and says, "Tell me another story about your brothers. Tell me about the day you met—a happy story."

I smile through tears, because I have so many of those—I have so many joy-filled stories. Stories about Lark helping me build dens with magical drawings on the walls, Kin pretending to tame fire while cooking ramen in the kitchen, and Ira keeping my feet warm in winter and chasing the gray mouse out of our apartment in spring. I have enough happy stories to chew on for the rest of my life. Stories that are warm like the rainbow colors of autumn or a sunset in an apple orchard.

Enough stories to wipe away the sadness that hangs on to my soul—so I won't be blue anymore.

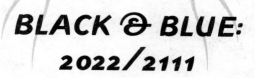

BLACK & BLUE:
2022/2111

*It is time for parents to teach young people
early on that in diversity there is beauty
and there is strength.*

–Maya Angelou

1

True

If I close my eyes tightly,
I see blue. If I open them
and look at my hands
for a moment, they are blue too—
     but that's only true for a second.

Sometimes the truth felt like a secret.
     If I locked it tight in my stories
          I could rewrite history
               with a story—
but that's not how stories work.

You can love something,
     present tense,
even after it's gone.

I love Lark.
I love Kin.

I love Ira.
Because I love them
I keep trying
and learning
and growing.
I am on a healing journey.
I am as free as a bird soaring
or a giant whale jumping from the sea—
    I am Imogen—Black girl who feels so much.
        Feeling is my magic, my folklore—
        I've gone wolf.

Author's Note

The series of events and characters in this book are fictional, but the ideas are inspired by true events. For example, when I first started writing this story, we were living through a pandemic, which is still not resolved, even with vaccines. Below are the actual dates of events referenced in *Gone Wolf*. I hope this book inspires you to learn more about these historical events so that history never repeats itself. I tell this story as a reminder that human rights are always worth fighting for.

- **Coronavirus Pandemic 2020:** The 2019–20 coronavirus pandemic is an ongoing pandemic (COVID-19) caused by severe acute respiratory syndrome coronavirus 2 (SARS-CoV-2).
- **Generational Trauma:** Trauma that is passed down genetically from generation to generation. Heightened vigilance, distrust, and other health conditions can be the result of generational trauma.
- **Slavery in the United States:** The first enslaved Africans arrived in North America in the early 1500s. Slavery was abolished in the United States in 1865. Slavery was legal in what would become the United

States for over 300 years; it has only been illegal for 157 years.

- **Fugitive Slave Act** (1850) or the **Bloodhound Law:** This law was passed by Congress in 1850 and required that all escaped slaves be returned to their owners. It was used in an attempt to keep the United States *united*.
- **Jim Crow Era:** 1870s until the late 1960s. Sets of laws that enforced racial segregation in the South were passed during this period.
- **Emmett Till's Death:** August 28, 1955. An African American teenager from the North was kidnapped, viciously beaten, and lynched (or hung) in Mississippi while visiting family. He was accused of flirting with a white woman.
- **Underground Railroad:** Created in the 1700s, this system reached its height in the 1850s. It was a secret network of homes, churches, businesses, and routes that helped enslaved Black people in the South escape from slavery by going to the North or Canada.
- **Civil Rights Movement in the US:** 1954–1968. The movement in the United States to obtain equal rights for African Americans.
- **Selma Marches:** March 1965. A series of marches from Selma, Alabama, to Montgomery, Alabama, during which activists peacefully protested for the right to vote. On March 7, 1965, African American protesters attempted to cross the Edmund Pettus

Bridge but were met with violence. The day is now known as Bloody Sunday. On March 21, 1965, protesters started the march again and made it to Montgomery.

- **March on Washington:** August 28, 1963. A march to stand up for civil rights for African Americans. Martin Luther King Jr. delivered his now famous "I Have a Dream" speech during this peaceful protest.

- **Harriet Tubman:** Born between 1820 and 1822, during her life she saved hundreds of slaves as a conductor on the Underground Railroad. She died on March 10, 1913.

- **Reverend Martin Luther King Jr.:** A prominent Civil Rights Movement leader, pastor, and human rights activist. Born January 15, 1929, he was assassinated (killed) on April 4, 1968.

- **Charlottesville Protest:** On August 12, 2017, Elitists—white nationalists—and neo-Nazis protested against the removal of a Robert E. Lee statue. The protest turned violent, resulting in the deaths of three people. The president did not condemn these protesters.

- **"I Have a Dream" Speech:** This speech can be found on the website of the National Archives: archives.gov /files/press/exhibits/dream-speech.pdf.